NINE LETTERS

BY THE SAME AUTHOR

Lotto

Nine Letters

John Webb

PENGUIN BOOKS

Published in 2020 by Penguin Random House South Africa (Pty) Ltd
Company Reg No 1953/000441/07
The Estuaries No 4, Oxbow Crescent, Century Avenue, Century City, 7441, South Africa
PO Box 1144, Cape Town, 8000, South Africa
www.penguinrandomhouse.co.za

First edition, first printing 2020
9 8 7 6 5 4 3 2 1

ISBN 978-1-4859-0413-7 (Print)
ISBN 978-1-4859-0460-1 (ePub)

Cover design by Georgia Demertzis
Cover images: paper crafting by Andrew Gibson; maps by Orange Smile;
crested myna by tinyfishy, Flickr; envelope by Diana Akhmetianova, Unsplash
Text design by Fahiema Hallam
Set in Bembo

Printed and bound by Novus Print, a Novus Holdings company

To my mother

'The truth is not a set of facts which can be recounted. It is a landscape through which we travel in the dark.'
— ANDRÉ BRINK *Looking on Darkness* 1973

One

Argue? Yes, she could argue. She *liked* arguing.

Some people might have said that all she *ever did* was argue, but that would have been unkind (if not altogether undeserved). Even if her argument might have been untenable, and even if she knew it to be so, she was heard to say, 'It doesn't matter if I'm right or wrong, at least I'm right'.

Well, it was hard to argue with that.

She phoned me on a Wednesday afternoon to tell me that she'd be going into hospital.

'Oh, Val, I'm sorry to hear that. What's wrong?'

'No need for melodrama, Teddy. It's just hospital. Plain and simple. I've been having stomach pains. Cramps. Constipation and a bit of diarrhoea.'

'Constipation and diarrhoea?'

'Yes,' she confirmed flatly.

'At the *same time*?'

'Yes,' she confirmed again. 'And don't sound so doubtful. It's a perfectly common condition. People have it all the time.'

'Right,' I concurred. After all, I'd often described her as a woman of contradictions; her medical condition was yet another succinct validation of this opinion. 'Well, I'll come to see you,' I said. 'I'll drop by tomorrow.'

'That would be lovely.'

I returned to my reading. *Smollen v Smollen and Another.*

But I couldn't read. Instead, I found myself thinking about what gift I might take to the hospital. Flowers, of course. But I couldn't be sure of her reaction. She might examine them closely and find some bruised petal or wilted sprig in the arrangement and conclude that I'd been frugal – bought something for a discount that the florist was about to mulch. Or she might say nothing and with a simple roll of her eyes accuse me of a lack of imagination. Or she might be positively delighted and spend an inordinate amount of time ruminating over her garden – the one she used to have on the North Coast. This would have led to a discussion about how people no longer appreciated gardens and the world, as we know it, has gone to shit.

Maybe a book. But that would have been even more fraught. She might accuse me of peddling in left-wing propaganda, or right-wing hatred, or the tedium of the political centre. Even if I chose something that had no political consequence at all – something harmlessly inspirational – I might be regarded as some wayward fool promoting the misguided, soft-headed, florid musings of the Self-help Age. 'It all started with that man who wrote that book about birds. Seagulls. What was it called? It doesn't matter. Selfishness. That's what it was all about. A celebration of selfishness,' she once said. 'And what else might that lead to but self-*help*? And self-help to the selfie!' she scoffed. 'Poor lonely beasts, the lot of you!' Sometimes Val did not regard herself as a member of the human race. *We* were, but *she* wasn't. She was above us, looking down at us with an unmistakeable frown.

Maybe a book of quotes. She liked those, but I'd have to inspect it closely, just in case there was a quote in it from someone she didn't like. Invariably there was. Bertrand Russell? Godless. Winston Churchill? Warmonger. Groucho Marx? Too full of himself. Bob Hope? Frivolous. Marcus Aurelius? Paedophile.

'That was Hadrian,' I'd corrected her.

'It doesn't matter. They were all the same, those Romans. Hanging around in the nude, buggering things until the whole place burned.'

If only someone had published a book of Margaret Thatcher's quotes, nothing but Thatcher quotes. She liked Margaret Thatcher. Never had an unkind word to say about her.

I can't deny that she didn't look well. The usual sheen to her hair that made us all describe it as 'silvery' was now just an ashen grey, spread out over the hospital pillow. Soft, wrinkled skin hung over the sunken recesses of her face. But it was her eyes that gave it away. They shone dimly, had lost that familiar molten glow. It was as if everything around her was suddenly at a grave distance. Even me, holding my flowers and a small hard-covered book called *The Joy of Smiling*, even me – regarded as little more than a distant phantom hanging around the doorway like a shadow, scarcely worthy of concern. She looked at me vacantly, resigned to the growing space between us.

Or perhaps it was just me. Hospitals have always made me feel uneasy. I looked about and, yes, the room was most assuredly decorated in warm pastel colours, had beige walls, cream curtains and a sunny print of yellow flowers above her bed. But still, it had not rid itself of that greenish gloom that invariably pervaded hospital rooms. It was unshakeable.

'I brought you flowers!' I said happily, but not without effort.

'Oh, yes,' she said. 'Give them to me.' She lifted her arms from the bed, reaching weakly towards me. A shiny plastic tube was inserted into one of her wrists. I handed her the flowers and she inspected them, sniffed them. 'Lovely!' she said.

I exhaled with relief.

'Arum lilies! Too lovely! You know we used to have banks of arums at the farm. Banks! They just used to spill out from everywhere! Everywhere! They'd literally sing on their little stalks. Sing with all the beetles! And the hydrangeas! Do you remember the hydrangeas, Teddy? Such proud fellows they were.'

'Yes,' I admitted. My recollections were utterly without passion and I felt aggrieved, as if I were missing out on something. 'I remember the hydrangeas.'

She inspected the flowers once more. I detected a sudden frown. Might she have spotted some defect? I couldn't tell. She placed the flowers on the table, alongside a jug of water.

'And I brought you a book,' I added. 'Just … you know … a book, something to read.'

'Oh, yes.' Val took the book and placed it next to the flowers without looking at it. 'Something to read. That's very kind of you.'

It was as if she were speaking to some nebulous character in the service industry – a bank manager who'd given her a free pen, or a travel agent who'd offered her a free plastic pouch for her ticket.

I was relieved. She'd hate the book. At least now we weren't going to discuss it.

'So, what's up?' I said brightly, almost choking with anxiety. Hospital bedside banter wasn't my thing. It's not anyone's *thing*, I suppose. Perhaps it wasn't anxiety that I felt. It was more like fear. I wasn't sure if it was a fear of her dying or simply a fear of her.

'Oh, I'll be fine. They're doing some tests. Probably be out of here in a day or two. It's just a check-up. You can't be too careful at my age.'

'No. Right. Absolutely. Good idea.'

We looked at each other for what seemed like a very long time. And again, that warped distance, full of tension, was there between us.

'You're not still in pain? I mean, the cramps.'

'Not a bit,' she said with satisfaction. 'You know how it is – the moment you check into these places you suddenly feel a whole lot better.'

'Yes. Of course. Exactly. You're on the mend already.'

'Yes, on the mend,' she said vaguely. Her eyes darted about, from the flowers to the jug and its matching glass, the telephone, the window, the blank sheen of the TV on the wall, the ceiling, and back at me. 'Well, no need to keep standing there like an imp. You look as if you've done something wrong. Pull up that chair. I want to talk to you.'

I didn't want to sit. Standing was my thing. Always geared for a quick escape. I pulled the chair towards the bed and sat in it, helplessly.

'Now look,' she said, 'I asked you here because I want you to do something for me.'

I could have made the point – I felt myself rising to the challenge, blood pounding firmly through my head – that she hadn't *asked* me here. I had *offered*. I had offered out of the *goodness of my heart* to visit her in her … her hour of need, if that's what it was.

'Right. Of course. What is it?'

'I've been up all morning, writing letters. You know, I have many friends, Teddy, and I like to write to them.'

I didn't know that Val had many friends. In fact, I scarcely believed that to be true. The people at The Cedars all seemed to hate her and she them. She regarded all her fellow 'inmates' (that's exactly what she called them) with such scathing derision, it was impossible to describe any of them as her friends, or even as *friendly*. Poor things. We'd sit at a corner table in the dining room, hunched over our soup bowls, assiduously avoiding them. Those lunches were unbearable. I was often pressed to take a massage afterwards, replete with forest music or the sounds of the sea, just to rid myself of the lingering tension that had seized me so fiercely over the lukewarm soup.

Val pushed herself up against the pillows and leaned towards the side table with a groan. With a trembling hand, she reached for the drawer and opened it. She dug around in the drawer, fussing and hissing, trying to get hold of something.

'Here,' I said, standing up. 'I'll help you.' I began to walk to the other side of the bed.

'No!' Val snapped. 'Sit down, for heaven's sake. I can manage perfectly well.'

I sat down. I watched her as she leaned forward and fumbled blindly in the drawer, one arm tugging at the plastic tube that was connected to the drip. Finally, she produced a bundle of letters. She placed them on her lap and rested back into her pillows, breathing audibly.

'Don't ever do that again,' she said.

'Do what?'

'Stand up like that. Trying to help. I'm perfectly fine.'

'Right,' I replied. How often had I thought of hating her? More often than I cared to remember.

'Now,' she resumed, regaining her composure. 'I want you to take these letters to the post office and post them for me. You will do that, won't you?'

'Yes, of course. No problem at all.'

'I mean, you'll do it right away. You won't put them in the cubby hole of your car or in your briefcase and forget about them, will you? You won't simply throw them away?'

'Of course not!' I protested. Why would she think that? Did she think I didn't care? Yes, I might have thought of hating her from time to time, but I still ... you know ... cared.

'Well, I know, that's what everyone says and then suddenly they're so busy, they run out of time, have other things to do and so nothing gets done.'

'I'll do it. I'll go to the post office right away.'

She offered me a slightly sly, crooked smile. 'You're a good boy.'

Val looked again at the bundle of letters in her lap. 'Such dear friends,' she mused, as if I might not even be in the room. 'Here,' she held up one letter. 'This one's for Caroline. Caroline Beaufort. Dear girl. She has the most beautiful daughter. Trisha. Or Tina, or something like that. She sent me a photo once. Such a pretty thing.' She offered me a curious smile – slightly playful, slightly mocking. 'Although, of course, that's hardly your cup of tea,' she added loftily.

'My cup of tea? No,' I agreed indignantly and then with sudden playfulness of my own: 'I prefer a cocktail to a cup of tea.'

She smiled again, showing her grey teeth. I could tell she wanted to laugh, but she withheld it as if she were avoiding some dreadful kind of pain. She looked away, at the window, thinking, no doubt, of everyone out there. Her expression stiffened and, returning to me, she added with grim steeliness: 'Try not to be lewd, Teddy.'

We were interrupted. A doctor stood at the door. He beamed at us. 'Good morning, Mrs Dickerson. Ah, I see you have a visitor! Very good!'

Val replied glumly: 'He's my nephew. Teddy.'

I stood and shook the doctor's hand. 'Dr Hoosen,' he said. He had the most stunning white teeth.

Dr Hoosen had test results. No sign of any cancer. He seemed mightily pleased. But still, there was something else, some unmentionable thing had been discovered. We all knew it, even if it's not quite what he said. 'I want to do a few more tests,' he said. 'We'll get you down to the cardiac wing.'

'I see,' said Val.

Dr Hoosen left the room with his white coat splaying out behind him.

'Can you believe it?' she said to me. Her mouth hung open with incredulity.

'Believe what?'

'They sent me an *Indian*!'

'Oh, right. Well, I can't say I noticed.'

'That's the trouble with all of you. Totally blind. Colour blind. It'll get you into all kinds of trouble.'

'Oh, I ... I ...' I stopped. No, I didn't want this conversation. I knew how it would end. There'd be a squabble, a quarrel, a tiff – something neither of us needed just then.

Val could sense my discomfort. With a surprising note of forgiveness, she said: 'Well, it doesn't matter.'

'Yes,' I said with relief.

Val stretched her hand out. 'Come, hold my hand.' I held her hand. It was surprisingly cool and fragile, almost bird-like. Looking again at the ceiling, she said: 'It doesn't matter. Very little matters.'

I had nothing to say. True, if I'd said anything – anything at all – it wouldn't have mattered.

'Well.' She faced me again. 'At least I don't have cancer!' she said smugly.

She seemed quite suddenly emboldened, triumphant. She gave me her usual crooked smile and I saw her usual ugly vanity. It almost made me feel sorry for cancer, as if it were some feckless mutational aberration that had no chance against her vivacious fighting spirit.

I eventually stood to leave, claiming (falsely) that I had a meeting to attend. Looking down at the small woman shrinking discreetly under the pale sheets, it struck me that the vast distance that had intervened between us when I arrived had briefly disappeared. We'd been chatting in the way that we always had – as if nothing spectacular was happening or ever would happen; as if whatever controversy might assail us, assail the world, could ultimately be dismissed with little more than the nod of a head or the wave of a hand.

'Don't forget to post those letters,' she said.

'No, I won't. I'll drop by again tomorrow.'

'Yes,' Val said, 'that would be nice.'

I gave her cool hand a gentle squeeze. She looked up at me. I let go of her hand and that vast distance immediately returned. It stretched and yawned and flexed in the space between us, driving us ever further apart. It would never go away. By the time I left, it was as if I had never been in that room and we'd never talked.

I posted the letters. I did my duty. I stood in the queue at the post office, bought the stamps, affixed them to the envelopes, and slipped the envelopes into the post box. Feeling good about myself, I returned to my chambers and to my reading. *Smollen v Smollen and Another.*

Again, I couldn't read. I was thinking about the letters. Who were those people? What was in the letters?

I had glanced cursorily at the names and the addresses, but now I can tell you them by heart:

Mrs Darshini Poonam: Pandeshwara, India
Ms Wilma Straughan: Vancouver, Canada
Mrs Glynnis Warburton: Johannesburg, South Africa
Mrs Tiffany Medford: Melbourne, Australia
Mrs Caroline Beaufort: Summertown, United Kingdom
Mrs Nawal Hassan: Alexandria, Egypt
Mrs Jennifer Steenkamp: Harare, Zimbabwe

Thus far, it seemed as if Val was in touch with the last remnants of Empire – keeping a thread of the old beast alive with these handwritten letters, delivered around the world, not by Union Castle mail ships (much to her chagrin), but more urgently by American-made jet aircraft. It surprised me that she'd addressed Jennifer Steenkamp as a resident of Harare. She still insisted on calling it Salisbury.

But then there was one addressee who was not from the Empire:

Mrs Candice McKinney: Phnom Penh, Cambodia

Eight letters in all. Val had described these people as her friends and it astonished me that there were as many as eight of them. I'd never heard Val speak of any of these people. In general, she liked to speak of people. She liked to point out their travails and their woes (and sometimes to point out, with her usual smugness, that they only had themselves to blame). She could talk for hours. Dorothy Gerneke flirted with all the men at the club – no wonder her husband left her. Lydia Bullen was a selfish, petulant woman who thought she was better than everyone else – no wonder her son was a drug addict. Walter Schneider consumed too many vitamin tablets, never ate properly – no wonder he was a psychopath. Hendrik Cloete should just come right out with it and admit that he's an Afrikaner. There were a thousand others. But not once had I heard Val speak of any of the addressees marked on the eight envelopes that she'd given me.

Two

I was surprised when I walked into her ward the following day and saw a nurse in the process of making up the bed. She was diligently tucking crisp sheets under the edges of the mattress.

'Where's Val?' I demanded. 'Mrs Dickerson. Where's Mrs Dickerson?'

The nurse looked up at me. She blinked and had nothing to say.

Grief thickened inside me. I turned to the corridor and spotted Dr Hoosen striding towards me through that green gloom, his coat flowing out behind him. It was a relief to see him. He'd be able to explain, offer me something palatable, amid what must be my misplaced alarm.

'Dr Hoosen!' I said happily. 'It's me – Teddy. We met yesterday. I'm … I'm here to see Val. My aunt. I'm here to see Mrs—'

'Oh yes, of course. Yes, I remember,' he said and put his hand out, not for a handshake but a gentle pat on my shoulder. He looked at his shoes and then up to face me. I knew it then. 'I'm so sorry,' he said. 'We couldn't reach you. We rang The Cedars. The number she gave us on her admission form was for Aubrey, Aubrey Dickerson, but we couldn't reach him either.'

'Aubrey?'

'Yes. She'd put him down as next-of-kin, but we couldn't reach him.'

'Well, that hardly surprises me. Aubrey was her husband. He's been dead for thirty years.'

'Dead?'

'Yes. Quite dead.'

'Ah, well, that explains it. I'm very sorry, Teddy. It was her heart. The tests we took for the stomach pains revealed some cardiac complications. We had her sent to the cardiac ward, but she succumbed to a cardiac arrest before we could get her there. We did everything we could.'

Outside, I leaned against the side of my car and looked up at the grey-white sky. I wondered what Val would make of all this. Nothing spectacular has happened, she would have said. Nothing that cannot be dismissed with a nod of the head or the wave of a hand.

An Indian myna flew overhead, shrieking as it went, and issued a creamy dollop of shit that seemed to hang, suspended in the air, taunting me, before landing on my shoulder. I recoiled as I examined it, noting the glisten of its oily green streaks as it slid down the front of my blazer.

'Val!' I cried. An *Indian myna*! Who would have thought it!

I took the old road – the coastal road, or what was left of it – heading for the North Coast.

Beyond the townhouses that had sprung up (and were eternally springing up) along the beach of Umhlanga Rocks, I passed the little nature reserve with its lagoon and white egrets, where nature-loving men used to strip off and offer admiring glances at one another's genitals (and if anyone got lucky, they got more than a glance). It had often confounded me how few people saw the fun in that.

The farm, Estantia, was a coastal sugar estate, just north of Shaka's Rock. Val had preferred to describe it that way. More accurately, it was just north of Sheffield Beach, but Val had never liked the name. 'People will think we're living in England,' she'd said. 'I prefer to say "Shaka's Rock"! More exotic!' I can still see the glimmer in her eye as she'd said that.

Estantia always made me think of Aubrey. I'd once mentioned this to Val. She was incredulous. 'Aubrey? No one ever thinks of Aubrey!' And she was right. No one ever did think of Aubrey. He was a frail balding man and carried himself about as if he'd never been anything but a frail balding man. It was impossible to imagine Aubrey as young. Quite impossible. I'd seen photographs, black-and-white photographs mostly: Aubrey standing on a rock holding up a fishing rod and a dead fish; standing in the garden holding a cricket bat; sitting on the veranda with a cigarette between limp fingers and a dog at his feet. He was in his twenties then, but still … frail and balding. He spoke in monotone, thinking himself to be interesting while people slept in their chairs.

I took the Sheffield Beach off-ramp and headed onto the gravel road. How long had it been since I was last here? Twenty years? It all seemed pleasingly familiar. And *familial*. It was all about *family*. Tennis matches came to the surface. None of us could play. Well, my sister, Clarah, might have had a thing for it, but the rest of us were all elbow and knee, rigid with tension, hating it. Still, we bounded down to the court with our wooden rackets, resplendent in 'tennis whites', for hours of constrained merriment on that bloody hot court. I remember being the object of envy when someone (I don't remember who; might it have been Val?) bought me a new tennis racket made out of some extraordinary metal – titanium or plutonium, or whatever it is that they make rackets out of. It didn't do much for my game. I remember flinging the racket across the court, hoping to strike Clarah after she'd won some hotly contested point. It might have been the last time I ever used it.

That reminded me of the arguments. Far from the sunny expanses of the front lawn and the view of the sea that quivered in the heat, there were those darker recesses at the back of the house, the guest rooms with shuttered windows where my mother used to sit on the bed and smoke after an argument. My father and Aubrey, two brothers, sat on the veranda, grinding their teeth in manly silence. Clarah and I would mostly dither about, ambling this way and that, hopelessly in search of some kind of distraction, aching over the slow passage of time.

And just – just! – at the point when time had done its most valuable work (my mother appearing on the veranda with brushed hair and reddened eyes, my father patting the cushion on the sofa inviting her to sit with him; Aubrey blithely patting one of the dogs or his knee or the side of the chair; and Clarah and I assembling with the rest of them in some kind of rapprochement, all of us drawn together by the comforting tinkle of teaspoons and tea cups), Val would start up again, while pouring the tea with disturbing ceremonial grandeur.

'All I'm *actually* saying is that you can't really trust the Spaniards! I mean, look at the Armada. They're tricky. Always been tricky. For as long as anyone can remember.' She spoke with great authority, as if she might have witnessed the Armada herself.

They were talking about the Falklands War. Well, *she* thought they were talking about the Falklands War or the dastardly deeds of the Mau Mau, or nuclear proliferation, the rise of China or the fall of Empire or whatever it was. But the rest of us weren't. These were just pretexts. It took me years to realise that people like talking about politics for one reason: we need to exaggerate our grasp of the things that scare us. And the thing that we were most scared of was one another. We sat on that veranda, drinking tea, utterly appalled by one another. Still, Val soldiered on, with her clarion call for justice and order and peace, as if nothing spectacular were happening.

I arrived at the gate. This had changed. The columns on each side of it, freshly painted in white, were still there, but the right column had a metal plaque affixed to it with the logo of an American tractor company and the words, *Ray and Marsha Henderson – Estantia*. I knew what the plaque concealed. It concealed the names of Aubrey and Valerie Dickerson forever carved into the plaster beneath it.

Just beyond the columns was an electronically operated steel gate. Its steel bars offered a blunt unwillingness to let me pass. I was shut out from Estantia. Emphatically so. Peering through the gaps in the bars, I could see the driveway curving away towards the house, trimmed lawns on either side of it. The house itself was concealed by dishevelled mounds of bougainvillea and delicious monsters and deep green swathes of forested garden. I could spot the old cement water tower, smothered in creepers, and the Norfolk pines on each side of it, but the house itself remained hidden.

Why was I there? I couldn't really be sure. Val had just died and perhaps I was feeling unusually sentimental, but I'm not sure that explained very much.

As I was contemplating my indecision, my car idling outside the gates, a large farm truck appeared behind me. It was one of those enormous shiny Americanised trucks with electronic everything, and it stopped in a dramatic cloud of dust. I heard the slamming of a door. I suddenly wanted to flee, but I was trapped between the gate and the truck.

A short man with blond hair and an impressively square face approached my window. I wound down the window. He seemed relieved. Might he have been expecting a black person? Or an Indian? A long-legged, big-boobed blonde – his most asphyxiating fantasy?

'Hi,' he said. 'Can I help you?'

'I … um …' I was sitting way down in the bucket seat of an expensive German sports car and felt utterly hobbled looking up at a man so obviously shorter than me. I opened the door and stepped out, pleased to offer him my impressive height. Now, looking down at him, I continued: 'I was just … I mean, this farm … My aunt has just …' I swiftly put out my hand. 'I'm Teddy Dickerson.'

The man was, as I had surmised, Ray Henderson, the owner of Estantia. He was about my age, and everything about him seemed short. His hair, his fingers, his neck, and most likely (although I had no intention of finding out) his temper.

Two large Rottweilers appeared at the gate. They gambolled about on the other side of it, their jaws salivating with a slightly depraved sort of hunger, not for food, but for something – anything – to rip to pieces.

'Caesar! Shaka!' Ray barked. Turning to me with a steely smile, he added: 'Ha! Rotties!'

Yes, Ray was the kind of man who called Rottweilers 'rotties'. What did he think they were? Sausage dogs? And what of those names? Caesar? Shaka? Yes, I knew this kind of man, had known him all my life. If there were two kinds of men in the world, then I was the other kind. It was obvious to both of us that we'd never really like each other.

'Of course!' he said. 'I remember the Dickersons. Can't say I've ever met them. My dad will remember them, though. Come in and have a look around.'

Now I *really* wanted to flee.

Ray was married to Marsha. She too had an impressively square face, but with a much broader forehead. She had weak blue eyes and thin inward-pointing lips. She liked to gossip. That much was obvious. She'd just been sewing in the sewing room, she told us. *She likes sewing*, I thought. *Oh no.* And there, on the veranda, were terracotta pots, each of which contained some neglected-looking succulent. Val would have been outraged, and I might have been in agreement with her.

A few remarks on Estantia: the house was built in 1922. The veranda was supported by a row of handsome Doric columns. The roof was grey tin. The floor was black-and-white tile. The front walls of the house were thick, white-washed, slightly skew. This was no place for terracotta pots!

The pots would not have been Ray's idea. Ray didn't look like the kind of man who had *ideas*. Ideas clearly exhausted him. It must have been Marsha. What was she thinking? This was a classic colonial-era homestead situated on an English sugar plantation. They needed blue-and-white Chinese glazed pots that spoke of the British East India Company and its many trappings, not bloody orange Italian pots! I fumed in my usual silent, stiffened way.

'Come and take a look inside!' Ray said.

But I stopped. I realised I didn't want to go inside. It wouldn't be the same. No, that wasn't it. Even if it were the same, I still didn't want to go inside.

'I … uh … I actually just came to see the garden. No need to wander about inside. I mean, I'm not here to intrude. It's very kind of you. Thank you. But I just wanted to see the garden, that's all. My aunt was very proud of her garden.'

So that is what we did. The three of us, Ray, Marsha and I, stood on the veranda and looked at the garden. A steel wire fence dissected the front lawn with exacting, gleaming precision. Ray seemed proud of it. The efficiency of it. The *cost* efficiency of it.

He knew what I was thinking and hastily offered an explanation. 'We had to put the fence up, obviously. Couldn't honestly expect it to follow the original boundaries of the garden. I mean, it's nearly eight acres! What are we going to do with eight acres?' he laughed hopefully.

'Exactly,' I said. 'A garden of eight acres!' I could feel Val glaring at me. I was tempted to look up and see if an Indian myna might be in the vicinity. 'And the tennis court?' I asked innocently. 'You still use it?'

The tennis court was outside the prickly security perimeter, no doubt neglected.

'Not really,' Ray admitted. 'Tennis isn't really our thing.'

'No. No,' I added glumly. 'Not mine either to be honest.'

Now *that* was a spirited moment. We had something in common. Neither of us liked tennis!

'We should get you some tea,' Marsha said. 'We want to hear all about it!' she said and disappeared through the front door into the cool gloom of the interior.

What did she want to hear about? The Dickersons? The Dickerson family? Was it a family worth *knowing*? Wasn't there a *Judge* Dickerson? How many of them – Dickersons – might be left? (I don't normally have any objection to talking about the Dickerson family, but I wasn't going to indulge Marsha – Marsha and her sewing and her terracotta pots.)

I didn't want tea. I wanted a gin. No, I wanted a tequila. More than one.

'Tea would be great,' I said.

Ray and I sat on white plastic chairs with thin yellow cushions. I suppose, to their credit, the chairs were made in China, much like the blue-and-white glazed pots that Val used to have on the veranda, but there's a distinction between the two that I don't need to go into.

'Ja,' Ray confirmed. 'Eight acres. Of flowers!' He laughed and looked at me keenly, inviting me, with slightly threatening insistence, to join in.

I did join in. 'Flowers!' I scoffed. 'I mean, for fuck's sake!'

After our very jolly laugh, Ray added: 'It's only me and Marsha and the girls. We've got two girls. Tilly and Jenny.' He turned to face the open front door (a mighty carved thing with bevelled panels made out of yellowwood). 'Hey, Marsh! Where are the girls?'

Marsha's voice, enfeebled by the thick historic walls of the house, returned: 'They're in the TV room!'

Whenever there had been an argument in that house, one of those hideous heavy insoluble arguments, Clarah and I had never had the sanctuary of television available to us. We'd had to wander around the garden searching for 'interesting things' like deranged little people. Television in those days only started broadcasting at six in the evenings. Half of the time it was in Afrikaans, a language that I (and anyone I knew) had no interest in speaking. Now, the Henderson children were in the TV room at eleven in the morning at the end of their summer holidays flicking from one channel to the next – hundreds of them. I hadn't met them, but I knew I already resented them.

'Hey, Tilly! Jenny! Come out here – we've got a visitor!' Ray announced and then looked at me with a wink.

It was obvious he was waiting for me to offer something about myself. Did I have children? I'm here on my own, so my wife couldn't make it?

But all I gave him was a slightly off-putting wink in return and proceeded to take a long look at the garden.

Tilly and Jenny appeared. I couldn't deny it – they were in every way those healthy angelic children for whom every parent must ache. They could easily have been cast in advertisements for soaps that are gentle on the skin. Shiny blonde hair, flawless golden skin, bright blue eyes – that sort of thing. They climbed onto their father, hugging him with their delicate arms. He embraced them and reddened, and I got the distinct feeling he was uncomfortable with such a blatant display of affection.

'Come on, girls. Don't be rude. We've got a guest.' He held his hand out towards me. It seemed as if they'd been assiduously ignoring me. I knew that kind of shyness; I had it myself. 'Say hello to Teddy.'

They both giggled. It was charming.

'I've got a teddy called Teddy,' said one.

'Oh, I bet you have,' I said. They gave another giggle and I added: 'I suppose a lot of little girls have a teddy called Teddy.'

That was a blunder. Evidently, the girl, Tilly or Jenny, I had no idea which, thought she was the *only* girl in the *whole wide world* to have a teddy called Teddy and now I had upended that little fantasy with a thoughtless remark that would change her life forever. She stared at me for an inordinately long time, as if in some haunting meditative pose – was she about to cry or disparage me with some scornful remark?

Where was that tequila?

The children returned their attention to their father – the man who called Rottweilers 'rotties'.

There was another thing I noticed about the girls. Yes, they were beautiful human beings; it couldn't be denied. But they wouldn't stay that way forever. I could, on further examination, see that beauty was already in the process of abandoning them. One clearly took after her father and was bound to end up plump, with a thick, rubbery neck, her curly hair growing frizzy and unmanageable and the bane of her life. The other took after her mother, and would grow into an insipid bookish creature with thin lips, a famously flat chest, and sunken cheeks. One day it would all be over, and sooner than any of them might have imagined.

Mercifully, someone to whom I had most assiduously not been introduced – a round middle-aged Zulu woman – carried a tray with tea things and placed it on the plastic table in front of us. She gave me a glance; I gave her a nod. This wasn't unusual, but I immediately knew she was the only person among the Hendersons whom I might like.

The children raced away, back to the TV, evidently bored of their father and his guest. Marsha returned and we drank tea on the veranda (and ate shortbread, and looked at the garden).

And we engaged by any measure in what is known as convivial banter. Yes! The Dickersons! Aubrey died thirty years ago. Cancer. His wife, my aunt, died last night. Heart attack. Two sons! Yes! One in Canada, a surgeon. One in San Francisco, has something to do with computers. Apparently he knows Bill Gates. Goes to parties at his house!

Neither Ray nor Marsha had considered how utterly insufferable a party at Bill Gates's house might be. They were most impressed.

We laughed and laughed and laughed (and ate a ridiculous amount of shortbread – the Zulu woman had been summoned to refill our diminishing stock).

I knew why they liked me – Ray and Marsha. Or perhaps, it wasn't so much that they *liked* me as much as they didn't have any precise objections. First, I drove an expensive German car. Then there was that wonderful revelation that none of us liked tennis, followed by my haughty dismissal of an eight-acre garden filled with flowers. Flowers! Of all things! Of course, I was white and English was my mother tongue.

I was already forming a view as to how they might have met. It would have been at an after-party on a field next to King's Park (or what did they call it now? Absa Stadium? Named after a bank?). Fold-up picnic chairs would have been hauled out of an suv, gas propelled barbecues ignited and cans of beer cracked open. Thousands of them would have milled about on that field, talking about the game. Marsha and Ray would have been introduced to each other by a mutual friend whom neither of them really liked. Marsha would have been impressed by Ray's knowledge of the game. He would have said things like 'Snyman should never have made that pass', and 'When Klippie got hold of the ball at the twenty-two, that was game over'. Everyone would have agreed and Marsha would have felt a chill of stunning titillation run through her – from the top of her head to the balls of her feet. She would have known it then. She would have known that she was *in love*. Yes, she had noticed his strong arms, bristling with blond hair, and she would have known how they might comfort one in an embrace or alarm one in a throttle. Still, she was in love. No one was at risk of being throttled. Not then.

And even now, I wondered if the two of them weren't already growing tired of each other. Their effortless congeniality seemed to conceal a grim, almost oppressive kind of boredom, a realisation perhaps that their whirlwind romance had fizzled into little more than a dull routine. I pictured these two people attending to one mundane triviality after the next, through each passing day until one of them (or both of them) screamed. Where would it all end? Would there be a dot of violence? Would Tilly and Jenny be placed in the care of some distant aunt while their parents tried to *work things out*? Would it finally be resolved by order of the Durban and Coastal Local Division of the High Court of South Africa in the matter of *Henderson v Henderson*?

But, of course, that was all for later. How could I possibly know?

Right now, this is what *actually happened*. Fernando arrived. That (that!) was the beginning of the end.

Fernando wore no shirt. He was from Mozambique, I guessed – a Shangaan with an exotic touch of Portuguese ancestry. He was responsible for maintaining their hamstrung garden. The muscles on his upper body, the pectorals and the torso, shone in sepia hues and his nipples, drawn in pristine dark ink, were firm and pronounced. His obliques curved suggestively towards each other as they converged in that hidden mossy tuft beneath his trousers. And yes, his trousers were baggy, but still it was obvious that he dressed to the left – perfectly obvious, practically all the way down to the knee! I remained silent. I'm sure I did. Or might I have let out a little gasp?

Fernando carried a spade and was enquiring of Ray (that little ray of sunshine) whether he might be permitted (or instructed) to dig up the sweet potatoes at the back of the house.

But Ray found that he could not speak. He looked to Marsha and Marsha could not speak either. They'd both been staring at me.

And I know what they saw.

'Later! Later!' Ray eventually spluttered.

The only person who hadn't glanced at anybody was Fernando. Notably, he hadn't glanced at me.

With darting eyes and pounding hearts, it was a credit to all of us that we managed to regain our composure.

Marsha said: 'Well, we will be praying for your aunt.' This was as good as saying goodbye.

I noticed she had a little gold crucifix dangling from her neck, between not particularly interesting breasts. A sewing room and Jesus. What more could she want?

'Well, that's very kind of you,' I said.

I suppose I must be off. Must press on. It's a work day after all. I have no idea if I said that. It must have been something like that. I was soon in my car, free of Estantia.

I took the freeway back. The coastal road could manage (forever) without me.

It was the end.

Three

There was a ninth letter.

Terry Winstanley was a smug little prick who needed to be cut down to size. It pleased me that most of my colleagues thought the same of him. The senior partner of an eminent firm of attorneys, he had a dogged way of ingratiating himself with people he despised.

And speaking of people he despised, yes, Val was one of them. When Aubrey was alive and that branch of the Dickerson family was thought to have money, Terry Winstanley had been adept at securing his appointment as his executor.

On the morning of Val's funeral, Terry rang me. 'Teddy! How goes the feisty young Teddy this fine morning?'

'It's Val's funeral today, Terry. That should give you a clue.'

'Oh yes, of course. Funeral. No good. Really sad. Couldn't help loving old Val.'

'I don't suppose you'll be attending. It's at the Manning Road Methodist.'

'Of course, I'll be there!' Terry stammered. 'Of course. Wouldn't miss it for the world!'

I didn't believe him for a second. He made it sound like some kind of venerated sporting event, a grand final – well … it was a grand final in a certain sense, one where the loser gets a large rectangular box instead of a silver plate. Val might even have smiled at the thought, but only if it were for someone else's funeral. Her own funeral was no laughing matter.

'Right. Well, that's kind of you, Terry. Thanks.'

'Not a problem at all. Now look …' He took on a more bumptious business-like tone – the kind of tone that kept him safe. 'We're still waiting for the papers from the Master of the High Court, so we're not formally appointed yet, but I had a clerk nip over to The Cedars, just to get preliminary arrangements under way. You know those people at The Cedars, they don't like to wait, if you know what I mean. Need to get the place cleared out, refurbished, and back on the market ASAP.'

'Right.'

'So, we found a letter. It says, er, let me see.' He paused for a bit, no doubt placing his reading glasses on the tip of his fleshy nose. 'Er, it says, "For Teddy Dickerson. My nephew. The lawyer". So, I suppose that's you.'

'A good guess,' I said.

'Yes,' Terry seemed pleased with his crisp deductive reasoning. 'It's sticky-taped to a box. "DO NOT",' that's in capital letters. The word "NOT" is in capitals, ha, so like Val. "DO NOT open", it says. Formalities aside, I thought I might have it delivered to your chambers.'

'Good idea, Terry. Go ahead.'

'Righto, will do.'

'Thanks, Terry. See you later … at the funeral.'

'Yes … ah … yes. I'll just check my diary, but yes, I'm sure I'll see you at the funeral. Absolutely.'

I had phoned my mother in Zürich. This was not something I did often.

'Died?' she'd said cautiously.

'Yes. Last week. Thought you'd probably want to know. I mean, I know you never really *got on*, but still …'

But still … *what?*

'Well, thanks for telling me, Teddy. I suppose I did want to know. I'm sort of glad I outlived her. The least I could've done.' My mother had given one of her customary caustic laughs which then descended into a series of painful-sounding coughs. Gathering herself, she'd added: 'You might as well go to the funeral to … you know … make sure that she is actually dead. I mean, you never know with Val.'

I'd also phoned my sister in Sydney. 'Oh, poor thing. You were very good to her, Teddy. Always visiting her at that place. What's it called? The Cedars. You were very good to her.'

'Well,' I'd said, plummeting into a state of helpless self-deprecation, 'you would have done the same.'

'Oh hardly!'

We'd had so little to say to each other, it was as if we no longer knew each other. Had never known each other.

'And you, Teddy? Are you all right? You sound a bit ...'

'A bit what?' I'd said. 'I'm fine. Absolutely fine. Never been better.'

I couldn't phone my father. He was dead. Long dead. He was six years younger than Aubrey, and died six years after him. They died at exactly the same age. It was two years after my mother had left him and moved to Switzerland with a man called Uwe.

The Manning Road Methodist Church was no longer on Manning Road. It was on Che Guevara Road. The church hadn't moved, of course. Val had always held a dim view of communists. I wondered how she might have felt about the idea of having her grand final on Che Guevara Road. It was impossible to fathom. She might have been outraged, or have said it was perfectly 'exotic'.

I suspected that she would have had more of a complaint over the religious denomination that would preside over the ceremony. She wasn't a Methodist. Aubrey had been a Methodist (same as my father) and that had seemed as good a reason as any for Val to regard herself as a Methodist too. It was something she seemed to have followed blithely. No, she wasn't a Methodist. She wasn't a *churchgoer*, she wasn't religious. But to say that she wasn't religious was not to say that didn't like speaking about God. Arguing about God. Or arguing *with* God. She often had things to say about God – the blue-eyed, silvery-haired, Christian version, of course. Any other version, according to her, was at the very least misleading if not downright fraudulent. God, she said, was love. It was an unhelpful definition. It was hardly the kind of proposition that would stand up in court. Still, 'God is love' is what she used to say. She exhorted people, all of us, to love one another and then she would berate us in the nastiest way possible for failing in this mission. The whole idea of it seemed implosive and led us in no discernible direction (except, of course, in acrimonious circles).

Still, she liked to speak about God, but had little to say about church. Perhaps that is why I suspected her discomfort at being the subject of religious ritual. She might have preferred it if her body was simply tossed into the sea, the sheets whipped away by a brisk wind, flapping off in the spume, while she sank, naked, to the greenest depths with palpable relief.

As I stood in the doorway of the old red-brick church, I was sorry I had never offered her one of Emerson's quotes: 'God builds his temple in the heart on the ruins of churches and religions'. She might have liked that. Or she might have said she knew it already and had strong reason to disagree with it. You could never tell with Val.

People gathered in the small tropical garden outside the entrance. The first person I recognised was Hilda, the German manageress of The Cedars. She hugged me hesitantly and pecked at the air around my cheeks. 'What a sad day. Poor *Fell*. Poor *Fellerie*. I know you *luffed* her.'

'Thank you, Hilda. Thank you for everything. She was …' I was about to say that she was very happy at The Cedars, but Hilda would never have believed it. No one would have believed it. I was a bit stuck.

Hilda didn't press me. She was a regular funeral-goer, familiar with the dreadful complexity that funerals concealed.

'She was very well taken care of!' I said at last, exhaling with relief.

'Oh! Ja,' Hilda paused, 'very good. We had the lawyers over yesterday. Winstanley *unt Smyde*. Very good. We'll have her apartment all sorted out in a *yiffy*.' She seemed pleased by this.

The Cedars was a little gold mine – getting things done in a jiffy (or a *yiffy*) was part of the business model, selling and reselling those plush carpeted apartments to an endless stream of people who were all nearly dead. It was a no brainer.

'Excellent.'

While Hilda and I were speaking, I noticed that she was accompanied by three of her inmates. They made slow progress climbing out of the minibus. Walkers and sticks and special platforms sparkled around the sliding doors as one decrepit inmate alighted after the next, each of them taking tiny shifting steps towards solid ground with their hands reaching out for the unfailing Zulu staff.

I recognised them. One of them was Esther or Ethel or Elspeth – something like that. She had made aggressive use of rouge that morning, which I took to be a sign of early senility, and her coiffed purple hairdo was fixed by enough hairspray to kill a small horse. The other was a man in a suit that offered a powerful scent of naphthalene. The third was a stick-like woman who appeared to have been born well before the war – the South African War, as we now call it; the one between Boer and Brit. I'm sure she was the one whom Val hated the most.

Craig arrived. Val's son. The surgeon from Vancouver. I was surprised I still recognised him.

'Craig! It's me. Teddy.'

This was of no help to him. He looked at me askance, as if I were trying to sell him something.

'Edward,' I continued, 'her nephew. Bernard's son.'

He swayed backwards, slightly startled, and then smiled weakly. 'Oh yes. Uncle Bernard. Yes. Teddy. Of course. Gosh. You're still here?'

What he meant by 'here' was the country. South Africa. It surprised him that anyone was *still here*. What on earth were we all *doing* here? Why hadn't we *left*?

'Yes, yes,' I said congenially.

Craig and his brother, Vaughan, were born to escape. By all accounts, their happiest days had been at boarding school in the Midlands. Holidays at home had been spent smashing tennis balls at each other on the court at Estantia, happily avoiding their increasingly doddery parents whose tennis days were already over. From boarding school, they leapt at the chance to study in Cape Town and from there Craig hurtled off to Vancouver and Vaughan to California. I knew what they were escaping from. It wasn't the end of Empire; it wasn't a communist revolution. It was Val.

'Gosh,' Craig continued, 'you were, what, knee-high to a grasshopper when I last saw you.'

'Well, not quite,' I said. I wasn't exactly enamoured of the description. It lacked imagination. And I wasn't *knee-high* to anything. I was probably twelve or thirteen. Tall for my age. I couldn't have been *that* forgettable.

Craig was a man in his fifties with grey, wavy hair and a pinkish, blotchy face. He seemed tired. Tired from the long journey? Tired of his two ex-wives? Tired of his offspring, their endless pleas for … *direction*? Tired of the ceaseless queue of patients that revolved around him, bleating over their pulmonary disorders? Whatever it was, it didn't seem as if all was going according to plan for Craig Dickerson.

'Vaughan couldn't make it, unfortunately. He's, you know. I mean, he's done incredibly well. Silicon Valley and so on.'

I wasn't quite sure what that was supposed to explain. Was he trying to tell me that Vaughan had been pressed into another soirée at Bill Gates's house? Was that supposed to be a good reason not to attend his mother's funeral?

'Yes. So I've heard.'

Craig had his mother's nose. It had a swollen nodule in the middle before tapering off into a slightly more delicate, reddish tip. 'It's a sign of good breeding,' Val used to say, sometimes adding: 'It's an aristocratic thing.' And when it suited her, she claimed it was also a sign of intelligence.

There were nine people in the church, including me and the priest.

Embossed with gold thread on a satin parament over the pulpit were the words, *God Is Love*. Val might have been pleased.

No one cried. Not a drop. We all filed out of the church with our heads drooping, as if we'd all just been admonished by a headmaster at a particularly arduous school assembly. It was no more despairing than that.

Back at my apartment that night, shoes off, whisky glowing in a tumbler on the side table offering me its smoky fumes, I opened Val's letter.

> *Dear Teddy,*
>
> *I know I'm dying. I don't know how I know, but I am. I've never been more sure of anything in my life. And you know me. I'm sure about a lot of things.*
>
> *I know you've probably spent quite a lot of time hating me, Teddy, and that makes me a little bit sad, but, in the end, it's* your *hatred and you're the one who'll have to live with it. As you know, Teddy, I'm a simple sort of soul and all I've really been trying to say all these years is that we should love one another. You'd think I've been asking people to chop their arms off! You wouldn't believe how many people have picked an argument with your poor aunt over my simple plea. Poor old Jesus tried to say the same sort of thing and look what they did to him!*
>
> *Of course, you and I have had our fair share of squabbles too. You've always been so young and so clever and that can be a truly frightful combination. You've probably forgotten, but there was a time when I told you about the importance of love and you accused me of peddling in mumbo-jumbo. You had hurt me and yet it rather annoyed me that I never had a retort. I have spent all the years since trying to work out why I had nothing to say.*
>
> *I suppose now that I write this letter, all I can say is that you probably ought not worry too much about the facts, Teddy. It's what we feel about the facts that count. Call it mumbo-jumbo if you like, but the last thing you should want in life, Teddy, is a world that <u>makes sense</u>.*

Love is silent, Teddy. The moment it is put into words, it becomes a folly. Not everything needs to be explained. Just ask the poets, poor tormented lot.

You were always such a sweet boy, Teddy. I remember how delighted you were by all the little fish in the ponds down at the seashore in front of Estantia. You used to love skipping from rock to rock, looking at all the colourful sea life squirming about, creeping into their hiding places. I'm a bit disconcerted by what's become of you. Never could see what might have made you into the kind of person you are, but there it is. I saw on television recently that you're all allowed to marry. Well, go off and get married, Teddy. You don't have to tell anyone. There's nothing wrong with a bit of privacy, even if everyone thinks it's old fashioned. Heavens! The world today! Everyone has to know everything. It's a tyranny, I tell you.

I'm asking you to do two more things for me, Teddy. Firstly, I've put it in my Will, which is in the custody of that odious little creep, Terry Winstanley, that my remains are to be cremated. I want you to take my ashes and throw them into the sea. I know you won't want to go far out on a boat. You couldn't stand that sort of thing. So, you might just go along to the beach in front of Estantia and deposit them into one of the little ponds that you used to love so much. Thank you for doing that, Teddy. You're a good boy.

Secondly, I'll be giving you some letters to post. I have many friends, Teddy. I know that probably comes as some surprise. A lot of people think I'm a hateful, spiteful old thing. Of course, anyone who thought of me that way was obviously wrong, shamefully so, but I think you'll find, as you look back, that I've actually been quite a forgiving soul. I want you to post the letters. In each letter, I have told them about you and given them your address. If you hear back from any of them, then write to them and tell them that I'm gone. Tell them that I loved them. Love, Teddy! It really is the only way out. It doesn't matter if you don't even know what love is, if you can't define it. Love is wonderfully irrational. It's a shame no one took the time to listen to your poor Aunt Val!

I'll be sticking this letter to a box of correspondence. I've kept all their letters. More than three decades! Hard to believe. I want you to keep their letters safely and maybe one day, when you know your time is up, you can leave them to someone special too.

I'll sign off now, Teddy. One last time!

I suppose I might say one more thing. You know me! I always like to say one more thing! Well, let me say that I know it hasn't always been easy for you and Clarah – that whole terrible episode with your father. Quite frankly, his death wasn't that easy for me either. Although, despite all that, I cannot say that I'm not proud of you, dear boy, for the way you've soldiered on, become a successful lawyer and so on.

I'm never one to forsake the last word, so I'll say one more thing: good luck, Teddy!

With all my love,

Val

So, one tear was shed on the day of her funeral. It rolled slowly down my left cheek. And then I sprang from my chair and poured myself another whisky, looked at the view of the city, scratched my head, and then I thought of Xanax.

The following day Hilda rang me. 'We have the ashes!' She seemed almost euphoric.

'Ashes?'

'*Ja*. The crematorium delivered them this morning. You can come to collect them.'

Well, *that* was certainly efficient. I wondered at what temperatures they burnt corpses. A thousand degrees? I could only surmise that the ashes would still be warm.

'Thank you, Hilda. I'll be right over.'

'Good! They will be at the front desk!'

'Super.'

Yes, it was *super*. Those Xanax could do wonders.

Walking to the front desk at The Cedars, I was approached by the stick-like woman from the South African War – the one who, out of spite or out of sorrow, had bothered to attend Val's funeral.

'You're the nephew,' she said, leaning on a stick and staring at me from hooded eyes.

'Yes,' I said, 'Teddy.' I put out my hand.

She ignored it and leaned ever more emphatically on her stick. 'Your aunt was very kind to my daughter.'

'Oh? Kind?'

'Yes,' the woman said, 'kind. My daughter. She lives in Canada. On the other side of the world.'

'I see … How interesting,' I said, as if I had no idea where Canada was. 'Well, that's very good. I'm very pleased.'

'Yes,' the old woman said. 'I was very grateful to your aunt. She was very kind and I was very grateful.' She turned and shuffled towards the dining room, her head nodding forward.

The woman at the reception desk handed me a purple satin box – something made in China. Inside was the glass urn, so I was told. She smiled at me and told me to have 'a nice day'. Well, perhaps she meant it.

I skipped out of The Cedars for what I thought to be the last time – or was it? As I drew nearer to my car, a deflating thought occurred to me, reducing my purposeful pace to little more than a slightly deranged meandering stagger. Indeed, I might one day return to The Cedars, not as a visitor, but as one of its inmates. Was that my ineluctable fate? Did I have any alternatives? Not really.

Four

I spent the next two weeks with the Smollens, well, the Smollen *case*. This was my work. This was my venerated career. A career could explain a lot of shortcomings. It was the reason we were always too busy. It got us the car, the townhouse, the holidays, and the retirement benefits. It was worthy and just and proper. While everyone might be dying around me and (as was obvious to me then) they would keep on dying in ever-greater numbers, I had my career. It was all I had. All that was left to Teddy Dickerson.

The Smollen case.

Janet Smollen was a short, tubby woman with round cheeks and fat painted lips. She had a giggly face, even though I never once saw her giggle. Regrettably, Janet was more inclined towards crying than giggling. She had very pale skin and, if the light from the window caught her at a certain angle, it seemed almost translucent. Her hair was a vibrant, fiery ginger, greying at the temples, and aggressively drawn back from her forehead into a short ponytail of little aesthetic value. I suspected that she might once have had piercing blue eyes, but now they were an insipid watery colour, totally without drama.

When I first met her she had said: 'We used to be very rich. Unimaginably rich!'

'Oh, how super,' I'd replied.

And then she'd burst into a fit of sobs.

It might have been insensitive of me. She had spoken of her riches in the *past tense* and I should have deduced that she was now unimaginably poor (or at least unimaginably *not rich*) and that could distress a lot of people.

'I mean, gosh, it was probably super *at the time*, but *now*, well it must be quite a … a different kettle of fish, I'm sure. You poor thing.'

She was no longer listening. Our first consultation hadn't exactly got off to a swimming start.

My instructing attorney was a man by the name of Ben Williamson and he seemed wondrously untroubled. He sat grinning at the two of us as if a distressed, sobbing client and a blundering, reddening counsel was a sign of exceptional progress. He was a large bearded man with a pink face and thick glasses, the lenses of which grew progressively darker as the day grew brighter. I liked Ben, mainly because he shared in my detestation of Terry Winstanley.

As I was to discover, Janet *herself* had never been rich, but her *father* had been.

The story was not without its intrigue. Her father, Randolph Smollen, was born an only child on a farm outside the town of Kitwe in what was then known as Northern Rhodesia. At the age of nineteen, he moved to Southern Rhodesia and promptly joined the 1st Battalion Rhodesian Light Infantry. Proving himself to be an outstanding soldier, he was decorated with illustrious military honours by the penultimate British Governor of the Federation of Rhodesia and Nyasaland, Sir Humphrey Gibbs, in 1962. In 1965 he found himself on the wrong side of history, backing Sir Humphrey after the government of Rhodesia declared independence from Britain. The governor would not budge. His instructions from London were to charge the new government with treason. Roundly laughed off, Gibbs remained a defiant occupant of Government House, insisting that he was the lawful representative of Her Majesty. With the lights, water and telephone lines to Government House cut, Captain Randolph Smollen provided surreptitious assistance, secretly managing communications between the governor and London.

Janet spoke proudly of her father's early accomplishments.

At that point, the story had become a little vague.

In 1968, Randolph moved to Johannesburg, married Jill, and together they produced their first child, a boy called Robert. Very little else appeared to have happened.

In 1970, the family moved to a small farm in the Natal Midlands at the end of an isolated dirt track with a view of the Lions River valley. There, Randolph and Jill produced their second child – my client, Janet.

What did they do on the farm? Nothing much, so it seemed. A few horses. A few cows. A few sheep.

Randolph spent extended periods away from home attending to business.

'And what sort of business was that?' I'd asked.

'Oh, you know… the usual sort of thing.'

'I see.'

'I mean, you know he had investments. Mining mostly.'

'Ah! Mining. Right. Please go on.'

As Janet had recounted these early years, I'd suspected at any moment that she would conclude by saying, 'and so we lived happily ever after'.

I had been almost inclined to yawn.

Janet spoke little of her mother, except to say that she was a mouse. She said this with such indifference, I wondered if she might have meant it literally – if she might have been seized by some sort of Kafkaesque delusion.

Certainly, there were others who expressed doubt over Janet's sanity. Ben was one of them. He'd known the family for 'some time' (as he put it) and, yes, Janet was known to be 'imbalanced' every now and again, but this was nothing that a litany of psychiatric interventions hadn't been able to resolve. 'She's fine. Completely recovered,' he had assured me before our consultation.

What was missing from Janet's account was how Randolph Smollen had made them all unimaginably rich. A small farm with a few horses, sheep and cows, and some opaque 'mining investments' hardly explained unimaginable wealth.

'Let's go back to the mining investments,' I had suggested.

'I don't know anything about them,' Janet had said.

'No?'

'Yes. No.' She'd looked at Ben, pleading with him to intervene.

'You'll need to tell him everything, Janet,' Ben had said. 'If we're going to run this case, we'll need to know. Can't be caught by surprise.'

Janet had paused and looked at the floor.

'He was involved with *them*!' she'd finally cried in exasperation.

There was a hint, just a hint of her fabled madness, when she'd said that. What did she mean by 'them'? Them who? It sounded as if she might be speaking of aliens, or phantoms – the voices in her head.

'Them?'

'Yes!' she'd pleaded. 'Plunkett. That mob.'

I'd looked at Ben and he'd promptly looked out the window. Neither of us, so it seemed, could speak.

'You mean, *James* Plunkett?'

'Of course I mean James Plunkett!'

James Plunkett was notorious in many countries for many different reasons. A graduate of Sandhurst. Started some kind of investment fund in Texas that was investigated by the FBI. Went missing for a spell. Last seen in a bar in Marrakesh. Resurfaced in South Africa about a year later. A warrant for his arrest was issued by police in Belgium, where he'd been charged with fraud. When the police converged on his house to serve the warrant, he'd mysteriously fled. Thereafter, he was nabbed by the gendarmerie in Pointe-Noire, trapped on a boat full of guns. Incarcerated in Congo on charges of plotting a coup, he was released a few months later through a deal generously brokered by the French government. Curiously, the allegations of fraud seemed to have died a natural death – lost in the sands of time, one might say. By the 1990s James Plunkett was back in full force. He owned the largest fleet of Rolls Royces in Hong Kong, was beaming in the pages of social magazines, and especially gratified when described as a *China insider*.

'Oh, right. I see.' I had maintained an appearance of calm.

'They're all connected. The whole lot of them. We got Africa. The Americans got South America and bits of Asia. The Middle East was divided up between us. We got Jordan, Oman, and the Emirates. The Americans got Saudi, Iraq, and Iran. The French got whatever was left over.'

'What do you mean, "we"? Who is "we", as in "we" got Africa?'

'Us! The British. The bloody English. The inventors of the gentlemen's agreement!'

'I see.'

'And if you don't believe me, go and see for yourself. You'll find the paymasters. Google it! They're all there! The bankers and the oilmen! The mining magnates and shipping tycoons. Shooting grouse in Scotland. Taking a punt at Royal Ascot! Orgies on their yachts!'

She'd suddenly picked up her handbag and placed it on her lap. It had seemed as if she was ready to leave. She'd said too much, was worried I didn't believe her or, worse still, that I was one of 'them'. Her delicate fingers – with reddened tips and bitten nails – had visibly trembled. She'd looked around my chambers, suddenly disconcerted. It was a messy room, I'd grant her that. Enough to disconcert many of my clients. But hers was more than disconcertment – it was more like terror.

'They're probably listening right now,' she'd quavered, looking down at her bag, it's broken zip now visible. 'This room is probably bugged.'

'Oh, I am sure it's not!' I'd said affably. 'You're perfectly safe here, Janet. Quite secure.'

'You don't know anything about security, Mr Dickson.'

'Dickerson,' I'd corrected her with a faltering smile.

'What?'

'Dickerson, my name is Dickerson.'

Janet had placed a hand to her forehead and begun to cry.

Since then, I had cause to meet Janet Smollen on many more occasions. As the case progressed and some success was had, her confidence in the system of justice (and in me, as an officer of the court, I hasten to add with some pride) had grown and afforded her a little hope.

And what of the case? Randolph, the father, went off and died, which, the family all agreed, was a most preposterous thing to do. As it turned out, the brother, Robert, received the entire family fortune, promptly divorced his second wife, married a third, and fled on a private jet in pursuit of indescribable pleasure, leaving Janet and his mother in penury.

Janet had reason to believe that Robert's good fortune (and very large fortune at that) was simply the result of a fraud. Testamentary documents had been forged. During Randolph's dying days, Robert had spent a lot of time with him, shooing other people away, sometimes even nurses and doctors. Janet was sure that he had been contriving some terrible injustice during those final days. When her father eventually perished and the entire estate was found to devolve on Robert, Janet flew into a terrible rage.

But she did nothing. Not a thing. A year passed and then, for whatever reason, she decided to consult Ben Williamson, and Ben instructed me.

Our initial investigations were promising. Our handwriting expert had reached an incontrovertible conclusion that the signature on Randolph Smollen's Last Will & Testament had been forged. Of the signatories who had purported to witness Randolph's final execution of the document, one had since died and the other refused to talk. A nurse who attended Randolph also confirmed how Robert had jealously (sometimes angrily) guarded his father's room. She was prepared to testify that she had seen various testamentary documents on the table and that both of the witnesses had attended his room on multiple occasions before he died.

So, things were looking up.

We launched the lawsuit, alleging that Robert was a fraud, a man uncon-strained by even the thinnest moral sentiments.

Robert spent much of his time aboard his private jet, flitting from one high-flying jetsetter's landmark to the next: Dubai to St-Tropez, Hong Kong to the Maldives, Johannesburg to the Seychelles. It wasn't easy to pin the fel-low down. In order to commence our noble proceedings, we submitted an application to the KwaZulu-Natal Provincial Division of the High Court to *find and confirm* jurisdiction over Robert Smollen, as a foreign defendant. He still owned the stud in the Midlands, even if the racehorses (which were, by all accounts, more expensive than the stud) had long since been shipped away. This was followed by an application for the trial to be heard in Pietermaritz-burg and then an application for the right to sue by *edictal citation*, granting us the right to serve a summons in a foreign country. That was all well and good.

Thus far, the process had taken nearly three years. A mere doddle.

At this point things hit a snag. Janet could not pay us. And this was becoming expensive. We needed lawyers in London and Hong Kong and investigators in other parts of the world. The family fortune was indeed unimaginable — just as Janet had said. But it would cost us money just to find out what exactly it was that we were suing them for.

Ben Williamson rang. 'Got a bit of news.'

'Ah!'

'Meet me downstairs. We'll go for a drive.'

Ben pulled up outside chambers in his old silvery-blue Mercedes. I jumped in. He swerved into the traffic and headed inland, taking the freeway towards Pietermaritzburg.

'This is big,' he said after a long silence.

He was unusually anguished. I dared not do anything as frivolous as ask him a question.

'Someone came to see me last night. At my house.'

'Right.' My heart began to beat a little faster.

'They know everything. They know exactly what we're doing. They know about Janet and Robert and Plunkett — the lot. And they want to help.'

'Help?'

'Yes,' Ben confirmed glumly, accelerating past a slow lorry as we headed up Botha's Hill. 'They know we need cash. He said he'd give us what we need. It doesn't matter how much.'

'Oh, well, that can't be a bad thing.'

'Come off it, Teddy. You're smarter than that.'

'Yes. I suppose I am.' The car reached the top of the slope and was now hurtling down the other side. I couldn't be sure that Ben was properly in control. 'Do you know anything more about him?'

'He's Canadian.'

'Well, that's a relief. I mean, you know, he's not Russian or North Korean or, you know … Italian.'

'Italian?'

'Well, you know, someone who … doesn't speak English.'

Ben laughed. 'We need the money,' he said grimly.

'I'll leave that to you, Ben. I'd prefer to be none the wiser. It's your trust account. Your cock on the block. Not mine.'

'That's not what I was expecting of you,' he said, more glumly than ever.

I felt a little ashamed. No, it ought not to be what he expected.

'I'm expecting your wise counsel.'

It took me some time, looking out of the window at the passing trucks and cars with vague disinterest to formulate something that might pass for 'wise counsel'. 'What does the Canadian want?'

'Justice. Apparently.'

That was hard to believe. It was always hard to believe.

'Well, look,' I said at last. 'Think of Janet. Think of her story. Think of her … you know … *situation*. It couldn't be right. We should do what we can, you know, without screwing anyone. Isn't that the point of all this?'

Was it the point of all this? I wasn't sure.

Ben smiled and headed for an off-ramp that would lead us back to Durban.

'That's the funny thing about you, Teddy. You're not really that concerned about the law. You're more concerned about,' he paused thoughtfully, 'the clients, their stories.'

I suddenly felt myself sweating.

Our snag, the first of many, appeared to have been overcome. Ben and I never discussed the mystery Canadian again and, in the ensuing weeks, we received more evidence as to the nature and scope of the Smollen family empire. There was the real estate: the house in Mayfair, a vineyard in Spain, condos in Hong Kong, and a tea estate in Sri Lanka. But most notable (and most valuable) were his stocks in the 'extractive resources' sector. These were held by dozens of companies registered in Panama and the Turks and Caicos Islands. They all had unusual names that revealed little about what they did: Matlan Ventures, Tiblin Investments, Vinford International. These obscure entities were tiny, almost inconsequential shareholders in very large joint ventures that owned mining and energy concessions in Africa's most conflict-ridden countries. Governments, some of the world's most notoriously corrupt, were the joint venture partners.

And yes, I did do a bit of googling. There they were – James Plunkett and Randolph Smollen! Smiling in a restaurant in New York, standing among a group of Chinese dignitaries on a rig, sitting in the office of an African dictator and, yes, at Royal Ascot, just as Janet had said. I did not, I'm pleased to report, find any pictures of them involved in an orgy on a yacht.

With the assistance of outrageously expensive counsel in Hong Kong, we served a summons on Mr Robert Smollen while he was drinking champagne in a VIP suite at the Happy Valley Racecourse, ordering him to appear at a court hearing in South Africa. Robert promptly responded by divorcing his third wife – a voluptuous twenty-something Argentinian beauty by all accounts – awarding her a generous divorce settlement. That old con! So we brought a further application, joining the mysterious Argentinian as a co-defendant in the suit, alleging that the divorce was little more than an amateurish attempt to conceal the contested assets.

Nearly four years had now passed.

I am still addled by the appalling complexity of it all. Why is the pursuit of justice such an exhausting affair? What has it done to us? What does it *say* about us?

But still, it should be noted that Janet's confidence in the justice system had positively ballooned. Why would it *not* have? Ben and I were adept at pointing out what stellar progress we'd made.

'We'll be setting the matter down for a hearing soon. Probably for June or July,' I told Janet with much in the way self-congratulatory satisfaction.

Robert Smollen had hired an army of attorneys and great brassy Senior Counsel to defend him. They were all boys from Johannesburg. Many of them wore silk braces. Most of them were overweight, and, as I once pointed out to Ben as we drank heavily in a bar, none of them would know a thing about how to suck a cock. 'They wouldn't know where to start.' I'd said this with great pride and Ben Williamson had laughed so hard, he'd slipped off his chair, tears running down his face. It was his funniest moment in years.

The defence team was headed by a man called Fanie Boshoff SC. I had never met Fanie, but people liked to describe him (and Fanie had no objection) as an 'eminent jurist'. No one had ever called *me* that. Perhaps one day, I mused. Perhaps if we win the Smollen case.

As the trial approached, the two legal teams exchanged an increasing volume of documents. Among the documents received from Fanie's team were various references to Janet Smollen's mind, more specifically, suggestions that she might have lost it. There were letters and statements and even old medical records that alluded to paranoia, hyper-anxiety, delusions, personality disintegration, and other psychotic conditions. One letter even revealed that Janet had received psychiatric treatment at Townhill – the architecturally splendid yet notoriously creepy mental hospital in Pietermaritzburg.

'Townhill?' I said to Ben over lunch. 'Why didn't you tell me she'd been to Townhill?'

'It was as an *outpatient*!' Ben fumed as he picked his way through a salad that he had no interest in eating. 'She was seeing a psychiatrist and he happened to have his rooms there. What was she supposed to do? Not go because she didn't like the address?'

'And what about all these records that speak of delusions and paranoia?'

Ben pushed his salad aside and looked at me grimly. 'Teddy, she's fine. Absolutely fine. I've known her for a long time and she's fine. Strong as an ox.' He called for the waitress and ordered a T-bone steak with pepper sauce.

I wasn't convinced. If she was somehow incapacitated, Fanie Boshoff might well be tempted to file a special plea, claiming Janet Smollen to be insane and legally incapable of litigating the suit. That would be the end of us. We'd have no plaintiff. No client. No case.

'I think we need to talk to the Mouse. Get our hands on a second plaintiff, just in case. That is, of course, assuming she hasn't flirted with psychiatric intervention as much as her daughter.'

Ben grunted dismissively. 'That'll never work,' he said. He seemed too hungry to discuss the matter any further.

At our next consultation with Janet, I mentioned with much in the way of tentative delicacy that it might be a good idea if we had a little chat with her mother.

'The Mouse?' She reddened right through to the tips of her translucent earlobes. 'She'll never do it.'

42

'Just a chat,' I countered. 'See where things stand. No pressure.'

'She doesn't want to have anything to do with Robert. Or my father. Or the money. Nothing.'

'Well, I wouldn't try to change that, but I'd like to meet her nonetheless. I mean, just a cup of tea. You know, and then she can continue on her way.'

Janet began to chew on her inner cheek. 'Hmm, I'm not sure. I mean no. Never. Don't ask me again.'

Five

The first of the letters came from Darshini Poonam in India.

It was three weeks since Val had died and I had not given her much thought. The purple satin Chinese-made box that contained her ashes was still sitting on a shelf in the entrance hall of my apartment. Val's box of letters remained unopened next to my collection of black leather shoes in my wardrobe.

> *Dear Mr Teddy Dickerson,*
>
> *I am writing to you to enquire about the health and good fortune of Mrs Valerie Dickerson. I am informed by Mrs Dickerson that she is your aunt. Mrs Valerie Dickerson also informed me by recent mail correspondence that she had been feeling unwell and at her urging I hereby contact you to enquire of her well-being.*
>
> *Mrs Valerie is my closest friend in the world. Please help me Mr Teddy. With felicitations and my warmest regards,*
> *Darshini Poonam (Mrs)*

My first reaction – I have to admit, even if it is slightly shameful – was that I really did not have time to deal with Darshini Poonam (Mrs). This was something I would have to get to … *later*. I was famously busy.

I put the letter down and then I picked it up again. I re-read it. For some unfathomable reason, I found myself pushing aside the psychiatric reports, the medical reports, the pharmacology reports, the scathing witness statements that implicated Janet Smollen. I pulled out a sheaf of paper from the printer and wrote to Darshini.

> Dear Mrs Poonam,
> Thank you for your letter which I received today.
> I am very sorry to inform you that my aunt Valerie passed away on 2 February 2015. I am informed by the medical staff who attended to her that she was not in pain and was well taken care of. It appears that she had endured some cardiac complications which contributed to her most unfortunate demise.
> I am very grateful to receive your letter and your good wishes. Val was a ...

Val was a what? I couldn't think. I considered crumpling up the note and starting again. I'd never given a tribute to Val, not even at the funeral. There was no eulogy. Now I had barrelled into this sentence and couldn't finish it. Then it came to me.

> Val was a special person to many of us and we will all miss her.
> With my kindest regards,
> Teddy Dickerson
> Chambers
> Durban

I sealed the letter, walked to the post office, and sent it on its way to Pandesh-wara. As I walked back to chambers, I wondered what might have prompted me to say that Val wasn't in any pain when she died. How did I know that? I didn't. I had made it up. She might have been in agony. But then I thought of Darshini and I was sure that I had done the right thing.

Two more letters arrived the following day. 'Bloody hell!' I was heard to expostulate.

> Dear Mr Dickerson,
> I have just received the most alarming letter from Val, your aunt. I am at a total loss as to what to do. Val and I have been writing to each other for more than twenty years and now she informs me that she is not well and,

to quote her, she 'might not be around for long'! Can you imagine it?
She gave me your address. Please write to me and tell me how she is.
Please do so immediately. Val mentioned you in quite a few of her letters
and I have every reason to believe that you are a gentleman and will at-
tend to my request with promptness.
Yours,
Wilma Straughan
Vancouver
P.S. I am sorry if I sound a bit pushy, but I'm overwhelmed by concern.
I'm sure you're very nice. Thank you.

A bit pushy? Well, possibly, but then she did assert that I might be very nice. I concurred fully and so was prompted to reply (immediately).

Dear Wilma,
Thank you for your letter which I received today.
    I am very sorry to inform you that Val died on 2 February 2015. She
had succumbed to some unfortunate cardiac complications while in hospital
being treated for stomach pains. I am pleased to report that Val was in the
best possible medical hands and was in no pain or discomfort at the time.
Sadly, nothing more could be done.
    It's all come as a bit of a surprise, as Val had always been in rather
good health.
    I note from your letter that you and Val had corresponded for a long
time. Allow me to express my deepest sympathy to you for the loss of a
friend.
With my best wishes,
Teddy Dickerson
Chambers
Durban

I was quite wrong to have said that Val had always been in 'rather good health'. She hadn't been. Val was seventy-nine. And for each of those seventy-nine years (I have it on good authority), she managed to complain about an atrocious malady of some sort or another.

The second letter of that day:

Dear Mr Dickerson,

I was very saddened to receive a most distressing letter from your aunt, Valerie, last Monday. I have been very slow to reply as I've been in a rather terrible state of shock. Your aunt and I have corresponded since the 1970s and now she has informed me that she is unwell and on the brink of death. You can only imagine my shock. She instructed me to direct all further enquiries to your good self.

I would be very grateful if you could inform me of her present condition and to convey to her my most heartfelt wishes for her speedy recovery.

In the years that we have corresponded, I have lost a husband, my eyesight, quite a few dogs and am soon to lose a leg. Valerie's letters have been an eternal source of comfort and inspiration to me over these difficult years. I always recall, with a sense of dreadful remorse, how I had at first resisted her companionship and still it is with an abiding relief that she persisted with her letters and that we became such wonderful friends. I have often thought of this to be something of a miracle.

You're probably an intelligent man and can probably see what I mean, even if I can't. (That last sentence was intended to be a joke, of course. I'm blind, you see. This letter is being dictated to one of the staff — a very kind soul called Thembi.)

I won't detain you for another minute. Valerie mentioned you are a lawyer and so I suppose you must be very busy, running about and catching all the criminals or setting them free or whatever it is that you lawyers actually do.

I await to hear from you.
With my best wishes,
Glynnis Warburton
Orange Grove, Johannesburg

Glynnis Warburton's letter did offer me an idea. I might dictate a pro forma response, have it typed by Thandi, my secretary, and simply sign it along with all my other correspondence as soon as the remaining letters came in (and, by now, I had no doubt that they would). But Darshini and Wilma had both received personal, handwritten replies, and I couldn't bring myself not to do the same for Glynnis.

> *Dear Mrs Warburton,*
> *Thank you for your letter which arrived today.*
> *I am sorry to inform you that my aunt Valerie passed away on 2 February 2015. She succumbed to cardiac failure after a considerable period of ill health.*
> *Allow me to convey my condolences to you for your loss. It is evident from your letter that you were very fond of Val and I am most certain that Val was very fond of you. Loss is never an easy thing to overcome. Val had taught me many years ago (when teaching me the game of chess) that one plays to win, but, more importantly, one must learn to lose. Or one ought to, I suppose.*
> *As to your question about what lawyers actually do, I am pleased to say that we ensnare criminals and set them free in roughly equal measure. That is what lawyers do and I suppose it explains why we're such a jolly bunch.*
> *Good luck with the loss of your leg. I was going to propose that amid all your grief, you might want to put your best foot forward, but now I see that would be an impractical recommendation.*
> *With my very best wishes to you and my thanks to Thembi,*
> *Teddy Dickerson*
> *Chambers*
> *Durban*

I won't deny it. I was pleased (utterly thrilled – not to put too fine a point on it) when the next two days passed without a further letter from any of Val's friends.

Instead, I sustained a weekend of tireless boredom which involved my couch, some beers and chips, and a passing interest in a televised test match. I also spent quite a bit of time wondering why I had told Glynnis that Val had taught me that one 'plays to win, but, more importantly, one must learn to lose'. She hadn't taught me that; Aubrey had taught me that. Aubrey had taught me how to play chess, not Val.

On Monday, there were three more.

> Hi Teddy,
> Your aunt Val wrote to me and told me that she wasn't well and was heading to hospital. She said I should send a letter to you because she might not be picking up her post.
> I know you don't know me, but I am interested in one way or another to know how she is. I never actually met her, but I guess I'd like to know how the old busybody's doing.
> Email me if you want. It's much easier! She was such a fuddy-duddy with her snail-mail. My email address is tiffany.medford@zinbank.com.au. Thanks.
> Tiffany (Medford)
> Melbourne

I instinctively took a dislike to people who used words like 'busybody', 'fuddy-duddy' and 'snail-mail'.

> Dear Tiffany,
> Thank you for your letter. It just arrived this morning. Sadly, poor Val passed away last week. Monday. I was told to expect your letter.
> So, now you know.

I wanted to end there, but it seemed a bit too brief – terse even. Even if Tiffany didn't like Val, I felt compelled to say more.

> She often used to say that it's not the death of another that shocks us, but the fact they we're still alive. I think there's quite a bit of truth in that. I suppose, in some strange sort of way, we would do well with an occasional reminder of our vulnerability.
> Wishing you all the best,
> Teddy Dickerson
> Chambers
> Durban

And from Egypt:

Dear Mr Teddy,

I cry and I write. How is the lovely Valerie? Is she great? When I was receiving her letter, the tears just fall from my eyes. I cry a lot about the news of her sickness. She wrote to me all the time for many years. I love to get her many letters. It is the most special thing I had. Please write to me a letter and tell me about the lovely Valerie. I miss her all the time.

She is better?

Good wishes to you and all of your family. Valerie said many things about Mr Teddy. How is your wife and your daughters and son? Six children! You are a very lucky man.

And with love, I say,

Goodbye

Mrs Nawal Hassan

Alexandria, Egypt

My wife and six children? Still, she was at least right about my being a very great man.

Dear Mrs Hassan,

Thank you for your letter which arrived in the post this morning. I am sorry to inform you that Aunt Valerie passed away peacefully on 2 February 2015.

I wish I had words that could help to dry your tears. Perhaps there are no words that can do that, only time. Val's departure is a terrible loss to so many (more than I had realised). I am pleased that you enjoyed receiving Val's letters. I am sure she would have been very happy to know that.

As they say, suffering is the source of all wisdom and if we are to get to the end of our stories with even the slightest modicum of grace, then we'll need all the wisdom we can get.

Thank you for asking after my wife and six children. I am quite sure they are all perfectly well.

With my best wishes,

Teddy Dickerson

Chambers

Durban

As *they* say? As *who* says? I was being highly inventive. As I sealed Mrs Hassan's letter something new struck me about Val's death. She knew very well that she was dying. I don't know *how* she knew. She had never trusted doctors. Still, despite all that, she did manage our last meeting with her usual propriety – knowing what she knew. Was that grace?

> Dear Mr Dickerson,
> I am a friend of your aunt Valerie, and received a letter from her last week
> telling me she was ill. She told me to write to you for further information,
> as she expected that she wouldn't be able to collect her post.
> Please tell me how she is. Thank you.
> Valerie told me that you are a lawyer and haven't been very happy.
> My husband used to be a lawyer. I know how it feels to be unhappy.
> With warm regards,
> Mrs Jennifer Steenkamp (née Millard)
> Highlands, Harare

She knows how it feels to be unhappy? Or to be an unhappy lawyer? Or to be married to an unhappy lawyer? And why the 'née Millard'?

> Dear Mrs Steenkamp,
> Thank you for your letter.
> Unfortunately, Valerie passed away on 2 February 2015 as a result
> of heart trouble. She had told me that I might expect to receive a letter
> from you.
> I am glad that you counted Valerie as a friend. She had many friends
> in many parts of the world and I know she will be sorely missed.

I thought I might slip in the comment about playing to win and learning to lose. Or, 'it's not the death of another that shocks us …' etc. But no, neither of those would do for Mrs Steenkamp (née Millard).

> Loss is painful and yet an essential part of our experience. I suppose we
> reach a phase in life where we are compelled to bear it with whatever
> dignity we might be able to salvage from our tortuously misguided youth.
> It becomes something of a truism that happiness is scarcely the point.

When I think of the last time that I saw Valerie, the day before she died, I am convinced she understood this perfectly well and honoured the wisdom of her years with courage.

With my best regards,

Teddy Dickerson

Chambers

Durban

Six

Returning from the post office, having dispatched missives to Mrs Medford, Mrs Hassan, and Mrs Steenkamp, feeling good about myself, I took long assertive strides through the lobby of my building and reached into my pocket for the key to my room.

'Er, Mr Dickerson.'

I turned. Thandi sat at her desk and offered me a slightly nervous glance as if something terrible were happening and I was blithely unaware of it. She nodded towards the row of seats in the lobby. 'Someone's here to see you.'

So there was. I hadn't noticed. I'd walked right past her. A small aging woman with a grey shawl over her shoulders sat on one of the pinkish armchairs, her feet not even touching the ground. She looked at me with narrow searching eyes. Her arms were folded across her chest and her mouth was clamped shut in an expression of obstinate silence. Yet there was also something explosive about my small visitor, as if the obstinate silence wasn't about to last very long.

'Ah! I see,' I said, swaying on the balls of my feet. 'How nice. May I help you?'

The woman took a furtive glance at Thandi and Thandi gave me a resigned shrug (and the very slightest roll of the eyeballs).

'I'd like to have a word,' the woman said. 'In private.'

I wasn't inclined to invite strangers into my room.

'Well, might I ask who you are?'

The woman frowned and looked at her scuffed brown shoes, her lips once again pursed shut. No. She wouldn't say another word.

I turned and unlocked the door. 'Please come in,' I said with deliberate resentment.

With the door shut and taking my place behind my desk, I saw the woman survey my room with evident distaste.

Looking at me, her formidable obstinacy had now given way to a more plaintive, pleading expression.

'I'm Jill Smollen. Janet's mother.'

I was enormously pleased. *This is who we need. This is exactly who we need*, I was thinking. I wanted to smile, but she wore such a grim expression, I felt compelled to do the same.

'Right. I see.'

'You need to stop this,' she said at once. 'I don't expect to have a long discussion with you, but you need to stop this. Today.'

'Stop the trial?'

'Of course.'

'Mrs Smollen, I'm afraid I really cannot discuss the trial with you at all. You know, as lawyers, we have all kind of rules—'

She cut me short. 'I know about all your rules, Mr Dickerson. I've been surrounded by lawyers all my life. I know more about your rules than you do.'

I gave her a slightly caustic laugh. 'Well, that's highly improbable!' I scoffed.

'But not impossible. I know Boshoff and that crowd from Johannesburg. I know them all. They were Randolph's. And now they're Robert's. We can't have anything more to do with this. You don't know anything, Mr Dickerson. You don't know anything at all. That's the only reason why you've got as far as you have.'

What an impertinent woman!

Still, with flawless indifference, I said: 'I'm terribly sorry, Mrs Smollen, I really cannot discuss this.' I stood and added: 'I'm afraid you'll have to leave. I'd very much like to speak with you, but only on the instructions of Janet's attorney.'

She crossed her arms defiantly, as if inviting me to physically carry her out of the room.

I continued: 'I can talk to you as a potential witness or as a potential plaintiff, but only if Mr Williamson is present. Otherwise, I cannot talk to you about the case at all. I'm very sorry.'

'Sit down,' she replied calmly (it was exactly the kind of thing Val might have said and exactly in the way that Val might have said it).

I sat.

'Forget about Mr Williamson. He's a cowboy. The only reason why I'm here is because you're new on the scene. I've never heard of you. Of course, I know Williamson. How do you think Janet thought to instruct him? Members of the Smollen family have had more to do with lawyers than we have with one another. It's almost as if the moment one is born and christened a Smollen, you're assigned your very own personal legal counsel to guide you through the rest of your life. Other newborns get little silver mugs or teaspoons. We dish out lawyers. It's abhorrent. It's an abhorrent family.'

'I see,' I said, readying myself for something further to say, but I had nothing. I leaned back in my soft leather swivel chair and let her speak.

'I'm here as Janet's mother. I'm here to protect her – in *her best interests*, to use a lawyerly phrase. And that must count for something – even to you. Janet is …' She paused and looked at the ceiling in search of an answer. 'She's always been a bit … wobbly. Her father had no time for her. Her brother was taught to do precisely the same. They hated me. They hated us with venom, Mr Dickerson. Venom. And what could we do? We had the rest of society to contend with. So, what could we do, but keep smiling?'

This wasn't consistent with what Janet had told me. She'd told me about happy Christmases, holidays in Switzerland, her father frolicking with her and her brother and a colourful blow-up ball in the pool. She'd said nothing of any venom.

'We don't need the money, Mr Dickerson. I have a brother in England, not a rich man, but he sends us a little money every few months. I work at an antique shop twice a week …'

'You work, but you … you're—'

'Only seventy-one, Mr Dickerson. Perfectly capable. And Janet, when she's stable on her medication, manages to work at the horse-riding school in Howick.'

'Horse-riding?'

'Yes.'

'Oh. I see. She never told me.'

'Yes. They have a programme there for street kids. They teach them how to love and take care of horses.'

'Street kids? Horses?'

'Yes. She earns a little money from it too, which is helpful.'

Janet had never struck me as the kind of person who took much of an interest in street kids.

I returned to the case. 'Well, look, Mrs Smollen, the point is that I've already explained—'

'It doesn't matter what you've explained, Mr Dickerson. Your explanations don't count. Janet is easily addled, scared half to death in case she wouldn't understand something in *exactly* the way her father wanted. Your explanations have done nothing but confuse her. It's exactly what Randolph did. He tormented her. She was weak, asthmatic, diabetic and, worse still, a *girl*!'

'Are you suggesting, Mrs Smollen, that there was no fraud? If Randolph hated her *and you* as much as you say he did, then might he have deliberately excluded you from the will?'

'I have no idea. When Randolph was dying, he spent lot of time with Robert. Who knows what kind of vindictive, deranged plot they might have come up with? They might have wanted it to *look* like a forgery, test our mettle, see if we had the great big manly balls to take them on!' She held firmly onto the sides of the armchair, now visibly cross.

'Well, do you? I mean, not balls, per se, but do you have the ... you know ... the ...'

'*Guts*, Mr Dickerson. That'll be the term you're looking for. And Janet and I have the guts to stay put. To accept. *That* takes guts. In Randolph's last days, they were inserting tubes into him, into every orifice, mollifying him, soothing him with their syrupy anaesthetics, easing his pain. Nurses fluttered around him like butterflies. It was pathetic. He cried out for yet another operation and another and another. More life! That's all he wanted. More bloody life! Fool!'

'Well, in a way ... I mean, in a *certain* sort of way, that's hardly unusual.'

'It might not be unusual, but it's still pathetic. These kinds of people, Mr Dickerson, they are literally eaten alive by fear. Fear of each other. Fear of themselves. Fear of the future. They couldn't even face a sunrise without being scared to death. They're like cavemen. They grunt around their cave, walloping everyone with a stick, telling them not to go outside because there's a big ball of flame in the sky. They're afraid of the future. They insist on a static world. It's always been their job to stop the future, to ease us into it slowly, meticulously ironing out its uncertainty. They're good old-fashioned *conservatives*, Mr Dickerson, and they'll tear Janet apart.'

Ah, there it was! A sudden quaver to her voice. Emotion. It was like the first note of a particularly chilling opera. And not very mouse-like at all.

She straightened her shoulders and gathered herself.

'And if you're not careful, Mr Dickerson, they'll tear you apart too. They're ruthless. Their fear is limitless. Cavemen.'

Mrs Smollen stood and drew her shawl more tightly around her shoulders. 'You seem like a nice enough chap, a lawyer, but still … nice. Stop this, Mr Dickerson. It couldn't be a more fruitless exercise.'

'Even if we win?'

'*Especially* if you win.'

With her hand on the doorknob, she turned to face me. 'Janet might be wobbly, but she's stubborn. And that's exactly when she gets hurt.'

Mrs Smollen left. She left my chambers and she left me shaken. If there was anything that frightened me about the Smollen case, it was the Mouse.

I rang Ben Williamson.

'Might we have another one of your drives?'

Ben arrived in his Mercedes.

'We went west last time,' I said to him. 'Let's head south and I mean that more than metaphorically.'

We took the N3 South, heading along the coast.

'We won't be getting the mother involved any time soon.'

'No?'

'She came to see me. Not as a witness or as a party, but as … a mother.'

'Ah!' Ben suddenly wanted to smoke. He fumbled around in his jacket pocket for his cigarettes. I looked at him with undisguised indignation. With a sour grunt, he took hold of the steering wheel with both hands, resenting me. 'An inscrutable woman,' he declared.

'She suggested that if there *was* a forgery, it was left there for us to discover it. A taunt. A trap.'

'Oh, that's Jill. Everything's a trap.'

'Well? Is it?'

'Hardly!' Ben laughed gruffly. 'The estate is nearly a billion dollars. You wouldn't put that at risk just to taunt someone. That's ludicrous!' He started to fumble in his pocket once again.

'Oh, for God's sake, go ahead and smoke. Just open the window.'

'Thanks,' he said with relief.

'We'll have to tell Janet,' I continued, slightly enjoying the smell of the cigarette.

'She knows already,' Ben said, exhaling a huge purplish plume from his yellowing beard. 'She rang me this morning and told me. She knew exactly what her mother was going to say.'

'Well, bloody hell, you might have warned me.'

'I did. I mean, I tried. I rang, but that secretary of yours—'

'Thandi.'

'Yes, Thandi. She said you were already in consultation. I left a message.'

'Right.'

Amanzimtoti was sliding past the window. Its holiday blocks faced the sea with defiant angularity, slowly eaten alive by the corrosive winds of the ocean while stuffed with delusional, inexplicably jubilant holidaymakers.

'Have you ever wondered if the freeway is moving beneath us or if we are moving on the freeway?'

Ben looked at me with slightly condescending curiosity. 'No,' he said plainly. 'No, I haven't.'

We were silent for a while.

'So what do we do?' I asked.

'Let's go to a bar!' Ben offered with a laugh.

'No, I mean what do we do about the *trial*?'

Ben paused, finished his cigarette, flicked it out of the window, and said: 'Let's go to a bar.'

We took the off-ramp to Amanzimtoti and drank beer until the sun went down. It seemed, at the time, as good a solution as any. But it didn't seem like that the following morning. Pain swelled in my head, bruising the back of my eyeballs. I sat limply in my swivel chair, looking at the window. The blinds were drawn. It was the most palatable view I could think of.

I left my room and found Thandi engrossed by the screen in front of her, while her fingernails clicked dramatically over her keyboard.

'Could you ask Stags to deliver their fattiest, cheesiest, most bacony, most heart-stopping, most disgusting burger on the menu, with a side of the greasiest possible fries and a large Coke?'

Thandi did not respond. She smiled at me doubtfully as if I had no idea what I wanted. There was some kind of appalling truth hidden in her smile. It made me look away from her.

'Use your discretion,' I said. 'Just make sure it has nothing to do with fish.'

'Fine,' she said.

I returned to my room, lay back against my chair and mused aloud: 'I love Thandi. I love her. I'd marry her if I could.'

Stags did their finest. I began to gobble the burger with almost fetishistic excitement. And halfway through, I began to feel sick. I let the half-eaten burger drop onto the grease paper, took a sip of Coke, and rested once more against the back of my chair. I suddenly felt like I wanted to cry.

Turning away from the food on my desk, I thought of the new owners of Estantia. Ray and Marsha Henderson. Day after day, organising their lives, this way and that. I thought of the Smollens, the abominable family. All these people, they had their secrets, their obligations, their guilt and their dreams of freedom – dreams that angered them like nothing else. It was as if freedom was just another word for *risk*. We have an insatiable need to be liked, matched by an endless doubt that we're not worthy of it. So we act. We imprison ourselves behind an identity we can scarcely recognise. 'We still had society to contend with' – so said Jill Smollen.

And still there, that half-eaten bludgeoned burger, made by some hopeful teenager wearing a paper hat crushed into a mortified frown, implored me to find some kind of meaning – for me and for it.

'Sorry,' I said, as I tossed it into the waste bin.

I left early and bumped into Sidney Ngwenya in the lift. He had his court gown flung over his arm, was on his way to court. A hard worker. A brilliant man.

'Good weekend?'

'All right. Watched the test match.'

'Ah! You guys and your cricket!'

'What's wrong with cricket?'

'It's nuts. It's the only game that is designed to be played over five consecutive days in the sunshine. One wonders how England, where five days of consecutive sunshine is a rare, almost life-threatening event, would have invented such a game.'

I laughed. 'Well, that's true. But we have plenty of sunshine down here, so it suits us more than most.'

'Hmph!'

Sidney was always talking about us, as in 'the English'. And he was not trying to flatter 'us'. He was the son of farm labourers from Empangeni in Zululand. He'd attended one of those notoriously underfunded schools, those miserly offerings of the apartheid state. And now, here he was, one the most respected jurists in our group.

Once I'd asked him why he'd chosen to become a lawyer and he'd replied without hesitation: 'Money, power and status – in that order!'

There was often an admirable breeziness to the way Sidney spoke, as if he was always concealing a deeper, more troubling irony. He made me feel like an expat here, in Africa, on just a short-term contract.

Seven

Janet Smollen sat in her usual chair. Ben Williamson sat in his. It was strange how they did that. Sat in their usual chairs. There was no rule. They could have swapped chairs. They could have alternated from meeting to meeting. But they didn't. Without even the slightest hesitation, the slightest utterance, they took their usual chairs.

'Now, Janet, look,' I said. 'Your mother is worried about you. And that's not a bad thing ...'

Janet looked urgently at Ben, seeking his reassurance. He gave her a subtle nod, permitting her to intervene. 'Mr Dickerson, I want you to know that my mother has nothing to do with this case. It's my case, not hers. I've been cheated. Robert has cheated me and that's not right. It's against the rules.'

She looked again at Ben. Instead of giving her his approval, he looked at me and shrugged.

'Fine. I understand, Janet. Really, I do. But the point is this: you're about to face a room full of people wearing black robes who'll be pointing their fingers at you, accusing you of madness, delirium. What you need to decide – and forget about what your mother thinks – is whether you can stand it.'

Janet looked again at Ben, imploring him to offer some kind of consolation.

Ben looked out of the window and then at his shoes. 'He's right, Janet,' he said eventually. 'You'll need to be prepared. You're bright enough. You know I have faith in you. And I know Teddy does too. We both do. What Teddy is asking is if you have faith in yourself. It'll be tough out there. But you can do it.

What Robert did to you is unforgivable. You need to fight back, Janet. This is your chance.'

A long silence followed. Janet looked at her feet. She shifted one foot forward across the carpet and then withdrew it, now shifting the other foot. She alternated these shifting movements for some time and, yes, they did appear to have a slightly deranged kind of rhythm.

And I wasn't entirely sure if I understood either of them. Ben had spoken of faith. Janet had spoken of rules. Faith in oneself? Or faith in the rules? These were two very different things.

Eventually, Janet looked up at me. 'I'm doing this. I won't let Robert get away with it. Never!'

She ran out of the room.

Ben and I looked at each other. I was hoping he would fire me. He was, no doubt, wondering whether he might.

'She'll be fine,' he said finally. 'We'll see you next week. Do a bit of coaching. She's tougher than she looks.'

Eight

It had been several weeks since Val had died and I'd not yet heard from all of her correspondents. I was surprised at how much this troubled me.

My growing disquiet was somewhat assuaged when I received a letter from Candice on a bright Monday morning:

Hey Teddy!

I bet I'm too late! Is she dead already? I bet she's dead. Mercury's in retrograde.

Okay, if she's not dead, then you better tell her to get well soon. Look here, I'm a nurse. I've been a nurse for a long time, like five centuries. I've seen people dying. It ain't the prettiest thing in the world, most of the time. But sometimes there are folks who just seem to know how to do it. You know, they die well. I like that. I think we should all learn how to die well. Heck, you probably have no idea what I mean.

Now look, I loved your aunt. Val was one of the most beautiful human beings ever to have walked on this petty little planet. She told me a lot about you, about how you're gay and all sad about it. Heck, I like gays. They're the best! The straight ones are a huge fucking bore! Let me tell you. They're a fucking bore. But the gays I like. You're not always leering at women – even if you like leering at each other, but that's your business. Anyhow, the point is that we all need to learn how to die well. To die and to do it well.

It's amazing how few people get this. Here I am in Phnom goddamn Penh, saving the fucking world! You wouldn't believe how exhausting that is. This place is full of people trying to save things. Save the children. Save the animals. Save the trees. Save the planet. Save the women. Save the unmarried mother. Saving the fucking freshwater dolphin! You know what they're saving us all from? From us! Each other! No one gets this. No one ever gets this. There's irony in everything, Teddy. Everything. Just as the planets are both repelled and seduced by one another, there is irony in everything. Val got that. Oh, I really, really loved Val. I still love her, even if she's dead.

It's so weird to think that Val and I never spoke. Not once. We never met. We just wrote each other. Letters, that was all. You want to know how that got started? A couple of years ago your aunt was in California, visiting that son of hers — the one who's friends with Bill Gates. Woohoo! Bill Gates! So they went up to Sonoma County and did a wine tour. My son, bless him, he's thirty-five now. I can hardly believe that. He's thirty-five with a girlfriend and a daughter — my granddaughter! Anyhow, I digress. My son used to do those wine tours. He and Val must have hit it off. Next thing you know, he's telling her all about me — his mom, living in Phnom goddamn Penh. Val said that she'd like to write me, so she did and now we've been writing each other for — oh I don't know — seven years?

You ever been to California? It's beautiful. So beautiful and not a lot of people get that. You should try it one day. There are a lot of gays there, so you'll like it. You can stay with my son, if you want. He's no longer doing the wine thing. Now he's into craft beer! Oh God! What a kid! My granddaughter's name is Gracie.

Come and visit me in Phnom Penh sometime. Come stay! This town is full of assholes. It'd be nice to have someone new to talk to.

Heck, I got to go. Look here, if Val is still around, give her a hug for me, won't you? And if not, go say a prayer. Pray for her spirit. Her beautiful spirit. You've got a beautiful spirit too, Teddy. I can tell.

Okay, now I got to go. Take care over there in Africa.

Love ya!
Candice
Phnom goddamn Penh, Cambodia

Val bristled when people used bad language. How was it possible that she might have corresponded with a person who spoke of the 'fucking freshwater dolphin'?

And why did Val say I was all sad about being gay? *She* might have been sad about it, seen it as a problem that needed a solution. I saw it as perhaps the singularly most thrilling part of myself.

Faith in oneself? Or faith in the rules? Or perhaps it's a very different question. Perhaps it's faith in oneself or faith in *them*? In everyone else? In the *object* of the rules? As a solitary creature, my most titillating fantasies might have been the most pleasing thing about life. As a creature that is nothing but an inseparable part of some larger organism, my most titillating fantasies might have been an aberration, something deserving of a cure – so which am I?

Hi Candice,

I'm afraid you're right. Val died on 2 February 2015 – a day after I posted her final letter to you. I have no idea if it had anything to do with Mercury being in retrograde.

Thanks for your letter. I was pleased to learn how you and Val became acquainted and enjoyed writing to each other. I know Val made a number of trips to California. She never mentioned any wine tours, or meeting your son or indeed, she never mentioned you or, for that matter, Phnom goddamn Penh.

I can't be sure, but I suspect that Val did die well. She left me a letter and wrote that she knew she was dying, but she never said much more about it. Even with just a few hours to go.

No, I've never been to California, even if there are a lot of gays there (I can't say that's a particularly seductive proposition). And thanks for inviting me to visit you in Phnom Penh, even if there are a lot of assholes there (again, not such a seductive proposition).

I liked your comment about irony, the planets being seduced and repelled by one another. That's exactly how it feels. When people tell me that they don't care what others think, I immediately suspect that the opposite is true. Maybe we all carry that tension inside us – how much do we indulge the self, its dreamlike spaces, its inner fantasies and how much do we indulge them, their propriety, their morality and their creed? Selfishness or selflessness? I'm not sure anyone ever gets that right.

Anyhow thanks for your letter. I've got the feeling I'll be re-reading it for some time to come.

Take care of yourself, Candice, and your son and Gracie too (if not the rest of the planet).
With love,
Teddy Dickerson
Durban

Terry Winstanley rang.

'Teddy, my good fellow!'

I had no idea why Terry spoke to people in this way, with his tireless good cheer.

'Terry.'

'Just a couple of matters relating to the estate.'

'Right.'

'Well, you know, as the executor, I just need to make sure that I cross all the "i"s and dot all the "t"s, as they say.'

I immediately knew what this was. Terry was appalled by the meagre size of Val's estate. He'd presumed, since the heady days of garden parties at Estantia, that Val discreetly presided over a ton of money. But his presumption was ill-founded. He was incensed. His three per cent cut, after all that fawning and all those generous compliments, wasn't worth more than a big night out.

'I mean, you know, she didn't have much in the way of family,' he continued, 'and you were sort of probably the closest person to her. And we've been through the accounts. All looking good, I might add. All perfectly straightforward, so no complications. A few creditors. The pharmacy. The doctors, that sort of thing, but I just wanted to, you know, double-check the old asset column, if I may.'

'Val wasn't rich, Terry,' I said. I felt my hand quivering slightly as I pressed the phone to my ear. 'She was pinching through her last few pennies. They might have been rich once, back in the eighties, but, you know, that's a long time ago.'

'I see,' Terry said hesitantly (mortified!). I could hear him breathing audibly over the phone. He might even have been sobbing. 'But ...' he persisted. 'But Estantia! I mean, she must have sold that for a tidy sum. Suitably invested ... I mean, what on earth could she have spent it on?' He was clearly irritated. 'I mean, I'm sorry, I'm just, you know, making sure ...'

'I have no idea, Terry. But keep looking. There might well be hidden treasure somewhere. It's not something I know much about.'

I *could* have been more helpful. I certainly did not know much about Valerie's financial affairs. Money was something she seldom talked about. She regarded any discussion of money with evident distaste. But over the years she had revealed, distinctively sotto voce, certain facts that suggested all was not as it seemed.

'Aubrey was always worried that people thought him stupid,' she once said. 'And perhaps he wasn't very bright. Never matriculated from high school. Certainly never went anywhere near a university. I'm quite sure he had no idea what universities were really for. He bought Estantia with his inheritance. Spent his days driving around in a truck, looking at the sugar cane grow. Whenever he was with other men and they talked about politics or finance or business, he felt demeaned, tended to exaggerate his understanding of whatever it was they were talking about. On one of our trips to Johannesburg, he fell in with a Jewish man. A broker. Oh, he was a broker, all right. So much so that we landed up broke. The farm was mortgaged. Not a soul knows.'

Aubrey died a year later, broke and broken by a broker. It all added up. My father had tried to help, apparently. He had urged Valerie to hang on to the farm. It was still a profitable enterprise, even if the cane grew itself. He negotiated with creditors, even urged Valerie to convert her home into a bed and breakfast.

'Never!' Val had declared.

When my father died, Estantia was sold. At least there was enough left over for Val to retire at The Cedars (if she managed her affairs with caution and provided she didn't live to a ridiculously old age).

I could have told all this to Terry. But I didn't.

I thought about those years – the mid-eighties. I remembered Val driving around the farm in the farm truck, watching the cane grow. I remembered her sitting at the kitchen table calculating the labourers' wages, how they all stood in a long line at the back of the house, with their hats in their hands, waiting for their little brown envelopes. I remembered her talking about a water pump that had broken and how she had no idea how to fix it. Despite these travails, I also remembered her parties – her famous 'garden parties', as she liked to call them. Umbrellas on the front lawn. Tables bearing silver trays of delicacies – stuffed eggs and salmon mousse and tiny sandwiches. Everyone went. *Every-*

one! Val loved those days, even if they were all (myself included) a little bit scared of her. The British East India Company was alive and well in the gardens of Estantia, even if the rest of the country was about to be engulfed in flames (and Val survived on a diet of leftover stuffed eggs for a month).

They talked about England. 'Home' they used to call it. And Europe was 'The Continent', as if there were only one; as if they weren't already on a continent or they were on a continent that didn't count. It didn't matter that the people who said these things had lived in Africa for six generations. England was home. None of us knew what the hell we were doing in Africa. Yes, it might have had its charms, but if we cared to look closely enough, it awoke something in us that we weren't prepared to confront – some terrible thing … about ourselves.

Perhaps that is why people were still drawn to Val's garden parties. They took comfort from the big, white-headed scary lady who paid the labourers from her back door, like a defender of the faith.

My contemplation of Val's parties, and all the jingoistic, paper-thin bravado that went with them, brought me to the last of the eight letters I was expecting to receive. Caroline Beaufort's letter arrived on a Friday, at the end of another burnt-out week.

> *Dear Mr Dickerson,*
>
> *I hope my letter does not come to you as a surprise. Indeed, it might. I am a very long-standing friend of your aunt Valerie's. We've been corresponding for thirty years. I was terribly saddened to receive a letter from her recently in which she explained that she was unwell and was soon to be hospitalised. Valerie instructed me to send further correspondence care of yourself in case she is unable to collect her mail. Hence this letter.*
>
> *I know that she has suffered from cancer for many years and she has most certainly carried herself with great dignity and courage. And of course, at the impressive age of ninety-three one cannot forever offer the same old platitudes, imploring one to 'get well soon' and so on. At that age, one cannot but help suspect the worst. As I write this, I cannot be sure that poor Valerie is still with us. Of course, I pray that she is. Please do convey my very best wishes to her, affording her courage and fortitude and strength as she contemplates the ordeals before her.*
>
> *Valerie and I never met and I do regret that. In the eighties, when*

South Africa was all over the news and the revolutionaries were setting everything on fire, my husband and I decided to travel there. My husband is an ornithologist and was keen for a spot of bird-watching and, for my part, I wanted to meet Valerie and prevail upon her to return home at once. Of course, for us in England, we'd seen this kind of upset time and time again, what with the Mau Mau in Kenya and all the terrible things that happened in Congo and the Rhodesias. So, it was a perfect opportunity for my husband to do a bit of bird-watching and for me to rescue a dear friend from the clutches of a communist revolution. Alas, upon our arrival, dear Valerie wasn't to be found! Upon our return to England, I received a letter from her wherein she explained that she'd been on a holiday in Greece. Greece! In the wintertime! I'd never known of such an extraordinary thing! So, sadly, we never got to meet.

Here I am rambling away! I must apologise. I shan't detain you any longer. I know you must be a very busy man, a High Court Judge, no less!

I'd be very grateful if you would send me a letter and keep me informed of Valerie's condition.
Yours sincerely,
Caroline Beaufort
Summertown, Oxford

It was Friday night. I was the last person to leave the building. Even Thandi had gone. The world was, if only for a few hours, in search of good times, frivolous good cheer. They'd have to press on without me.

I gathered all eight letters and put them in my briefcase. And the letter from Val to me.

I turned out the lights and locked the door to the empty rooms before heading home.

Nine

Standing on my balcony, eleven storeys above the ground, above the shaded lumpy streets of the Berea, I regarded the harbour lights with a sense of disgruntled resignation. Durban. An old whore of a town. Ensnaring the money-men with a glimpse of her hot promise, she is dredged and flung open. They penetrate her warm lagoon, deposit their bits of poison on the hardening walls of her once muddy shores and withdraw, their propellers vibrating, tingling under the water, weighed down with her riches. They would return. They'd always return. Queue up outside, waiting their turn. A reliable old hooker.

In my survey of the city I saw all those old points of logic connected to one another by threads of evidence, tightly fastened, going this way and that, turning order into chaos, chaos into order. Who is right and who is wrong? Who is right and who is left? Who is a victim and who is a perpetrator? A freedom fighter or terrorist? A victim of terror or collateral damage? The endless explanations, the arguments, the words, constantly exploding and imploding, ballooning and withering, in the pages of books, announced at podiums and pulpits and bellowed on battlefields – all of them applauded and decried. All of them spirited by the promise of truth.

Durban. That old whore of a town. The pleasure she gave. The triumph! The riches!

And the loss and the poverty too.

I poured a whisky. What else is one to do?

Dear Caroline,

Thank you for your letter which arrived on Friday last. I regret to inform you that my aunt Valerie passed away on 2 February 2015. Yes, she suffered with great courage during her final years. The cancer had progressed to a point where even the bravest among us are finally afforded the wisdom of a dignified retreat.

I'm very sorry that you did not have the opportunity to meet Val. Yes, she loved Greece, especially in the winter. Strange, I know, but that was Val.

Fortunately, South Africa has not been subsumed by a communist revolution. For now, we are living in the midst of the revolution that never keeps on happening. All that aside, I cannot help but appreciate your concern for her and your visit to this country for the purpose of encouraging Val to return home. I have no doubt that you had her wellbeing at heart. Allow me to express my gratitude for the concern that you had for her safety.

Fortunately, for all of us, Val lived until the ripe old age of ninety-three. She was kept safe and comfortable, and ended her life with the same quiet dignity by which she had lived it.

With kind regards,

The Hon. Mr Justice Edward Dickerson

Durban

Val hated Greece. She'd never have gone to Greece, especially in the winter.

On Monday morning, as I slipped the letter into the post box, it struck me that in all the letters I had sent, I had written of friendship and fondness and loss and wisdom, but I had not written about love. Perhaps I did not need to say it *expressly*. They'd get the idea. They could *infer* it.

In any case, they were all strangers to me. It seemed somehow a bit too intimate to write to these people and speak of love.

Then again, it seemed as if all these people had been strangers to Val too. Some of them had made the point that they'd never met Val. I suspected this might be true of all of them.

Still, love is a strange thing to speak about. It's vague. It doesn't seem to have any kind of discernible meaning. It's the kind of thing that people believe in simply because there aren't any other ideas.

Val would have berated me for thinking such a thing. It would have infuriated her. She would have accused me of 'negative thinking'. We would have argued. Fiercely.

Well, what more was to be done about it? Val had had her last word. No argument was in the offing. The letters had all been sent. My duty done (as best as could be expected). All that was left for Teddy Dickerson was the exhilarating plunge towards decrepitude and a late check-in at The Cedars before calling it a day.

Ten

I did not expect to hear from Darshini, Wilma, Glynnis, Nawal, Tiffany, Jennifer, Candice, or Caroline ever again. Val was gone and, if they had the inclination, they'd have to find someone else to write to – preferably someone who used email so that they no longer had to bother themselves with post offices and queues and stamps and other primitive inconveniences. So it was with a mixture of surprise and intrigue that I received this letter on my desk some three weeks later.

Dear Mr Teddy,

I am so sad to hear about our lovely Valerie. She has passed to the Heaven! I thank you for the letter that you write to me. I cannot believe that my greatest friend in the world has passed to the Heaven. I pray for our lovely Valerie. Every day I pray that she is resting in the Heavens. I will pray for her every day until I die and meet her in the Heavens.

You are a very great and wise man, Mr Teddy. I love your words. What a kind man you are? Mr Teddy, one time Valerie asked me to send her a picture of me. I sent her one picture, many many years ago. She replied and made a joke about my nose. She said that I have a nose, just like hers! She said that I am beautiful and that my nose is the nose of the great Queen and the nose of an intelligent person. Oh, I was so happy to get that. Many people have said nasty things about my big, bumpy nose, but only Valerie said it is the nose of the Queen. Mr Teddy, please help me? I ask Valerie many times for a picture of her, but she never sent one to me. I think she forgot many times. Do you have a picture of Mrs Valerie? I will love it. I will put it on my wall. You can send me a picture?

I love you, Mr Teddy, and all of your six children. You hug the children tonight and say it is from Mrs Hassan in Egypt. Have a very lovely time, Mr Teddy.

With love, I say, goodbye.

Mrs Hassan

Alexandria

The nose. The nose! Of course. Oh God, Valerie and her secrets, her privacy, her impossible decorum! What it all concealed ... Nawal Hassan of Alexandria and Valerie Dickerson of Shaka's Rock were half-sisters!

Valerie's father had been an officer in Military Intelligence, stationed in Alexandria during the war. He'd had the big bumpy nose too – I'd seen it in photos. I pressed the letter to my breast and laughed out loud.

Did I have a picture of Valerie? I wasn't sure. I must have one somewhere. In an album. In a box. I'll have to check. Valerie hated having her photograph taken and never looked good in photographs either. She became unmistakeably tense, and looked as if she were undergoing electric shock therapy every time she posed for a photograph.

No, by all accounts, my duty was not yet done.

Dear Mrs Hassan,

Thank you for your letter. It is very kind of you to write to me.

Yes, our lovely Valerie is now high up in Heaven. I am sure she is looking at us with a smile.

Unfortunately, I'm not sure if I have a photograph of Valerie. She was never very comfortable with people taking photographs of her. She was unusually modest in that way. Nonetheless, I will hunt around for one.

It's funny that Val should have remarked on your nose. She said much the same about her own nose – how it was a sign of nobility and intelligence. I have no doubt that she was quite right about that!

Also, I should add that I omitted to mention something in my last letter to you. Before Valerie died, she asked me to tell you that she loved you. And I certainly believe that to be true.

With kind regards,
Teddy Dickerson
Chambers
Durban

'Good heavens!' I exclaimed as I sealed the envelope. 'Sisters! From Cape to Cairo!' I felt unexpected affection for Nawal Hassan. And for Val – so outspoken and yet so much unspoken.

Wilma Straughan came next, a few days after Nawal. She wrote from Vancouver and the depths of maudlin despair.

Dear Teddy,

May I call you Teddy? I hope so. Well, I guess I'd like to thank you for your letter and your condolences. I really cannot believe, cannot accept, that Val has died. I've cried so much, I don't know what to do with myself. Neither does my cat, by the way. My cat, Prunella, has been with me for fifteen years. She'll be the next to go, if I don't go first. And if I did go first, what would happen to Prunella? I don't want to think about that. Val was my dearest friend. We wrote to each other regularly for more than ten years. I never get any mail from anyone nice. It's all just junk or bills, but the thought that, amid all that tedium, there might be a letter from Val, was just enough to keep the kettle on the boil, the toast in the toaster, life humming along as if everything, even the unimportant things, still really mattered. Val told me that you're the 'gay one' in your family. Well, I'm the 'gay one' in mine. But how weird all that seems to me now. Once I had a lover. Twenty years younger than me. We bought Prunella together. She stayed with me for three years and I thought that maybe – just maybe – life was going to turn out okay, you know, like in a movie, an American one, not a French one. She was the daughter of a Spanish immigrant. They landed on hard times, here in Vancouver. I never had much money, but I took care of them all. And then one day I got home (I work at the library – yes, a lesbian librarian with thick glasses; you get the picture) and Tiffany had gone. Just vanished. Her parents wouldn't speak to me. They took the money, but never really liked me. Turns out Tiffany got hitched to someone else – a man! And left for Australia. All I got from her was a three-line note, telling me that one has to 'move on'

in life. What does that even mean? Move on to what? From what? When all that happened, well, I guess I realised that life really was as bad as a French movie, where people die in the middle of a sentence, but not just any sentence — it's a sentence uttered during an argument with someone you love. Only Val got me through that. The fact is, Teddy, that people are really disappointing. That's why I love animals. They always look at you with that weird kind of meditative silence and make you feel as if you're a bit hysterical. Val loved animals too. I loved all her stories about the animals on the farm. The chicken called Hennie Pennie and the cockatoo called Roger. Oh, and the pig called Walter! She shared so much of her life with me, so much of my pain. I will miss her. I was born in South Africa, grew up in Johannesburg. Val knew my mother from The Cedars. Next thing I know, I got a letter from her! Val was really a mother to me. A real mother. I feel like I've just lost a mother. You sound like a nice person. Val always spoke highly of you. So, sorry if I sound mad. I hope you're doing okay too. I'll sign off now, Teddy. Thanks for your letter and keep in touch if you care to.
With love,
Wilma
Vancouver

This was a lot to take in. I instinctively reached for my notepad and took to re-reading the letter, making notes of the most salient points.

Firstly, it seemed to me that Wilma was having suicidal thoughts. Her musing over what might happen to Prunella if she died was as good as trumpeting her suicidal ambitions from a rooftop. True, everyone has suicidal thoughts. Everyone. Life *is* a French movie. No wonder the French are such a jolly lot.

It wasn't clear to me how the Tiffany who'd written to me from Australia had ended up corresponding with Val, but there could be little doubt that this was the same Tiffany who once had loved Wilma, the lesbian librarian with a cat in Vancouver.

And finally, Wilma's mother was the woman from the South African War who had attended Val's funeral and who had told me how kind Val had been to her daughter in Canada.

Dear Wilma,

Thanks for your letter and, yes, of course you may call me Teddy — especially since you were a great friend of Val's.

Actually, I think I know your mother. Val and I quite often used to lunch at The Cedars and I would spot your mother there. She, frankly speaking, scared me a little; she was clearly the oldest person in the place and shuffled about staring at the floor without much to say. But I will tell you one of the most extraordinary things: I was recently at The Cedars to pick up a few old bits and pieces, and your mother approached me and said (I quote as accurately as I can recall): 'I am very grateful to your aunt for the kindness she showed to my daughter who lives in Canada.' The point of this, Wilma, is that your mother — your actual mother — approached me, completely uninvited, and told me that she was grateful that someone — anyone — had treated you, her daughter, with kindness.

I don't know why it's so hard for us to express these things directly to each other. We all seem to hurt and get hurt, and it all seems interminable, as you say. Just like a French movie! Animals are lovely until they want to nip you or eat you — either bit by bit or whole — and so we end up being afraid of them — afraid of dying between their jaws or pincers or germ-laden mandibles. But in one of the grandest ironies, humans are the ones who make us afraid of living. It does all seem perfectly insufferable. And amid all this outrageous tumult, you, Wilma, have written a letter to me, Teddy, and I couldn't be more grateful. Thank you for sharing your story with me. As you so rightly said, Val's letters kept life humming along as if everything — even the unimportant things — still really matter. I suppose they do. Your letter is testament to that.

I am sorry that Tiffany left you. I, like Val, share in your suffering. For every greeting, there is also a farewell. This is our challenge. I suppose it's a challenge that you and I share, and I am certain that the farewell we now offer to Val, even if we cry, is one of our greatest achievements of all.

Finally, I must add that I forgot to mention something in my last letter to you. Before Val died, she wrote a letter to me too, in which she instructed me to tell you that she loved you. I'm sorry I hadn't mentioned it before, but I'm pleased to have the opportunity to do so now.
With my very best wishes to you and Prunella,
Teddy

As I lay in bed that night, I even thought of flying to Vancouver to see Wilma, to make sure she was okay, that the kettle was on the boil and the toast in the toaster (and Prunella still very much alive). I had trouble going to sleep, thinking about Wilma.

The following morning, back at chambers, still thinking about Wilma, I received a letter from Darshini.

Dear Mr Teddy Dickerson,

Mr Dickerson, I wish to hereby express my sincere gratitude and deepest thanks for your letter. I am very sad to hear that your poor aunt, Mrs Valerie Dickerson, has passed away.

The letters between me and Mrs Valerie were a beautiful thing and went on for many years. In 1983, Mr and Mrs Dickerson were travelling on a holiday in Switzerland and it was there that they met my mother. They were at a restaurant in Pontresina. Would you believe, Mr Dickerson, that my mother was an Englishwoman called Mrs Gillian Pendergast? They were having a happy time together and then, suddenly, my father arrived. He was a doctor, by the name of Dr Rajesh Poovalingam. Mrs Valerie told me about her surprise that my mother was married to an Indian man. I knew exactly what she meant. It was like that for some people in India too. I was so happy to learn that no matter who was married to whom, Mr Aubrey and Mrs Valerie enjoyed a very happy time with my parents. When Mrs Valerie returned to South Africa, she wrote a letter to my mother, but she did not know that after their meeting at the restaurant in Pontresina, both of my parents had perished in a car accident on their way to Zürich. I received Mrs Valerie Dickerson's letter and I kept it. I did not answer it for many years. I was raised by my aunt too – just like you. Then, some many years later, in 1995 I decided one day to write to Mrs Valerie and express my thanks to her, and inform her that my parents were deceased and therefore Mrs Dickerson should not be upset about it or take it personally. So, from that day until the present time, Mrs Dickerson and I were happy writers!

I will always miss my very close friend, Mrs Valerie. She told me many truthful things. She told me that she raised you after your father had passed away when you were just a small boy and your mother had passed away during childbirth. I was sad to hear that. We are the same

age too, both born in 1979! She said many good things about you, Mr
Teddy, so I am pleased that we can write to each other. I know that Mrs
Valerie was very proud of you and I am sure she had many good reasons
to be – you have experienced much hardship in your life too.

Some years ago, when I was married to my husband, I was feeling
very sad about my life. I explained my sadness to Mrs Valerie. When she
replied to me, she said, 'No one really knows anything. Nothing is ever
really resolved. We all make a lot of noise though, as if the opposite were
true. The one thing that I like about writing to you is that it is done in
silence – only the scratching of the pen against the surface of the paper.' I
love her words, Mr Dickerson.

I say, people are beautiful people. Isn't it true, Mr Dickerson?
With felicitations and my warmest regards,
Darshini Poonam (Mrs)

No one really knows anything. Nothing is ever really resolved. We all make a
lot of noise though, as if the opposite were true. It stunned me to think that
the woman who claimed to know everything and resolve everything and, to
that end, made a lot of noise, was the same woman who penned those words.
I pictured Val sitting in her room at The Cedars, hunched over the table, hearing nothing but the scratching of her pen against the surface of the paper. She
endured that silence. Alone.

Still, *people are beautiful.* I agreed with that, even if it's not quite what I had
said to Wilma, to whom I had declared that people were generally worse than
animals.

Dear Mrs Poonam,
Thank you for your letter and sharing your story with me. I am very
pleased that you and Val shared so much during the course of your cor-
respondence. I am glad that Val comforted you during difficult times. No
doubt, you also comforted her.

I think she was always worried that people would invariably be unkind
to one another, that it would be safer if we stuck to our small groups. Now
that I have read your letter, I recognise that for much of the time Val was
alone and belonged to nothing at all. Perhaps love (she often spoke of love)
was all we had, is all we've ever had, but can we really trust it? I picture

Val, sitting alone in her room, writing letters to you in India, and I suppose in that silence and in that solitude and with the slow exchange of the words penned between the two of you she believed we could.

Before Val died, she wrote a letter to me too. I am sorry I did not mention this in my previous letter. It had slipped my mind. She had given me a clear instruction to tell you that she loved you. And I know she did.

With kind regards,

Teddy

P.S. Please do call me Teddy. No need to address me so formally. We're the same age, after all!

We weren't the same age. I was born in 1970. Darshini in '79. Val had me time-travelling in her letters. She had my father dying when I was a small boy (I wasn't; I was eighteen) and my mother dying during childbirth (she was still very much alive — with a terrible cough — but very much alive). And no, I wasn't raised by my aunt. To Caroline, my aunt was ninety-three and had cancer. To Wilma, there were farm animals named Walter and birds called Roger and Hennie Pennie. I was a High Court judge. I was a father with six children.

But I corrected nothing. If anything, I embellished the deception, added to it and polished it, and I did so quite joyfully. And I wrote to them about love! Something I did not understand. Not a bit.

On workdays some of my colleagues went to the gym, or ran along the beachfront, or took time out with a mistress. They had the time. When I received the first round of letters, my immediate reaction was that I didn't have the time. But now, as I drove to work in the mornings, I found myself looking forward to the letters, was imbued with an eagerness to read them and reply to them. Let my colleagues all go to their gyms or for their runs or their tawdry liaisons. I have my letters! I have time!

Dear Mr Dickerson,

Thank you for your letter. Thembi says that you have very good handwriting, just like Valerie. It's such a relief. Some people have terrible handwriting and it nearly drives me to drink, because Thembi can't read it and I can do nothing to help her.

So, Valerie has died. This is sad. It's always sad, isn't it? One can never really prepare for it. I remember saying this to Valerie once and she replied, saying, 'I'm almost ready and, when it happens, I'll be ready enough'. Tough old thing was our Val.

I've still got both my legs. The left one is off next week. So, I won't be able to put a 'best foot forward' after that! A week after my operation, I turn seventy-seven. The numbers get bigger, but the body grows smaller. I'm sure numbers are more deceptive than people realise. Or perhaps it's simply that we don't know what numbers mean. We know what they do, but we don't know what they mean. Val once said that a theory of everything must explain nothing. She also told me that she was impressed by humans, in that, throughout our story and throughout every cultural formation, we have submitted to the act of prayer. The essential symbolic gesture of prayer is to bow or kneel or even lie flat on the floor. This, she said, was a gesture to demonstrate our smallness. Sometimes we need reminding. I only mention this, Teddy, because I am growing smaller. Now with my leg being removed, this is an incontrovertible fact. I often think of the bits we excise, remove, lop off – the diseased bits. We seem pleased by our medical ingenuity, but, in the end, are we only ever contributing to our ineluctable diminution, our ever-increasing smallness?

The young will never really understand the old. Perhaps they're not supposed to. Being young is about growth, the body, its strength, its beauty, and its proliferation. This is the purpose of youth. Being old is about growing smaller and weaker, fading eyesight, collapsing organs, toothless heads, and recommitting the body to the earth. This is its purpose. If we seek to understand the purpose of life, well, the first thing we should accept is that there's more than one purpose. Knowledge is for the young. Faith is for the old. Straddling the two isn't easy. We call it a crisis, don't we?

Val and I never met. I used to be a lecturer at Wits. English literature. My husband was a professor at the medical school. My eyesight began to fail and I was forced to stop work. At the same time one of my students had a job as a waitress in a restaurant. Val was a customer. I can hardly imagine how it came about, but the waitress and Val got to talking. The waitress got teary-eyed as she explained the many woes afflicting her poor lecturer. So, Val wrote to me. I was annoyed at first. I told her that I was

perfectly fine and didn't need the sympathy of strangers. I made it clear
that she need not write to me again. But she did — only to apologise.
About a year later, my sight completely gone, I wrote back, offering her an
apology of my own.

It's a strange thing to progress through life in the dark. In some way,
it's made me appreciate that we are all in the dark, whether we have eyes
in our head or not. How much more is out there for which we have no
physical senses? One can only imagine.

And I have often felt that I have met Val. Sometimes I have been
sitting here in my front room and I have felt her standing right next to
me and even sometimes she is outside on the veranda. Sometimes I know
when she is driving along the street in front of my house.

So, it's leg off next week! Is it medical genius or just another kind of
prayer? How might I know?
Thank you for your letter, Teddy.
With love,
Glynnis

I had swiftly and keenly replied to all the letters I had received thus far. But now, this letter from Glynnis, well … I couldn't. The nib of my pen hung suspended above the paper in a state of startled inaction.

And speaking of doctors, of medical ingenuity, I was reminded of something Sidney Ngwenya had once told me at a Christmas party. He'd confessed to consulting a sangoma.

'A *sangoma*?' I'd said with a laugh, taking a large gulp of unspeakably sweet sangria punch. 'But you … you're, you know … What the hell are you doing visiting sangomas?'

I'd meant this flippantly, as a breezy Christmas-party, throwaway remark. But I could tell he was offended.

He looked at me sternly. 'When you visit a sangoma, you must kneel down. You should try it sometime.'

I'd forgotten that conversation, but was pleased that Glynnis's letter had reminded me of it. I suspect it was a timely reminder too.

As I drove home that evening, noting with pleasure the cool hint of another subtropical autumn, it was the word 'crisis' that loomed at me from the page of her letter. I had often joked that I had entered a midlife crisis at the age of around thirteen and would only be relieved of it at some point in my dotage, with just weeks to go before I popped off. That would be Teddy Dickerson's funny old story! Perhaps it was this rather light-hearted frivolity that had concealed what was, indeed, a very real crisis, one that seized me at this very moment. Yes, this is a crisis, I mused as I yielded for the oncoming traffic, watching the slow progress of the electronic gate that juddered on its little wheels, my face illuminated by the green glow of the flashing indicator light on the dashboard. I was going home, to my apartment, waiting for the traffic. I'd done this a thousand times. This was a crisis.

Eleven

It did strike me from time to time that, despite my laudable efficiency as counsel for the plaintiff, the Smollen case might be resolved through some means so simple, so plain that it escaped me altogether. Heading to trial struck me as a comprehensive waste of human intelligence. A more depressing squander of precious time could hardly be imagined. What were Janet and Robert thinking? What was Randolph thinking? What were we *all* thinking – us, the lawyers, Boshoff and Williamson and Dickerson? The only person in this fiasco who made any sense and for whom I had a growing affinity was Jill Smollen, the Mouse – the one who wanted nothing to do with it.

For now, the trial was in progress – set down for hearing before the Honourable Mr Justice Ncube in the KwaZulu-Natal Provincial Division of the High Court of South Africa for three days in June. What had to be done had to be done, I told myself (and then I kicked myself – I hated that kind of line. It reminded me of people who said things like 'It is what it is'. What does that even mean? Still, I did not relent). The case was yet another set piece that comprised my inescapable fate, just as my lonely, beer-drinking, cricket-watching weekends were, and just as checking in to The Cedars would eventually be. Crisis? What crisis?

And we had no other Will. Our handwriting expert had compared the signature on Randolph Smollen's Last Will & Testament to signatures on other documents, but not to any earlier *testamentary* documents. The question to be asked was, even if the signature on his Last Will & Testament had been forged, had Janet Smollen sustained any loss? Was there a divergence between his last

Will and any previous Will? If we asked the court to assume that there was no valid Will in existence, then Janet would inherit nothing. Everything would go to the Mouse. But the Mouse was not a party to the suit. Yes, we had a bit of correspondence, a few emails here and there that showed a previous Will to have existed, but without the actual document, we couldn't be sure, with any degree of certainty, what it might have provided for. If we weren't arguing for the court to find that Randolph Smollen had no valid Will, then what were we asking the court to find? There were another thousand things that worried me about the Smollen case.

And now there were one thousand and one things.

We were again in Ben's Mercedes. This time, we were on the N3 North. We were running out of options. We'd done west and south. There was no road east. 'Let's wait until we're on the open road,' was all he said when he picked me up. His resolute silence did not conceal a distinctive anger that had his reddish face redder than usual. Or maybe it wasn't anger. It might have been a festering anxiety. Or perhaps both.

As we crossed the bridge over the Mdloti River, he brought up one of our guys in London, doing some digging around on the estate – Panama mostly. 'A good chap, Toby Braithwaite, a very good chap …' It seemed as if Ben could not go on. He began to twist the steering wheel in his large pink hands as if trying to snap it in two. The car travelled faster. A sheen of sweat appeared on his temple.

'Yes?' I said. 'He's a good chap and …?'

'He *was* a good chap,' Ben growled. '*Was.*'

I felt a shot of adrenalin run through me, fizzing like hot ice in my veins. 'What's happened?' I said, looking straight ahead at the grey freeway curving through the cane fields, pressed flat to the ground like a ginormous dead snake.

'They're saying it's suicide. London counsel aren't convinced. He'd just fathered his first kid. Six months ago. A healthy, bonny little boy, so they tell me. There's a note, apparently, but that's in the hands of the police. The wife hasn't seen it. The wife says it's a fake. Couldn't possibly be true.'

'Well, she would, wouldn't she?' I said trying to comfort him, comfort myself.

'London counsel are worried. They think we're poking a beehive. They're saying we should back off.'

Just at the point when I was mulling over whether the entire case might be the most foolhardy escapade in the history of lawsuits (and there have been many), I was also told that it might be deadly.

'Do we know if he was on to anything? Anything ... you know ... meaty?'

'Wire transfers. Central African Republic. Equatorial Guinea. It isn't really where we want to go.'

'No,' I said.

We passed the Ballito off-ramp. Next would be Shaka's Rock and then Sheffield, the way to Estantia. If we kept going, we'd get to the bridge that spanned the Tugela River, the point at which the British Empire, during one of its heady expansionist exercises, decided to launch its attack on the Zulu kingdom.

'So, what is this? The empire strikes back?'

Ben grunted with approval.

'Let's back off, Ben. We have enough. This is about Janet Smollen. All she wants is the stud in the Midlands, not an offshore drilling block. I mean, we're not representing a fucking mining house or an oil company.'

We did back off. And although an inquest in the United Kingdom revealed that Toby Braithwaite had been shot to death in his car in the car park facing the beach in Brighton (a suitably emotive landscape for someone who wanted to end their life), there appeared to be no evidence that anyone other than Toby had done the shooting.

Before pitching the entire continent into a colonial stranglehold to which it could do nothing but acquiesce in a state of gibbering effusiveness, the British had at least established some fine-looking towns in Africa, and Durban was one – a better one – of many. The beachfront had its Golden Mile and here were the splash pools and funfairs and games arcades that once might have enthused the beachgoers in a place like Brighton. But this was no Brighton.

Like all of these places, the night offered refuge to its murky truth. Now I was sitting in my bucket seat in the midst of the murk, parked in the carpark at South Beach, facing the sea. With the hostile reddish geometry of the Addington Hospital behind me, the ambisexual casuarina trees swaying with meaningless grace above me, I was on the lookout for a hookup. This was where they hung out. I'd done this before. Before long, a shadow, a shape, a gulp, a nod, this whole titillating vile sequence of gestures, produced him, standing at my window – smiling, like an ad for deodorant. White teeth, a wisp of moustache on each side of his curling upper lip. I knew this one. He was beautiful. The next move was on me. Would I wind down the window? I did. Just a bit. He spoke. I couldn't stand it. I stuffed some money through the tiny gap and raced away.

At home, I was nude and standing in front of the mirror. Not a good idea. Not when you're forty-five. Not when you're forty-five *and above*. My paunch sagged subtly. The hair between my pinkish nipples was grey – in no particularly alluring shade. Just a static, immutable grey. *Nobody ever gets to see this*, I thought with relief. Maybe the crisis is already over. Maybe I just think it's a crisis, but it's come and gone. Maybe I'm okay.

I returned to my bedroom.

I took a Xanax.

There's this thing about death and sex – the way they're connected. The French have a word for an orgasm. Le petit mort, they call it. No wonder French films are such a lark.

Twelve

*D*ear *Glynnis,*
    It's taken me a bit of time to gather my thoughts and write this reply to your letter. I've been thinking about your legs – the one you've let go and the one left behind. About your growing smallness. How can smallness grow? But that's exactly what it does.

    Loss. Loss of a limb. Loss of the amenities of life. Loss of life itself. If we find that someone caused this kind of loss, then we can seek compensation. That's what lawyers will tell you. Compensatory relief. It's as if loss shouldn't really happen even if we know that everything gained is lost.

    I am sorry for your many losses, Glynnis. I'm sorry for the loss of your leg. I'm sorry for my own losses. I wish I might do more to comfort you, other than simply penning these words. But I have a vague suspicion that there is little more to be done. Even lovers will embrace each other with all their might, only to find, exhausted, that they are still alone. Still, an embrace will remind us of our connectedness, our influence, our meaning to others, even if our lives might have no clear meaning to ourselves.

    Perhaps we'd be better off if we simply all gave one another a hug, rather than sought relief in a courtroom, complained to the police, argued about our rights. This idea would make my colleagues laugh. It might make the whole world laugh. They would laugh with tears in their eyes. They would laugh until they cried.

    Everything gained is lost.

Tell me, Glynnis, if there is anything I can do for you. For now, I do have one duty to you, and that is to tell you that Val loved you. Before she died, she wrote a letter to me and instructed me to tell you that she loved you.

Thank you for writing to me and I would be pleased if you wrote to me again.

With hugs,

Teddy

Praying wasn't something I normally did. It wasn't something I'd *ever* done unless I'd been instructed to, when part of some vast obedient congregation of others. Sidney Ngwenya had once told me that I should try kneeling sometime.

And now I found myself kneeling in my bedroom, my hands flat against the floor. I leaned forward, my head dipping until my forehead brushed against the carpet. I considered my smallness with relief.

A week after writing to Glynnis, I received a letter from Candice! I tore open the envelope like a kid, as if it might contain tickets to a funfair.

Candice had dispensed with the niceties. There was no 'Dear Teddy'.

Oh crap! So, Val has died. I knew it! I just knew it!

I'm sorry, Teddy. I guess you loved her. Hey, I loved her too! I feel sad. I miss her. I will always miss my beautiful Val.

I hope you had a good ceremony. You know, the ceremony is never for the dead. It's for the living. We've got to acknowledge and, you know, thank them for their story. We're all still here, Teddy, muddling our way through each blinding day, blinking in the darkness each long night. It's unbearable if we don't go around and thank people for their stories. You know what I mean?

Look here, I've been a nurse for a long time and I know a thing or two about grief, and you've got to do the ceremony and you've got to do it right. We've always done the ceremonies, us humans. It's how the archaeologists distinguish between the bones of an ancient ape and the bones of an ancient human.

You know, Teddy, a lot of people come over here to Asia and they get all excited about it. They buy a wind chime and stick it on the balcony.

They slip a crystal under their pillow and they burn fragrant incense. They meditate and they even get into yoga. It's all mighty seductive, I'll tell you that. They get to feel good about themselves and they find themselves smiling, not scowling like the rest of us. They've found some kind of answer! It's here in the East! They breeze around in a kind of annoying, slightly lofty way with their little smiles and they think they've got it – some kind of beautiful answer. But all they have discovered is fate. It's goddamn bliss, I tell you (until it isn't). You know how I know this? Because I'm a nurse, Teddy. I've been sticking tubes into people, down their throats, up their asses, into their veins, trying to keep them alive. That ain't no fate, Teddy. That's us! That's us getting involved, muddying the waters, changing their course, intervening, dodging fate.

Fate is a cool idea until we realise how cruel it is. This place has known cruelty, Teddy. You better believe it. In the end, the East and the West, they ain't so different. Fate or free will, somehow we have yet to learn that we're not really getting along. But we could, Teddy. We could get along. You know what I mean?

Now that Val has gone, I am reminded of all this. Fate is great. It's a goddamn relief. And so is sticking a tube up someone's ass to keep 'em alive. But what really gets us out of bed in the mornings? It's each other, Teddy. It's not our rights. It's not our money. It's not our uniformity. Heck, we're not computers! Silicon Valley! Give me a break!

And here's another thing, Teddy. I'm in Cambodia and I love these people. You know how I know that? They have suffered. If you don't know the story of this place, then google it. These people have suffered. And when you learn more about their story, your heart will fill with sorrow and horror and admiration. You can't help it. This is how we are. And so they are loved. Heck, there you are in Africa and you've got your stories over there too, I guess. We need to embrace these stories, these tales of suffering. We need to do this to wake up and know that we are loved.

I sure am going to miss my Val. My beautiful Val who I never met.

Hey, come and visit. Stay with me! Yeah, Phnom goddamn Penh might be full of assholes but some of them are nice – nice assholes.

You take care of yourself, Teddy and, yeah, write me, goddammit!
Love ya, Ted!
Candice

I folded Candice's letter neatly and placed it back into its envelope. I looked out the window. There was a small patch of blue sky framed by the cool shadows of the half-empty concrete buildings that crowded around me. It made me feel as if I were sinking slowly into a grave. Grave or not, I was happy to receive Candice's letter, that little patch of pale blue sky.

And what of Val's ceremony? Was it a good ceremony? In the Manning Road Methodist Church that was no longer on Manning Road? I couldn't be sure.

Thirteen

I was in Pietermaritzburg attending to another case, a motion for the attachment of a farm to be seized in execution of an uncontested debt. Yet another failed dream. A formality. I walked out of court. The sunlight was a weak watery orange, but I enjoyed it as I stood on the steps, almost oblivious to the whooping and thumping of the minibus taxis that congealed around the rank on the other side of the street.

Angus Goddard was an attorney. He was known for his tweed jackets and maroon cravats and a tattered brown soft leather briefcase. He drove around in an old Rover. Now, he carried himself with a strangely defiant sort of totter, his wisp of grey hair at the back of his head illuminated by the pale sun. The future was no place for Angus Goddard. He shuffled up the steps of the courthouse.

'Angus!' I said.

He looked up at me and blinked. Nope. Nothing.

'It's me. Teddy Dickerson.'

'Ah, yes, hello, Dickerson.'

Angus had been on my mind. He'd acted for Randolph Smollen in years gone by. It was his firm that had prepared previous wills for Randolph. We'd subpoenaed them, but they'd resisted. He was an obstinate man.

'I'm glad to see you. I mean, to have a chance to chat.'

'Chat?' he said, as if slightly disgusted by the idea.

'Yes, chat. About Smollen. Randolph Smollen.'

'He's dead.'

'Yes, so I believe. You were his attorney. Helped him with a will.'

'What of it? You're not banging on about that subpoena, are you?'

'Hardly *banging on*. But frankly, it disturbs me that you haven't complied. What might be the matter?'

'Nothing's the *matter*, boy! Are you suggesting I've done something *wrong*?' A small dot of froth glistened on his lower lip.

'Wrong?'

'Smollen was a client. A damn good client too. I won't betray the man. Confidentiality. Privilege. That sort of thing. I won't release a thing.'

'You know how this is going to end, Angus. I'll get an order.'

'Do your damnedest,' he bristled. 'I'm on the bloody cusp of retirement! Why the hell are you doing this to me? His thin wisp of hair gleamed, a sudden golden blaze in the slanting sun, as if it were about to burst into flame. 'Now get out of my way.'

I stood aside and Angus hurried into the courthouse with brisk, agitated steps, as if he were suddenly at risk of collapsing.

Fourteen

*H*i Candice,
   Thanks for your letter. And, as requested, here I am writing to you, or writing you, as you Americans like to say. Val often criticised American English. She couldn't abide it, quite frankly. She used to describe it as a 'highly inventive summary' of the English language. She lamented what she called 'Americanisationalism'.

   Still, notwithstanding your dubious grasp of the Queen's English, I know Val loved you very dearly. She asked me to tell you that.

   I've read your letter many times, sometimes laughing and sometimes biting my lip — teetering on that familiar knife edge between fatalism and my celebrated free will. I suppose what unites all of us is not happiness, but suffering.

   I'm running a case at the moment and the scariest thing about it is that I've completely lost interest in it. I feel like telling both sides to go home, watch some TV, stare out of the window, relax. Hardly the duty of an advocate. I was once captivated by the idea of law, how it postulated a sublime orderliness to the ways of people. But I'm no longer captivated. I am simply captive. Held captive. Trapped in the rooms of these old sandstone edifices that house the contorted language of conventional wisdom. The rooms echo, one to the other. I suppose that the moment wisdom becomes conventional, then it is no longer wisdom, but just another deadening kind of creed. You're right — we're not computers. Computers don't get old. They don't suffer. They don't sit under a tree, trying to still the code inside them. They don't put tubes up one another's asses with a sigh of relief.

Thanks for writing, Candice. Give my love to your son and to Gracie and even to the assholes in Phnom Penh (but only the nice ones).

Maybe I'll come visit someday. I don't know. I don't know much, just at the moment.

With love,
Teddy

Ben ordered a rump steak with 'Thousand Island' sauce.

'No salad?' I enquired innocently.

'Stop bugging me about salad. Jesus, you sound like my wife.'

'I'll take that as a compliment.'

'Well don't,' Ben steamed, handing the menu back to the waitress without looking at her. 'So, it turns out that Toby Braithwaite never owned the gun. No one can work out where it's from. Not reported stolen. Not on any registry.'

'So, he shot himself with a mystery weapon.'

'The mystery is if he shot himself at all.'

Ben didn't really want to back down. He was to be paid a windfall if we came anywhere near to recovering even a fraction of the estate. Still, anyone who got too close to the money ended up dead with a mystery weapon in their stiffened grasp. Well, perhaps not *anyone*, but at least one … so far.

I didn't want to talk about Toby Braithwaite. He might have been tracking the family fortune, but I was looking for something else – justice, repentance, contrition? I wasn't sure, but something other than money.

I changed the subject.

'A funny thing happened to me the other day.'

'Funny?'

'Well, of sorts. I bumped into old Goddard, Angus Goddard, on the steps of the court.'

'Oh! Old codger. Why won't he give us that fucking Will? I hope you asked him.'

'I did. He behaved like a nutter, asking me if I was accusing him of having done something wrong. "Why are you doing this to an old man?" he said. As if he was trying to protect himself from some hideous scandal that'll upend his unblemished fifty-year career.'

'We better file a motion. Trial's in June, for Christ's sake.'

'He'll defend it. It'll turn into a trial itself.'

'Stubborn prick!'

Our food arrived and we ate in silence.

Someone else in the restaurant was celebrating a birthday. The staff gathered around their table and sang 'Happy Birthday'. They brought a cake with a sparkler. There was much merriment. I stared at them. It was a family gathering and they looked a bit hard up. The meal might have been a special treat. There was something heartbreaking about the whole scene.

I looked up at Ben. His moustache and beard were speckled with Thousand Island sauce. 'Ben,' I said solemnly. 'Why are we doing this? I mean this case.'

Ben's mouth hung open. He was enjoying his food. He resented any kind of conversation in the middle of a meal. 'It's our job!' he said. 'You know, this is our career.'

'Isn't the right answer that we're doing this for Janet?'

'Janet?' He seemed a little stunned by the question, as if he couldn't quite remember who Janet was. 'Of course, we're doing this for Janet. I mean, you know, she's come to us because this is our job and our job is to do this for Janet.'

'And for a dot of money.'

'A dot of money? More than a bloody dot, let me be clear about that,' he said gruffly, cleared his throat, and resumed eating with almost life-threatening relish. After a long slightly troubled silence, he added: 'What's wrong? What's with these questions? You're sounding a bit soft headed.'

'I don't know. I'm just … you know … thinking about things.'

'Huh! Next thing you'll be telling me you're having a midlife crisis!'

'Well, you're older than me …'

'A bit.'

'A bit, yes. So, you ever been through a midlife crisis?'

'Oh, don't be ridiculous!' Ben scoffed. It was as if I had asked him if he'd ever worn women's underwear. 'A midlife crisis is for people who've screwed up. And we haven't screwed up. Look at us, we're successful. We're eating steak. Have nice houses. Cars. Wives, families … you know.'

That slightly troubled silence re-emerged. It was evident to both of us that

I didn't have a wife or a family. I was the last remaining Dickerson in the country. And I wasn't eating steak. I'd ordered fish.

'Is this about your aunt?' said Ben, swallowing his last bloody morsel. 'I saw old Winstanley the other day. He's doing the estate, isn't he? He said you were mightily cut up about it. Almost in tears.'

'Tears? He's the one in tears. The estate isn't worth a penny. He thought she was rich. Ha!'

Ben looked at me earnestly. The remnants of creamy sauce were drying on his plate (and on his beard). 'But you miss her, right?' For the first time, Ben seemed almost sincere.

Did I miss Valerie? Did I care for her? Did I often think of how much I hated her? Had I ever considered that my memory of her was gradually being discoloured by a blessed rosy hue? Would it eventually turn blood red? Crimson? An asphyxiated scarlet? Did I ever have moments where her empty apartment, not far from where I lived, seemed to have hollowed out a slightly haunting empty space inside me?

'Yes, I miss her,' I said finally. 'Come on, let's get the bill.'

'But dessert!' Ben protested. 'We haven't had dessert. It's a set menu!'

After that miserable lunch I was pleased to return to Chambers and discover a letter on my desk from Jennifer Steenkamp (née Millard). It was precisely the kind of distraction I needed.

> *Dear Mr Dickerson,*
>
> *Thank you for your letter. I am so sorry to hear that Val has passed away. She really was a special friend to both of us. I used to read her letters to my husband whenever they arrived and we both enjoyed receiving them immensely. It's rather sad for us to think that we shan't hear her 'voice' in our home again.*
>
> *There's a joke doing the rounds in Zimbabwe these days: 'What did they have before candles?' The answer? 'Electricity!' I don't suppose it's terribly funny, but I only tell you that because I'm writing this letter by candlelight. Probably not good for the eyes. We do indeed have electricity at the moment, but I rather prefer candlelight.*
>
> *You may be interested to know that we never met Val. Our correspondence arose a bit strangely. My husband and I enjoyed a brief spell*

of rather horrid notoriety. Just more than ten years ago we retired to a farm just outside Harare. My husband had spent his professional life in the law courts, but he was also the son of a farmer and wanted nothing more than to return to the 'land'. After a few years of being happily settled on our farm, we were confronted by a group of ululating, machete-wielding war vets. You can guess what happened next. On the day of moving, packing everything onto the back of a flatbed truck, the BBC arrived and wanted to interview us. Evidently, Val saw the story on television and she put quite some effort into tracking us down. The next thing we knew, she had written to us and asked us if we were quite all right.

We were quite all right. We'd lost the farm, but still had enough to buy ourselves a comfortable house in town. We have our bits of silver on the sideboard and our three children — Richard, John, and Molly — are all well, as far as we can tell, all making a go of their lives in the UK.

Val's letter turned into nearly fifteen years of correspondence. We have really treasured that.

It's all about land here in Africa, isn't it? It's where we place our feet in the mornings. It's where we grow our food. It's where we lay our bodies to rest ... eventually. Val often said: 'Well, you've got to live somewhere, can't live in the air!' How right she was.

None of us has any money here, well, none of our own. We use other people's money. Rands and dollars. We printed our own out of existence. What always amazes me is how the people of this country simply carried on. It was the same when we got rid of electricity. There was a bit of disruption, certainly, but most people simply got on with their lives with little more than a murmur. It was Conrad's 'inborn strength'. It stunned me. It still stuns me. We got rid of money! I think that might always have been the idea. Yes, we still use other money, other currencies (nothing to be done about it, I suppose), but the idea of getting rid of money might always have been the objective.

I suppose if anyone cares to understand something of this Mother Continent, this mother to us all, then Mugabe might give you a clue. Mandela will give you a dance.

When I was a child growing up in Matabeleland, the old chiefs used to caution the young: 'Beware of money,' they used to say. 'The cost of money is something we are unwilling to admit and incapable of paying.' The measure of a man is not by what he has but by who he is and he will never know who he is. Only others will know that.

I once wrote to Val and gave her my interpretation of the parable of the prodigal son. The parable, so I argued, was a story about humanity. Mother Continent. It is from here that the Son of Man must depart on his journey. Imbued with much pride, he would seek riches and grandeur and jollity, while the brother stayed at home, tending to his people, and observing his rather prosaic duties. One day, the prodigal son would return, famished, filled with shame over his misguided adventure. The father would celebrate his return and that would leave the brother indignant. Somehow it is the challenge of humanity to unite once again, here on the Mother Continent – one part of us filled with shame, the other filled with indignation.

I remember Val's reply very clearly (and it came after nearly a year of distinctively prickly silence): 'What rot!' she wrote. But at least we had resumed with our letters.

In her final letter to me, she said: 'I'll be ruined by the great Zimbabwe after all!' I think she loved living on the southern tip of Africa. It awoke something in her, something she wasn't sure she wanted, but she knew she needed. Inborn strength. She appreciated the land, resolved that we could not live in the air, and was grateful to the place for letting her put her feet on the ground.

Thank you for writing, Teddy. I know I mentioned in my last letter to you that my husband used to be a lawyer. He was never so happy as he was on the day he left the profession. I hope you're not too blue about it. Frankly, you sound far too nice to be a lawyer.
With love,
Jennifer and Riaan Steenkamp

Fifteen

I did not go as far as explaining Jennifer's unusual interpretation of the parable of the prodigal son. But I did ask Sidney if he thought that the whole objective of the Zimbabwean story was eventually to print money out of existence.

He nodded and rubbed his chin, careful not to disturb the perfect triangular shape of his clipped beard. 'You know what's got us all by the balls?' he said.

I shook my head.

'Money. We call it liquidity, you see?'

'Do I see what?'

'Liquidity! It's liquid! It moves. It's unstable. It's a trick.'

'But I thought your whole career was for the money! Isn't that what you're always telling us?'

He laughed with enviable lightness and said: 'I'm not stupid enough to try to change the world. I go to court in one of your gowns, reciting your Roman code, earning the notes printed by your central bank, but the truth will emerge eventually, for each of us. And it's bound to hurt.'

He walked to his car and I walked to mine.

I liked Sidney very much, but I always got the feeling that I might irritate him, that he resented me, the angelic English liberal whose ilk tormented his, took all the gold and left an accountable, transparent constitutional order as a parting gift – a tinsel crown if you like. I could see how that might be annoying.

Now I was in the bucket seat of my sports car. It could travel at a top speed of three hundred kilometres per hour. But here it was stuck, idling in traffic, churning out its invisible fumes while hundreds of protestors danced and sang along Dr Pixley KaSeme Street. What were they protesting about? What's with the song and dance? Was it really about jobs, or public housing, or overtime pay? Or was it just about money, the true nature of money, its fluidity, its liquidity? It's always priced slightly out of reach. It's never quite enough. Does it delude us with its numerical precision? Why does it move the way it does? I looked forward to writing to Jennifer and putting this to her.

Finally extricating myself from downtown Durban and its jubilant horde, I drove along Lambert Road and parked outside the house where I grew up.

Ostriches. That's what it was all about for the Dickersons. My great-great-great-grandfather had an argument with a business partner somewhere in the Eastern Cape. Taking his share of the business, he headed north, by ox-cart. Some thousand kilometres later, fording over crocodile-infested rivers, traversing mountain peaks and through sweltering thorn-scapes, he arrived in Estcourt near the Drakensberg. He acquired a huge swathe of well-watered ground from the colonial government which was actively in the business of dishing out land to almost anyone who could sing for it. With yardsticks and measuring tapes they proclaimed title over these bits of African turf in the name of Queen Victoria, who, as the title deeds noted, also happened to be 'the supreme chief of all native peoples'. No one, so it seemed, might have contemplated what a spectacular political convenience that was. Here, my doughty old ancestor built a house that he called 'Wykeham Hill'. His share of the business? Fifty ostriches.

In later years he'd be praised for his acumen, his uncanny prescience in predicting the near-frenzied demand from French fashion designers for ostrich feathers. I had always surmised that the man knew nothing of the French, of fashion or of designers, and I guessed that a bit of old-fashioned luck could easily be mistaken for 'acumen'. His flock of birds multiplied as did his fortune, and by the end of the 1920s his successors were enjoying copious amounts of gin as if it were something as unassailable as a human right. In 1929, the feather business collapsed. They took to cattle. They took to vegetables. They took to wild animals. Nothing worked. It was all too hard. Aubrey and my father inherited the land in the 1960s. They sold it immediately, before it became worthless once again. Aubrey bought Estantia and my father bought this house in Lambert Road.

Now, it was just me. The only Dickerson left.

For this reason, I could be sure that I did miss Val, even if I couldn't quite decide if I ever really liked her. A few weeks ago, there'd been two of us. Now there was just one. And I was indisputably the end of the line. It really was the *end*.

I couldn't see much of the house now. It hid behind a big cream-coloured wall, with thin electric wires stretched like the strings of some finely tuned instrument along the top. I remembered the veranda. The red polished floor. The white Doric columns. The view of the city below. The kidney-shaped pool surrounded by slasto tiles that some owner, in a pique of perfectly mundane inspiration, had installed in the sixties. The TV room where Clarah and I would watch the one channel, broadcast in two languages for no more than three hours a day.

That reminded me of my first album. It was the soundtrack to *The Graduate*. Val had given it to me for Christmas in 1977.

I used to lie on the floor of the living room playing and replaying it. I had no objection to the Simon & Garfunkel songs – a bit gloomy, perhaps, but what thrilled me were the tracks composed by Dave Grusin. I'd never seen the movie, of course, but the Dave Grusin tracks had my imagination unfurl in vivid Technicolor, permitted me to arrange and rearrange my interpretation of the world in slightly varied, always dizzying compositions. I twirled and swirled around the living room, distinctly alive and delightfully bamboozled by the possibilities of the future.

My mother once claimed – in a manner unmistakeably scathing – that I was 'terribly musical'. I wasn't sure what she meant by that, but I knew she wasn't referring to my love of music. And to any observer, musical – in the more conventional sense – is exactly what I was. Music – all music – filled the otherwise empty spaces of my life (I did, notably, draw the line at Christmas songs and Country & Western – this was the kind of music that was aching to be forgotten, the sounds of the anti-future). From the Bee Gees to the Beach Boys, Perry Como and Bing Crosby, to the Rolling Stones and Led Zeppelin, my record collection swelled along the lower shelves of the living room, neatly catalogued and lovingly regarded. Sometimes Clarah would meddle in the collection, misplacing an album or, worse still, scratching a record. This had me sobbing with rage.

My parents eventually bought me my own stereo system and they had a builder install shelving along an entire wall of my room. These were soon filled. Orchestral Manoeuvres in the Dark, the Pet Shop Boys, Erasure, Air

Supply, Tears for Fears. It was the age of the VCR, and I recorded every broadcast of *Pop Shop*, a weekly music-video extravaganza featuring men in lipstick, wearing tight pants, with shocks of long blond hair and voices like girls. If this is what my mother might have meant when she said I was 'terribly musical', then I could do little but agree.

I recalled the parties too. It seemed as if they were all having the most incredible fun – my parents and their friends. They'd joke and drink and eat and pat one another on the back. There was one kind of cheese. Cheddar. There was one kind of coffee. Instant. There was one kind of right. Right. There was one kind of wrong. Left. Everything had been worked out with stunning precision. All one had to do was go forth and enjoy it. It made one eager to grow up.

But what were the bits that I had missed? I might have taken a clue from my father. Nearly subsumed by the merriment, he'd occasionally glance away from the others, towards a window, towards the opening of another dark night, as if vaguely mesmerised by its secrets, quietly outraged by his cowardice. Called back to the reddish beaming faces before him, my mother would accuse him of being sullen, to which everyone would laugh uproariously just in case she was right. He would smile with effort. I got the feeling he secretly hated all those people.

Wealth, money, land. None of us is to be trusted.

Dear Jennifer,

Thanks for your letter.

Honestly, I have no idea what to make of Val. I often told people that she was a woman of contradictions. I still think that. Maybe we're all a bit like that. Or a lot like that. I can't say that there were all that many people who liked her – certainly not among those who actually met her. And this was a fact that she almost regarded with some pride. It seemed to be a quite proper validation of how misguided they were. There were many times when I was outraged, apoplectic over the things that she said. I cannot describe her as having been honest in her dealings with others. I cannot describe her as having been patient. Or respectful, and yet, somehow, I do find myself missing her more severely than I would have thought possible when she was alive. I used to visit her at The Cedars. Nothing too regimented. Maybe once a month. Maybe more. Sometimes I sat outside in the car, contemplating a quick escape. A phone call. An excuse. *Something's come up! Sorry, we'll have to have lunch another time! But I never did.* I'd walk into The Cedars like the hobbled servant of a despot, bringing her news of the outside world.

I had some kind of duty to her, I suppose.

We speak a lot about our rights these days, not so much about our duties.

This brings me to your letter. Whenever I meet a white Zimbabwean, the first question I ask is: 'So where do you live now?' I never presume that a Zimbabwean should live in Zimbabwe — not a white one. But there you are, with your husband, writing letters by candlelight, admiring (if that's the right word) what has happened. No money. No electricity. I've never considered whether that might have been the objective. But everything that is gained is lost. Is that what the dark penniless nights of Zimbabwe awake in us? Is that what it awoke in Val?

I have a colleague here, a superbly intelligent fellow. He's Zulu and spent his formative years herding cattle across the hills and through the gullies of old Zululand. He tells me that money is liquid, inherently unstable, and I suspect that when people protest about not having enough, what they're really protesting about — what enrages them, has them so easily angered — is that they should believe in the value of money in the first place. 'It's a trick!' so my colleague says. Val once told me that anger — all anger — is anger at the self. Whenever I saw her angry — which was frequently — I'd remind her not to be angry at herself, to which she'd reply: 'That's my line!'

Fluid, unstable.

I should mention that Val wrote a letter to me too. She told me that, if I was to hear from you, I should write to you and tell you that she loved you. Despite her contradictions, I firmly believe this to be true.

And I'm quite sure you're right about one thing: I am too nice to be a lawyer.

Give my best wishes to your husband.

With love,

Teddy

Sixteen

The grass was crunchy underfoot. Frost had already begun to deaden the landscape and it was only April. It promised to be a cold winter.

Janet Smollen had insisted that all she really wanted was the stud in the Midlands. It was a small thirty-hectare estate called The Millhouse. I don't know why it was called The Millhouse. There was certainly no millhouse on the property. By all accounts, there never had been. Perhaps it was just another cute English name that someone had picked out from a book. Dickens. Or Austen.

But it was a fine piece of ground. A meadow sloped gently away from us, its grasses a flattened brown and burned by the early frosts. The vestiges of a primordial forest, with brooding greens and purple shadows, curled around each side of the meadow, matching its gentle contours, softening its edges. At the foot of the meadow was a small dam. A solitary willow leaned towards it, dipping its fronds in the dark water. Weavers nested in the bulrushes. Dots of silvery light sparkled on the lily pads. 'Oh!' Janet cried, biting her lower lip as if suppressing memories of unutterable joy. 'Daddy and Robert used to go fishing in the dam. Fish and fish and fish! Oh, they loved it.'

It all seemed a bit unreal.

The gatekeeper had let us in. He lived in a small redbrick hut with a chimney and an asbestos roof near the gate. We were, by all legal accounts, trespassing, but he knew Janet. He might have been told that she was no longer allowed here. Still, old Mister Smollen, so he had heard, was dead. The young Mister Smollen had vanished. So who was he to remonstrate with us – two unstintingly polite white people, here with Janet?

He followed us at a distance with a slight smile.

We headed towards the house. The grey thatch roof sagged uneasily in the shade of large yellowing plane trees. Giant delicious monsters and grey-chested ferns clambered against the white flaking walls as if they were discreetly devouring the old edifice. Perhaps they were.

Janet walked briskly ahead, leaving Ben and me at our weary plod. Ben hadn't wanted to come. He thought it to be a miserly plot of ground. There was a vast fortune, dotted around the globe, to be carved up instead. Obsessing over this small abandoned farm was distinctively unambitious. I, on the other hand, had thought this to be a good idea. We still had no other Will. We needed to show that Randolph had adored his precious daughter, would never have done a thing to harm her, and up to his dying day had fully intended her to enjoy what was left of his earthly riches. A visit to The Millhouse, of which she had always spoken with a sort of breathless glee, might prompt memories that would add a tearful poignancy to her testimony.

'The door's unlocked!' Janet announced cheerfully.

As we approached the front doors, we could also see that the glass panes had been smashed. Janet pushed. The door juddered and the hinges squeaked. We stepped inside. The guard wandered away with a slightly mortified stoop, disinclined to enter the vaunted dwelling.

We were confronted by the smell of urine: rodent, cat, human – hard to say. Stray threads of thatch had fallen to the floor, the carpets pulled up, inner doors ripped away; crumpled knots of wire protruded from the walls where there'd once been electric lights.

'The place has been gutted!' I stammered.

'Not yet,' Ben said grimly. 'There's still the wiring. Embedded in the walls. They'll be at it with a chisel soon. I've seen it done. They chisel through the walls to get to the wiring.'

Janet seemed not to notice. She ran to the fireplace, the great hearth at the end of the long room, and rested her delicate hands on the stone. 'Oh! The fireplace!'

We moved through the house, following Janet as she explored the hollow trappings of her childhood. Ben and I said little as we surveyed the empty spaces where built-in cupboards, shelving, sinks, bathtubs, taps and light-fittings had once been installed.

'Oh, we used to have the most *terrible* amount of fun in here,' Janet said as we entered the billiard room. 'People used to come from all the neighbouring farms, from far away, from Johannesburg even! What parties! The grown-ups all hung about in the lounge, but all of us, the kids, we used to romp around in here. Amazing fun. All in our pyjamas! Giggled our heads off!'

The beams to the billiard room were at a particularly painful curve and the floor was covered in a heavy blanket of fallen thatch. I had the distinct feeling that it might cave in at any moment. I pictured the headline: 'Two Lawyers and Mentally Unstable Client Killed by Falling Roof While Trespassing in House Belonging to Billionaire Playboy.'

'Let's move back outside,' I suggested with subtle urgency.

We reached the back door of the house through the kitchen. Janet had little to say about the kitchen. It was as if she'd never been there before. No remark on the pleasing aromas of home-cooked food – pumpkin soups and cottage pies. Nothing. It was as if they never ate.

Through the back door, we approached the stables, along a stone pathway lined with gnarled oak trees. We crunched over their fallen leaves to inspect the place where Randolph Smollen had kept his famous racehorses.

'Oh! The stables! The horses!' Janet spoke as if she were stricken by a delirious kind of lust. 'I can remember all of their names!' she added and then began to murmur. Her pace slackened. Her murmuring grew more hateful. No, she couldn't remember their names.

'Well, we don't need to know their names,' I said hopefully.

'But I *can* remember them!' Janet protested hotly, turning to me.

'Oh, yes, of course you can, but you know, I mean I don't need to know them. You know, it's your … what … it's your secret.'

'Yes!' Janet said, enchanted by the idea of a secret. 'It's my secret!' She hurried towards the giant wooden doors that led to the stables. She drew a door open. It gave a mighty creek on its hinges. In the dank gloom was a long passageway that led through the middle of the building, where the million-dollar prize horses had once chomped innocently on their octane-fuelled grasses (or whatever it is that they feed horses). Janet broke into a jog, searching for something very particular. She looked like little more than a skittish sort of shadow, weaving this way and that, towards the furthest end of the building. We soon lost sight of her. Ben looked at me apprehensively. He was filled with words, remonstrations, but said nothing. We followed and found her in the furthest stall, kneeling, mussing up the rotten hay on the floor with her strange, translucent fingers.

'Here,' she said, looking at the floor. 'This was Blackforest. Blackforest was mine.'

'Blackforest,' I mused aloud, hoping to disguise my sudden and unexpected angst. 'A horse?'

Janet looked up at us. 'Oh, he *was* a horse. *My* horse!' Janet leaned back against the wall, into a sitting position. 'Daddy gave him to me. He said that he was the fastest racehorse in the world and he said he was mine. His precious Jan.'

This was followed by a slightly unsettling silence.

Ben spoke. 'When might this have been? One wonders what might have happened to poor old Blackforest …'

Janet looked at Ben with disturbing severity. It was obvious to both of us that Ben had committed a most egregious blunder.

'Daddy shot him,' she said, and then she looked again to the floor, patting the dead straw with her fingers and murmuring at it.

'Ah! I see,' I said. I didn't see. We needed to leave. This was indeed a bad idea. My idea. We needed to leave right away.

Ben shifted from one foot to the next. We needed to coax Janet back to the car.

Janet looked up at us again. She smiled in a strangely shameless way – the way mad people smile. 'You know? Once, when I was little, Daddy brought me here and he showed me how to make a noose.'

I didn't really want to believe what she had said. I insisted quietly that she must have said 'moose', like how to make a moose out of clay, or even 'mousse', how to make a mousse out of chocolate. Yes, how to make a chocolate pudding in a building full of horses. Odd, but that is what she must have meant.

But now, she repeated herself. 'Daddy taught me how to make a noose. Oh, it was many years ago! How old would I have been? Nine? Ten? He taught me how to do the knot and to sling the rope up over the rafters. Everyone should know how to make a noose, he said.' She looked up at the rafters and began to laugh as if recalling the happiest memory of all.

I ran from the stables. I was sick outside.

Everyone should know how to make a noose! And to sling it up over the rafters? Who was this man, this father? Why does he insist – to this day – that we witness his torment?

Seventeen

I was the prodigal son.

Driving around in my car, stricken by the idea that I didn't know where I was headed. There was nowhere else to go. We were approaching the end.

On TV I saw images of people on boats. They were sailing, no … they were *drifting* from Libya towards Europe on boats that were about the same size as Da Gama's caravels. Their arrival created much consternation. They were a threat to the nation state, to territorial integrity and national sovereignty and many other kinds of highly inventive concepts. There were crisis meetings. There was flag-waving and much in the way of yelling into megaphones. There were a few dead babies.

They wouldn't be let in. They'd be turned back. They'd be processed and discreetly returned. They'd be deployed as cheap labour. Whatever happened, this was the end. Pride had already mutated into shame, poverty into indignation. There was nowhere else to go.

Dear Mr Dickerson,

Thank you for your letter. My husband and I have just returned from a trip to northern Spain and so I must apologise for my slow reply.

How very sad to know that Valerie has finally passed away. What a brave and courageous soul she was! I will most certainly miss her. I see you do take after your dear aunt, with all your wise words and whatnot. What on earth is a 'revolution that never keeps on happening'? My husband and I have spent quite a bit of time trying to work out what that means and I'm afraid we're none the wiser!

I was never quite sure if I understood Val. I was never sure where she stood in relation to some of the important questions of our time. Once she wrote to me and said that she was against equality. I couldn't have agreed more, given that equality is a perfectly unnatural state of affairs. But then she went on to explain that arguing over equality will provoke an unnecessary obsession over wealth. To argue over capitalism and communism was to argue two sides of the same coin. It was to argue over different emphases of the same question. How much do I get, or how much do you get? The argument, so Val suggested, was interminable because the answer to the question was the same. The answer was always, Enough! And how much is enough? Too much!

Larry and I (that's my husband, Larry) were concerned, quite frankly. I mean, wealth is hardly something one should complain about, no matter who gets it. But then in her next letter she wrote about Margaret Thatcher and declared her to be the best thing for Britain since the bulldog! We were both relieved! Larry and I were both very fond of Baroness Thatcher. Heavens! You're a High Court judge, so you probably are too!

Oh well, I suppose we're all entitled to our opinions. Greece in the winter! As you say, that might be a bit odd, but that was our dear Valerie.

Speaking of holidays, we've just had a very pleasant stay in San Sebastien. We have a flat there and enjoy visiting in the spring, to relieve ourselves of the muddy English winter and before the beaches become too crowded. We are very much looking forward to a visit to Burma in July. (I don't know why they're trying to change the name to Mynamar, or something like that — what a strange name for a country!) Our daughter lives in Rangoon and is working on a project to bring clean water to the poor! I'm sure you'd be very fond of our dear Clarissa. She never married, sadly, but seems to be quite happy putting so much of her energy into helping those less fortunate than ourselves. It is a bit sad for Larry and me, in that we see very little of Clarissa, although she is very good about phoning us on the internet computer.

I wonder why people don't get married any more. Val mentioned that you never married either — too busy fighting for justice, I suppose! In my day, we all did it without a second thought!

I shall sign off now. It's been such a pleasure to write to you (as it always was when we wrote to Val). If you ever find yourself travelling to England, you will come to stay with us in Summertown. We have a very large house and it's just the two of us rattling around in it, so we're always jolly pleased to have a guest – a High Court judge, no less.
With warm regards,
Caroline Beaufort

The possibility of my travelling to the UK was remote. And now it was remoter still. Caroline Beaufort struck me as a paranoid, irritable, unimaginative woman who never stopped talking and only did something wildly unconventional if everyone else was doing it. She appeared to live in morbid fear of being exposed for not having an opinion. Even the most exemplary ignorance could be concealed by a strident opinion. I didn't want to go anywhere near her. No wonder Val concocted the winter holiday in Greece. (I'd probably avoid Burma too – didn't like the sound of Clarissa either.)

Dear Mrs Beaufort,
Thank you for your letter which arrived this morning.
Indeed, we are all saddened by Val's death. She certainly was a courageous person. In many ways, I suppose we are all courageous as we plod our way through life, unsure of what it means and slightly appalled by how it ends.
Val wrote me a letter too and she asked me to tell you that she loved you. Val often spoke of love, exhorted us all to love one another, and seemed confounded when a note of discord attended our many discussions. Being loved, I suppose, is not the same as being liked. These days we seem to use these words interchangeably, which produces its fair share of confusion. Being loved is a much harder thing to do and so I suppose its rewards seem slightly more dubious.
Since Val died, I have been mulling over what it is that sadness does, not to us, but for us. I suppose in some way it instructs us, quietens us down, coerces us towards solitude, compels us to examine what our lives might mean to others.
Yes, Val was very fond of Baroness Thatcher. I am glad that you had all that in common. And true too, Val had a curiously ambiguous view of

money, at one point telling us that it was nothing more than a supersti-
tious symbol, and at other times imploring us to go out and earn some.
As you say, we're all entitled to our opinions, even if we have more than
one, I suppose! Nothing is really that certain after all!

That might sound strange coming from a High Court judge, but believe
me, we spend an awful lot of time searching for certainty, only to find that
there's always one more fact, one more perspective, one more unexpected
peculiarity to send a perfectly plausible theory into little more than a smoul-
dering heap. It explains why the quest for truth is so cumbersome, so slow
and so expensive – what else might lawyers spend so much time squabbling
about? I suppose compassion, a way of sharing in the confusion, no matter
what the facts might be, helps us to muddle through it all.

I do hope you have a wonderful time in Burma with your daughter,
Clarissa. Clean water for the poor! Whatever will they think of next?

With my best wishes to Larry and Clarissa and of course, to you.
The Hon. Mr Justice Edward Dickerson
P.S. Please call me Teddy

I knew it wasn't very much like a judge to extol compassion, 'no matter what the facts might be,' but I was hopeful that Caroline Beaufort would be 'none the wiser.'

And Caroline and Larry Beaufort, rattling around in their large house in Summertown, missed their daughter, Clarissa, who lived in Rangoon. I can't say that I didn't feel a bit sad about that. I didn't know how old Caroline and Larry were, but I assumed they were hurtling towards the end of their con-scious experience at startling speed. No doubt, they might be troubled about what happens next. And Clarissa, the produce of their own purplish, shudder-ing loins, was nowhere near to comfort them. Rattling around in a large house! It sounded terrifying.

That's really the whole point. Why would anyone complain about Robert Smollen being a millionaire and Janet Smollen being a pauper, when Caroline and Larry were agonising their way to their ignoble end while Clarissa smoked pot in Rangoon and took Danish lovers who worked for the World Food Programme into her three-star hotel room? Caroline and Larry were lonely. Janet was lonely. I was bloody lonely! Sharing the planet with seven billion people, each pulling away from the other in pursuit of individual freedom.

Freedom from what? Each other? Millionaires and paupers! A fitting distinction (a well-deserved debate) for a species made up of little god-kings.

I stood in front of the mirror. Nude again. I made a mental note that this could hardly be a good habit to get into. My pectoral muscles were no longer muscles. They were just lumps of fatty tissue, sagging towards the core of the earth. I used to trim my pubic hair, celebrate the thickening tumescent mass of my penis as it rose steadily in throbs of arousal. How thrilling that all was! Now it hung, soft and redundant, recoiling slightly into the long curly hairs of my groin. No one would pay for that.

This was hardly a new story. But I was one of the lucky ones. Tragedy was passing me by. I wasn't the twenty-year-old who suffocated in his vomit during a big night out. I wasn't the teen who got whacked in a car accident after music practice. I wasn't the kid who got swept off the rocks by a freak tidal wave, never to be seen again. I was slowly outgrowing tragedy. My demise was fated to be unspectacular, if unsightly.

I was one of the lucky ones!

Eighteen

The trial was now only a month away. Angus Goddard had still refused to hand over Randolph Smollen's previous Will.

'We may simply have to have you arrested, Angus,' I informed him with blistering coolness.

'Do your damnedest, Dickerson!' he replied with blistering finality.

I put the phone down.

'What the fuck are we going to do?' Ben said.

'He's a stubborn old goat,' I said unhelpfully.

It turned out that we couldn't have Angus arrested. He'd instructed counsel to apply for the nullification of the subpoena. We might oppose it. It would become a trial in itself, just as I'd predicted. The Smollen case would be postponed. Fanie Boshoff and his client, Robert Smollen, would find all this mightily amusing.

'We can't postpone,' Ben said.

'No.'

'This is nearly year four of this goddamn junket and we're nowhere near a trial.'

'Right.'

I had a slight, vain hope that Ben was losing confidence in me. Maybe there were other advocates with a more spirited interest in the proceedings who could hasten things along. Maybe he could sense how my enthusiasm for the trial had waned. Maybe he could sense how my enthusiasm for the rule of law had waned.

Later that day, Ben phoned and said: 'No postponement. We have to go ahead with what we have. Those are my instructions. Crystal clear. We have to give Janet her day in court. It's as simple as that.'

Ben was talking about the man in Canada – the one paying the bills.

'It won't be easy,' I said.

'I know, Teddy. I know. But I've got faith in you.'

I was sad when he said that. Inestimably sad.

I knocked on Sidney's door.

He was dressed in a spectacularly gaudy outfit: purple silk tie with shiny tiepin, gold satin waistcoat, bright pink shirt with white collar and cuffs.

'All dressed up to the nines. What's the occasion?'

Sidney returned his attention to his papers. 'A funeral.'

This was a conversation-stopper. But what *should* he have worn? Conventional dark suit and white shirt? Or something even more morbid? Perhaps his black court-gown?

'Well what is it?' he asked while I dawdled at the entrance to his room without, it might have seemed, any special purpose.

'Actually, I wanted to see if you'd be interested in a matter; taking something over. I'm not sure I want to do it any more.'

'Oh? What is it?'

'It's a contest over a deceased estate. Sister suing brother. Fraud. Forgery. That sort of thing.' I could tell that the moment these words fell from my lips, Sidney would want nothing to do with it. He worked for insurance companies, banks, people who sued the government (he loved those).

'Not a chance,' he said. 'I'm overloaded as it is. Argue over the intentions of a dead man. That's your sort of thing.'

'I thought you might say something like that.'

Sidney studied me closely. I looked down at my shoes and then out of the window.

'Why, might I ask, would you want to palm the matter off to someone else? What's worrying you about it?'

I sighed deeply, wasn't sure I had a coherent answer. 'I don't know,' I said at last. 'I mean, I just feel the whole caper is … just that, a caper. A lark. The system, the whole system, seems to operate in a perpetual state of failure. I'm not really sure it's doing any of us any good.'

Sidney smiled and leaned back in his chair without taking his eyes off me.

'Don't worry too much about the system, Teddy. All systems are corrupt. Yours, mine, theirs.' He gestured weakly at the window as if referring to the rest of the human race – the addled masses who lived and cursed beyond the room in which he and I sat. 'We invent systems because we're unreliable and we corrupt them because we're unreliable. They go nowhere. They're a palliative. Not a cure.'

I eventually stood to leave. At the door to his room, I turned. 'Sorry for your loss,' I said.

'Right,' he said. 'Thanks.'

Friends of mine with children used to say that the responsibility of parenthood was always a bit scary. 'There's no instruction manual!' they used to say with a laugh. It's true, there was no instruction manual – not for the children, not for the parents. Life comes with no instructions.

And what was I saying about 'friends'? I didn't really have any friends. I'd given up on them a long time ago. I was forty-five – halfway to ninety. Not long to go and I'd do exactly what Val did. I'd take the corner table in the dining room at The Cedars and sit with my back to the rest of the inmates.

No, I didn't have any friends. I didn't even have a cat.

Wilma had a cat. Prunella. And all she could do was worry about what happened if she died before Prunella. Or Prunella died before her.

No, there was no instruction manual.

Yes, I'd do exactly what Val had done. I'd have my corner table. I'd have my back to them. I'd have my letters.

Val was born in Johannesburg in 1936. She was the oldest of four children. After the war, her father returned from Egypt and took up a job with an illustrious mining house. In 1961 her mother, a heavy smoker, died of cancer. It was also the year South Africa left the Commonwealth. And it was the same year that Val married Aubrey Dickerson. It was a terribly difficult time, Val confirmed wistfully. I was never sure if she was referring to the death of her mother, the end of the Empire, or her marriage to Aubrey. Craig was born in 1962 and Vaughan in 1963. Her siblings began to drift away in the 1970s. A sister moved to Australia, another sister to London, and a brother to the Caribbean. Her father died in 1973. Aubrey died in 1982. Craig moved to Vancouver in 1984 and Vaughan left for America in 1985. Val sold Estantia in 1988 and spent the following decade and a half in a strange sort of nomadic stupor, moving from one apartment to the next. We could hardly keep up. No sooner had she moved into an apartment, arranged her heirlooms on the shelves, settled into a comfortable chair near a window, than she was on the phone to an agent, appalled at her circumstances and in search of another place to live. Finally, in a state of what I assume to be exasperation, and much to my relief, she checked into The Cedars in 2005, a week after her sixty-ninth birthday.

A lot of effort, a lot of heartache, goes into the assembly of an unremarkable life. Val spoke a lot about herself – her opinions, her knowledge, her theories, how she knew everything. But for all the talking, I knew so little about her – not even enough to fill half a page.

The trouble with Val, the thing that annoyed me infernally about her, was how she betrayed suffering. Even when speaking of her family – the death of the father, the death of the mother, the siblings and the offspring drifting away to opposite ends of the earth – the only thing she could tell me was, 'The importance of family is not that it sticks together, but that it falls apart'.

People often praised her for being strident and forthright and stoical. Never once had her voice quavered. Never once had I seen even the tiniest speck of a tear forming in the corner of her eye.

Soon after she moved into The Cedars, I went to visit her. We sat at the corner table, neither of us aware that this would become her custom. I asked her if she was happily settled, if she had made any new friends. 'Life is sad enough, Teddy. The last thing one needs is a whole lot of people making it sadder still. They all make too much noise.'

This was the woman who'd prevailed on everyone she met to 'love one another'.

Why did we not cry? Why did we shield our eyes, stifle our sodden gasps? Why did they quickly rush around to find you a tissue? Why did they say 'Shhh, there, there, *don't cry*'? Why might it have been noble to suffer in silence?

'Love is silent, Teddy,' she had written. 'The moment it is put into words, it becomes a folly. Not everything needs to be explained. Just ask the poets, poor tormented lot.'

But Val was tormented too.

Nineteen

I sat in my comfortable swivel chair listening, again, to Janet Smollen.
'I'm not sure it will be helpful if you tell the court that your father taught you how to make a noose, how it was important that everyone should be able to make a noose,' I said.

We had emails and letters and birthday cards. 'I love you,' he had written. 'I only want what's best for you.' That was the kind of sentiment we were after.

'Of course he *loved* me!' Janet said. She had no idea what that meant. It was as if she were stating a banal truism. *All* dads *love* their little girls.

We had the nurse. Josephine Sangweni. She'd been into Randolph's room countless times during his final days. Yes, she had seen Robert in there. Many times. Yes, she had cleaned up the papers on the desk, just trying to be helpful. Yes, Robert had chased her our of the room. Yes, she remembered the document. Last Will & Testament. She remembered entering the room at night, when Robert wasn't there. Randolph was asleep with his reading glasses perched on his nose. He held the papers to his breast. She remembered the witnesses. How they had had an argument. One of them had left in tears, shouting at Robert. 'You bastard!' she had yelled and then brushed past Nurse Sangweni and stormed for the door.

One of the witnesses had since died. No sign of a mystery gun. The hospital records showed a perfectly unremarkable cardiac infarction. The other witness refused to speak to us. 'I don't want anything to do with this. It's a terrible business.' That was all we could use.

We had letters from Angus Goddard addressed to Randolph. His Last Will &

Testament had been drafted, so Angus had confirmed in one of these letters. An appointment for a meeting was set up at his offices for Randolph to attend and sign the document. An invoice from Angus Goddard's firm included a charge for the custody of the Will, so it must have been signed. This was all six months before Randolph died and after he became ill.

So, why would he have executed a second will, months later, with just two weeks to live, after Robert had so fiercely guarded access to his room?

'When he was sick, Janet, you visited him from time to time.'

'Of course I visited him! He was very sick! He was my father!' Another truism. *All* daughters visit their sick fathers!

But she had only visited him twice in the last six months.

'I was very busy,' she explained. 'Heavens! I had … you know … all kinds of engagements, all kinds of errands to run. I was very involved in the gymkhana in Johannesburg. I practically had to organise it single-handed!'

'And on those two occasions, the two visits to your father, Robert was not there?'

'I've already told you, Mr Dickerson. You've already asked me, and no, he wasn't there.'

'Do you know where he was?'

'The first time he was in Durban. The second time … the second time it was at the hospital and Daddy didn't have long to go. Robert was away. I think he was in London.'

'So during the last six months of your father's life, you did not see Robert at all?'

'No. Not at all.'

'Were you trying to avoid him?'

'Avoid him? No! Of course I wasn't! I loved Robert! *Loved* my brother.'

Right, all sisters love their older brothers.

'Janet,' I said sternly, 'what was the problem? There was clearly some kind of problem. Your father was on his deathbed. You loved him. He loved you. You loved Robert and Robert loved you back. Yes, you might have been busy with the gymkhana, but it would be absurd to ask the court to presume that there wasn't something gravely wrong with your family.'

Janet looked at me aghast. 'How dare you say such a thing!' Her blue-grey eyes flared for an instant.

'None of you had any time for each other! This isn't … it isn't … *love!*'

I had raised my voice. I was losing my enviable composure. I settled back into my chair uneasily, tapping a pen against my knee.

'I'm sorry,' I said after a long silence. 'But these people are going to suggest that your father had some kind of problem with you, that he preferred Robert to you and always had. There was nothing untoward in his final testament. We're trying to prove the opposite, and visiting your sick father twice during the last six months of his life when he was gravely ill, and only when you knew that Robert wasn't there, hardly suggests that you got along. Frankly, it suggests that you couldn't bear the sight of each other. That's *all* it suggests. Gymkhana or not.'

I stopped tapping the pen against my knee and leaned towards her, placing my hands on the desk. I glanced at Ben. He gave me a slow nod of his grizzled head.

Janet looked at the floor. 'Nothing happened,' she said weakly. 'He gave me Blackforest. Nothing happened.'

Something happened, I thought. *Something most definitely happened.*

My car sped up the hill, away from Pietermaritzburg, passing the Queen Elizabeth Nature Reserve on the right and World's View on the left, towards the Midlands.

Some kind of molestation is what came to mind, some kind of appalling sexual abuse. The father and the daughter? Might Randolph have hated her because she was a victim and a witness to his secret? What kind of tormented soul was he? Or might it have been Robert? Did Randolph molest Robert? Might that have explained the strange, almost obsessive attention Robert gave to his father in his final days? Seeking redress, protecting his father's legacy by fiendish threats of his own? Or might Robert have molested Janet? What about the Mouse? Were they all molesting one another – these millionaires – in orgiastic frenzies filled with spite and power and recrimination in the billiard room? Or perhaps this was just lurid, not very imaginative, speculation. Perhaps they were all terribly happy, fishing in the dam, riding their horses, sitting in front of the fireplace roasting marshmallows.

Perhaps my quest for the truth was misguided and foolish.

The old gatekeeper emerged from his hut. He saw my shiny car at the gate and blinked. I stepped out. He recognised me and I got the feeling he wasn't pleased to see me. I wasn't supposed to go running off on my own, investigating the twisted history of the Smollen family. I'm searching for the truth, I told myself, but I wasn't convinced. Fanie Boshoff was filing all these papers about Janet's mental health. I didn't know why. He had some kind of tactic to discredit Janet. Yes, she was an unusual woman, but I didn't want any surprises. I needed to know what had happened. I needed to *know*!

'I'd like to talk to you,' I explained to the guard, 'just a few minutes, if that's okay.'

The guard stood at the doorway of his hut. He did not move. He did not smile. He stared at me. It was almost as if his expressionless silent face might compel me to scamper back to my car and drive away, never to return.

But I was nothing if not obstinate. 'Um, I need to ask you a few questions. It's for the court in Maritzburg. We're helping the family. The Smollens.'

He looked at the car, to see if there was anyone else with me. Finally, with a slight shrug and murmur of resignation, he trundled towards me, drawing the keys from his pocket. He unlocked the padlock and unfastened the chain to the gate. I drove in and parked next to his hut and a small patch of withered corn stalks.

I stepped out of the car and walked up to him, giving him my most harmless smile. 'I'm Teddy,' I said, putting out my hand. He shook it in the way that Zulu men do, while holding his forearm with his left hand.

'I … um … as I said, I'm here helping the Smollens. You know, they have some problems and you have worked here for many years. I thought you might be able to help me.'

The man looked about him, at the ground, the sky, the forest in the distance − anything but me.

'I worked here for forty years,' he said glumly. 'I don't know much about them.'

'Forty years? Gosh, that is a long time.'

I looked up towards the house; the plane trees had shed more of their leaves, defeated once more by the seasons.

'Come,' I said. 'Let's walk around a little bit. What's your name?'

'Jabu,' he mumbled cautiously.

Jabu regarded me with unmistakeable mistrust. He didn't need to say anything. It was obvious to both of us; it was the same kind of mistrust with which I regarded myself.

'I'm a friend of Janet's,' I explained as we commenced our slow stroll up the driveway towards the house. 'Janet is very sad. I think she's been sad for a long time. She's been sick.'

Jabu offered me no more than a long, troubled sigh. His breath steamed in the thin winter air.

'She's been seeing doctors. Many doctors. Many of us are trying to help her.'

The house came into view. It looked even more dishevelled than I remembered it. I strolled leisurely. Jabu strolled wearily. He was sick of me, of people like me. There we were, walking close together on each side of the road, separated by centuries of misapprehension. I had the shiny car. He had the little patch of corn. I was looking for the truth; he was constrained only to accept it.

'When the family was living here,' I continued, anguish swelling inside me, constricting my throat, 'there were some problems. Some things happened here that made Janet sick. You know old Mr Smollen has died. Mr Robert, he's moved away. So you are the only man who can help. You are the only man who can remember the old days, when they were living here.'

Jabu gave a miserly grunt. He had wanted to laugh. I could tell. He'd wanted to laugh it all off. Forty years of treachery. But he could only grunt. Laughter had died at The Millhouse a long time ago.

'Let's go to the back. To the stables.'

We walked around the side of the house, past the towering rhododendrons and the garages where they once had parked their Range Rovers and Jaguars during those fun-filled sunny holidays as Janet seemed to recall them. I pushed open the stable doors.

'Here,' I said. 'In here, Jabu. Something happened. Something happened here that made Janet sick.' We entered the dark, silent passageway. I headed for the stall that once had accommodated Blackforest. Jabu's pace slackened behind me.

He gave another great sigh. He didn't want to go on. I reached the stall. Jabu stood some distance away, his woollen hat in his hand. He'd go no further.

'Aikhona!' he said eventually. He shook his head, looking at the floor. 'Nothing, nkosani. Nothing. I remember nothing.'

'Jabu,' I implored gently. 'You have a daughter? A son?'

'Khona.' He nodded.

'If something or ... someone made them sick ... wouldn't you want to know? Wouldn't you want to know, so you could help them? Make them better?'

Jabu stood in the passage, just a sagging silhouette of a man against the open stable door at the end of the building. He was again motionless, without words, wishing I was gone.

'There was a horse here. Do you remember? Blackforest?'

After a long heavy pause, he nodded. 'Yebo. I remember, nkosani.'

'And it was Janet's horse. Mr Smollen gave the horse to Janet.'

'Yebo.'

'What happened to the horse? What happened here, in this place?'

'Eish!' Jabu exhaled, shaking his head. 'I don't know, nkosani.' His voice was pitched at an unusual, plaintive whine. He turned and walked away, at a more assertive pace, mortified that he should have turned his back on me, furious at me for my questions, but he could stand it no longer.

I followed him, walking briskly to catch up. I was out of words.

He stopped under the plane trees and surveyed the meadow in front of the house. I caught up with him. Jabu might have mistrusted me, but he knew too that I meant him no harm. He knew that I was trying to help and perhaps he also knew that I wasn't helping at all.

He looked grimly ahead, memories awake inside him – memories he was happy to live without. He pointed to the end of the meadow, to the lone willow tree whose branches hung over the dam. 'There,' he said. 'The one who died. The sick one.' He turned and walked back down the driveway towards his hut.

I climbed over the fence into the meadow and jogged across the brittle grasses, down to the willow tree. The grasses around the edge of the damn were still a lush, fleshy green. I looked about. There, under the tree, was a mound of thick grass. I pulled away at it, plucking the roots from the soft damp earth. There was the stone. Slightly weathered.

Norma Smollen, 1976–1982, May Her Soul Rest in Peace.

Norma Smollen. Dead after six years.

Who was Norma Smollen? Most likely a sister. Why had Jabu pointed to the grave? What secret did it conceal? How might it explain Janet's trauma? Or Robert's villainous plot to defraud Janet and his very own mother of their lawful inheritance? Was he jealous because Janet got a horse and he didn't? Four decades later and he was still bitter? Was he really that petty? Over a horse? What did Norma's death have to do with Blackforest, the horse that Randolph had shot to death? And what was with the noose? Something awful must have accompanied Norma's early demise, something more than a tedious humdrum illness.

It must have been some hideous thing – enough to inspire a sickening derangement, enough to infect an entire life story. That brought me back to the rape, the molestation, the abuse.

I grew tired of the speculation and admitted that I didn't really need to know any of these things. There are times when a lawyer ought not to ask a question of his client. And where would that leave us? The case? In a state of emphatic defeat. No, I didn't need to know. If Fanie sprang some outlandish allegation at Janet, belittled her, shamed her, rattled her so that her last few smatterings of sanity were set adrift, into the ether, what might I do about it? Perhaps I was trying to protect Janet. I didn't want them to hurt her.

And Jabu had lived in that hut for forty years. He would have been just a boy when the Smollens bought that farm. He'd seen it all. When asked for the truth, he only pointed to what was left of it. The stone at the bottom of the meadow. That is where the truth resided – the corroding surface of the headstone, leaning imperceptibly, ever further to one side, cold at night, hot in the day, caught in the ceaseless movement of light, never still. It didn't seem to matter what he *remembered* of the truth, but only what was left of it – here, today. Perhaps the only certain thing about the truth is its dreamlike nature, that it happens and then it fades away.

Remembering the truth seemed to be just another way of recreating it, turning it into yet another fiction.

There was no one to talk to about my visit to The Millhouse and my conversation with Jabu. Ben would have been outraged. Janet would have been smitten by grave suspicion. I'd have to try and let it rest, pretend I'd never returned to the Millhouse and never discovered Norma's grave.

I returned to Durban and parked the car outside The Cedars, even though I knew Val wasn't there any more. But I parked there and sat in the car for about half an hour.

Twenty

I looked at the clock in the corner of the screen. It had been hours. It couldn't have been!

I'd been looking at porn. Scrolling this way and that, looking at clips and pics and blogs. My hand glued to the mouse, I was half man, half machine.

Porn still worked … sort of. This pleased me … a bit. There were endless categories. Twinks and hunks, bears and cubs, Latinos and Asians, hairy and smooth. I was reminded of an old joke: if you don't like watching me mastur-bate, then get off the bus. It was funny, yes, and I smiled at the image of it.

Trouble was, I didn't feel like masturbating, on a bus or otherwise. Yes, the porn was a pleasure to look at. Reminded me of old fantasies, fleeting images as good to me now as they were when I was young. But they were images, just suggestions, ideas, had no purpose, no currency in the world of warm, pulsat-ing, stifled organisms. The porn worked, but only enough to coax my organ into a state of limp arousal. Unamused by the same old deadening fantasies, it grew soft again, returned to its usual sluggish posture as if annoyed for having been wakened at such a late hour.

I had a boyfriend once. An Italian. I used to call him the Italian Stallion and he laughed very much, without any idea of what a stallion was. He worked at a not-very-good Italian restaurant. I was drunk and told him that the chef was better than the food. We hung about for nearly a year and then I stopped an-swering his calls. He got the message. Six months later, I threw his toothbrush away and hoped I would never see him again.

At Chambers, I had brought him along to the Christmas party. Everyone had been very civil. Even the other gay advocates who'd brought their own boyfriends and girlfriends had been civil to poor Basilio. But I'd felt stiffened and outraged, and we'd left the party early.

Why had I been outraged? I knew what people were like and they weren't really that nice, but boy oh boy, did they want to know. Thirty? Thirty-five? Forty? Not married? So, um, are you … I mean … you know … What would you … You don't mind me asking, but …?

And then they wanted to tell me how *fabulous* they thought I was, as if I were some kind of exotic pet. And true too, that's exactly what I felt like, an exotic pet – a novelty – a llama at a dog show. Ten points for originality but no points for failing to jump through the hoop. It was suddenly as if *being different* were little more than a fashion statement. Who needs to jump through a hoop anyway, they'd laugh generously.

And those were the *nice* ones.

Sidney had once denounced homosexuality when we were drinking together in a bar. 'It's disgusting,' he'd declared.

And I'd said, 'Yes. I'm sure it is. All sex is disgusting. Just think of what you do with your sweaty bits. What a revolting proposition!'

He'd smiled, laughed and patted me on the back, suitably silenced (for once).

So, there I was, half man, half machine, hooked up to the internet, looking at porn.

I unpicked my hand from the mouse. They were no longer fantasies. They were just *memories* of fantasies. There is a point in life when even fantasy shifts from the realm of the implausible to the realm of the impossible.

Could the future really be that barren?

I turned the machine off.

Terry Winstanley phoned me on a Monday to tell me that the Estate Late Valerie Joan Dickerson had been wound up. 'We'll be filing the papers with the Master this week,' he said chummily.

'Right. Well, thanks.'

'Just thought you'd want to know.' He paused. I could tell he still had plenty more to say. I taunted him with silence. 'So,' he resumed finally. 'You know, the thing is that there was nothing in the Will for you, I'm afraid. Everything went to the sons – the billionaires in America.'

'And Canada.'

'Yes, and Canada.' He paused again briefly. 'I'm sorry,' he said. 'I mean, I know how well you looked after her, all your effort. You were a good fellow to old Val, but I'm afraid nothing came of it.'

I detested Terry Winstanley. More than ever.

'Thanks, Terry.'

I had my letter. She'd left me a letter. She'd left me a legacy – a real legacy, but to Terry Winstanley a legacy was an entry in the asset column of a liquidation and distribution account. Letters were worthless.

I supposed that her bits of jewellery, the silver jug, the brass lamp stand, and her collection of tiny oil paintings were being packed and sent to her sons in North America, leaving Africa at last.

It's about time, I thought.

'Can you believe,' I said to Ben at another one of our steak lunches (where I, again, ordered the fish), 'that Terry Winstanley rings me up to say that I didn't inherit anything from my aunt? He tells me how sorry he is. He says that, despite my efforts, my *unstinting* dedication to her well-being, she didn't leave me a thing. It's as if that's all I was ever interested in – some fucking antique trinket!'

'Terry's a prick,' Ben said gruffly.

'Total prick,' I agreed. 'It's as if life is just a series of trades, swaps, transactions – everything tit for tat. Otherwise people are pointless. I mean, I might have been concerned for my aunt but for Christ's sake, it wasn't for money. You know, it was—'

Fortunately, our food arrived and I was stopped in mid-sentence.

It was for what? It suited me that Ben wasn't really listening.

'In any case,' I continued, 'she did leave me something. She left me a letter. It was a very kind letter. Well, *most* of it. I'm very pleased to have it.'

'Right,' Ben said between mouthfuls of food. 'That's what it's all about. You know, feelings.'

That might have been the most philosophical thing Ben had ever said. Neither of us really knew what it meant.

'So, we're up for our final coaching session with Janet this week,' Ben said, eager to change the subject. 'All good?'

I hesitated, poking at the grey lump of fish on my plate. 'I'm worried, Ben. You know that.'

'We can't postpone. We'll never get that Will from Goddard.'

'No, but we'll make it part of the trial. We can prove that the Will exists.'

'Exactly.'

'But we can't prove what it says.'

'No.'

'That'll be our problem.'

'Yes.'

We ate in silence for some time. My fish was undercooked – frozen in the middle. I pushed the plate aside. 'Boshoff is going to make the case that Randolph hated his daughter. Or maybe not *hated* her, but had some legitimate gripe – that there was nothing inconsistent between what he felt about her and what he provided in the forged Will.'

'He'll go down that road.'

'After The Millhouse I'm worried more than ever. Janet isn't telling us something. I get the horrible feeling that we're going in half-cocked. She keeps telling us that everything was magical. Well, you know what that means: if it was magical, then it wasn't real.'

'Yup,' Ben agreed.

'There's no sign of any … you know … discord. Never an argument, a disagreement. Never a harsh word. No trauma. No tragedy. No random nastiness. But then there's this inexplicable Will. We're in the dark here, Ben.'

Ben stopped eating. This surprised me. He looked at me intently. He placed his knife and fork on the edge of his plate. 'Well,' he said. He wiped his mouth with a napkin and looked at the brownish smear he'd left on it with satisfaction. 'There was a bit of a tragedy, actually. It's not something they talk about. Quite understandable, really. Nothing to do with the case.'

'Oh really? And when were you planning on telling me?'

'It's nothing, Teddy. The thing is that they had another daughter. Norma. Poor thing. She had Down Syndrome. Was a sick little thing and she died very young.'

I stared at my fish. I couldn't look Ben in the eye, couldn't let on that I knew about Norma, or knew, at least, that she had once existed and her body was buried at the bottom of the meadow.

'Norma?' I said with deliberate coolness. 'Down Syndrome?'

'She was sick and died. There was a funeral. No one likes to talk about it. The point is that it has nothing to do with any discord or any kind of controversy. Nothing to do with what Randolph put in his Will – decades later, I might add.'

'You think?' I said caustically.

'We can't go there, Teddy. I've known the family for years and I'm telling you they don't like to talk about it. Obviously. Losing an infant. Not easy.'

Ben resumed eating with his usual gusto.

'I'll bet Fanie will want to talk about it. He wants to talk about her mental health. That much is clear.'

'Well, let him. It won't go anywhere. It was just a death. A sick child. Traumatic. But it explains nothing.'

'You should have told me, Ben.'

He grunted. He was suddenly in a surly mood. His steak had cooled with all the conversation.

'I'm going to raise it with Janet,' I said.

Ben gave me a steely glance and then shrugged. 'Well, it's up to you. You're trial counsel.'

Twenty-one

To the eight letters that I posted for Val on the last day of her life, I had received eight replies. I had sent out eight replies to their replies, to which I received seven replies in return. One was missing. Tiffany Medford was missing. She was the one – the only one – who didn't seem that fond of Val. I had no idea how their correspondence had begun, but yes, Tiffany must have been the one who had abandoned Wilma and Prunella in Vancouver to pursue some dreary romantic ambition with a man in Australia. She was the one who worked for a bank, gave me her email address, and used words like 'fuddy-duddy'. Work for a bank! Who, in God's name, would want to do a thing like that?

> *Hello Teddy,*
>
> *Interesting to know that Val finally died. I didn't really have any plan to write back to you but then I thought of your letter and I realised what a pain in the arse you must be to write a letter like that. You sound just like Val with all her little 'wise words'. You Dickersons all sound so sorry for yourselves and so sad. Get a life! I don't need any more 'wise words' from a Dickerson. That's what you all do, you all meddle in everyone else's business, sticking your little noses where they don't belong. I'm moving on with my life. I'm having fun and I don't need you to tell me about all your sad stories. I've got a great job, great kids, I'm happily married and we're actually very successful, so I don't really need any letters from you.*
> *Thanks!*
> *Tiffany*

People who use phrases like 'get a life' should be shot.

I put the letter down. I did feel like a sad Dickerson. That was true. The last sad Dickerson of Africa. I had nothing to say. Letters, handwritten — only the scratching of the pen on the surface of the paper, taking days to reach their destination — were all I had, and I was grateful for that.

Yes, I resented Tiffany. I resented Val. I resented Tiffany for resenting Val.

Janet and Ben arrived. This was bound to perk me up.

'Janet!' I said, after they've settled in their regular seats. 'Not long to go now before we have our day in court, our day in the sun!'

She looked at me with her usual expression: pain, guilt, confusion, and hope. That about summed it up, summed *her* up.

'Wouldn't it be nice,' I said, reclining in my chair, looking up at the ceiling, 'if Robert simply looked you in the eye and said he's sorry and shared your father's things with you?'

I felt Janet was slowly shrinking in her seat. I felt her looking at Ben for some kind of intervention. I felt Ben looking out of the window.

'I … I don't think I could look *him* in the eye,' she quavered.

I returned to face her, gave her a profoundly penetrating glare. 'No? And why not?'

'I … I can't forgive him. Look at what he's done. Cheating me like this. I … I hate him.'

I reclined again and looked at the ceiling. 'Hate,' I said, mostly to myself. 'A most unfortunate thing.'

Ben upended my delicate repose, my nascent reverie. 'You won't need to look him in the eye, Janet,' he said. 'He's not coming. He won't be attending the trial. His attorneys have told me that he'll be in the Caribbean. Fishing for marlin apparently.'

I glanced at Ben. 'He's not testifying?'

'The plan is to sink our handwriting expert and, without that Will from Goddard, they'll argue there's no loss to the plaintiff and wrap it up.'

'Hmm, yes,' I concurred with a note of doom. 'A bit sad, though, that Robert couldn't simply pay a visit. You know, just observe the proceedings. I mean, say hello. If this is what the father wanted, then so be it.'

'I'm glad he's not coming,' Janet said icily. 'I hate him. Couldn't face him. Cruel, callous little man.'

I leaned forward with my elbows on the desk and pressed my fingers together. 'Let's talk about the hatred, Janet. It seems that there's hatred all around, in buckets. And they'll like that because it's exactly their point. They will be saying that you've hated each other for years; your father hated you. His Will proves it.'

'Oh!' Janet gasped. 'We've done this already! I've told you! Everything was fine. Everything was perfect. We were just the usual happy family. We had a lovely time. It was only when—'

'Norma?' I interrupted her.

Janet paused. A sudden weighty silence seemed to hang over us.

'Who told you about Norma?' She picked up her broken handbag from the floor and placed it on her lap. She began to dig through it with grave agitation, with no idea of what she was looking for.

'A lot of people know about Norma,' I said.

'Norma! Norma! Why on earth is this always about bloody Norma?'

'Well, isn't it?'

'No! It's not! I didn't know! What do you want me to say?' Janet began to sob. Her handbag miraculously offered her a tissue, which she snatched up fiercely. She sobbed with painful relief, taking in great convulsive gulps of air, her shock of ginger hair hanging messily over her downcast head.

Ben crossed his arms and looked at me accusingly. He did nothing to comfort Janet.

'This is about the truth,' I said to both of them.

Janet jolted upright and glared at me. 'The truth? What do you know about the truth, Mr Dickerson?' She spoke with such unusual ferocity, such bitterness, I couldn't help feeling disconcerted. It was a side to her I'd never seen. It was blinding rage, and it was about Norma, not Robert.

I opened my mouth; I closed my mouth. I couldn't answer her.

'The truth! The bloody truth! Everyone wants to know the truth!' She raised her hands as if offering herself to the heavens. 'Well, if you *have* to know the truth, Mr Dickerson,' she said scathingly, slamming her hands against the desk, 'Norma died. She was sick and she died. That's the truth. That's all there is.' She looked at me with shimmering eyes. 'Why does this *always* have to be about Norma?' She began to sob again.

Ben reached towards her and gave her a pat on the shoulder. She brushed him away, still staring rigidly at the floor.

'We're here to help,' he said with surprising tenderness. 'Teddy wants to help and sometimes it's a bit painful.' Speaking to Janet, but looking at me severely, he added: 'We won't speak any more about Norma. It was very sad and we won't speak about it again.'

Janet nodded and dabbed her eyes. It seemed as if she felt a little better.

Ben rang later.

'Look, Teddy, I know why you had to go there and I don't blame you. I mean, I had to talk her off a ledge ...' He paused and corrected himself: 'I mean, *metaphorically* speaking. She's fine now. She realises that, you know, we're trying to help and get this case over the line and that it will be tough. She's fine. She trusts you. She trusts us.'

I loved the idea of being trusted. There's no greater feeling in the world. No greater feeling, I said to myself, except when it's not deserved.

'Norma's at the nub of this, Ben.'

'Yes. I know.'

'Something terrible must have happened, something that shook that family to the core.'

'Yes.'

'And Janet and the Mouse are still paying the price.'

'That's how it appears.'

'And Fanie obviously knows and he's going to rattle her.'

'Don't be so grim. Let me assure you, Teddy, that, yes, Janet can seem a bit, you know ... wobbly ... but she's not stupid. She's smart. She'll manage.'

Ben had not assured me of anything.

And at the end of the day, there was still the matter of what to do over Tiffany Medford's letter. I had thought of writing to her to apologise for hurting her feelings or to tell her to go and fuck herself. I couldn't decide which might be more deserved.

Not writing to her at all wasn't satisfying either.

I thought little more of my letters and my letter writers until the day before the Smollen trial was due to commence. Mrs Nawal Hassan wrote to me from Egypt. Curiously, I had formed the view that I couldn't quite regard myself as the last Dickerson of Africa while Nawal was still there, in Alexandria (even if she was the descendent of a different bloodline).

Dear Mr Teddy,

I love to receive your lovely letter. Thank you, Mr Teddy. You are kind to say that Mrs Valerie loved me. I loved her too, very much, and I miss her every day. And every day I pray for her spirit high up in the Heavens.

Do you pray too, Mr Teddy? Mrs Valerie used to tell me that many people do not pray in your country any more. I know, it is like that in Egypt too. We have so many troubles here. Nobody prays. They go to pray, but they don't pray. Mrs Valerie made me laugh many times. She said that the big problem we have in the Middle East is because it has a foolish name. How can a place be in the middle and in the East? No surprise that there is so much conflict. She said that we should call it the Muddle East, then everyone can calm down, because everybody will know about the muddle. Oh, I miss my Mrs Valerie so much.

Do you know, Mr Teddy, I was a school-teacher? I was a teacher of history for nearly forty years. In Egypt we have this feeling that we are special people. We have the pyramids and the gods of Isis and Osiris. We are the place where the old books remark about the Red Sea and the beginning of the human journey. Egypt is the place of the first university and the first farms. We like to think that when people pray around the world, they think about this little place called Egypt. It is the place where humanity started to worry very much and began to wander around our planet, making it so small, as we search and search for something. What are we searching for Mr Teddy? Is it the truth? Do we need the truth to guide us? If so, why have we not yet found it?

I am an old lady now, Mr Teddy, and soon I will follow and meet my friend in the Heaven, my lovely Mrs Valerie. Even my own children, they do not listen too much to their old mother! So I tell you, Mr Teddy, because you are a lovely man, that we, all of us have a long story all the way from the times of Egypt. It is the same story in every place. We didn't like the superstitions. We didn't like the religions. We didn't like the monarchs. We don't like the republics. Then we are left only with the self. And, now, we are not sure if we like the self either.

I never knew my own father, Mr Teddy. He passed away during the war. My mother, bless her soul and rest in peace, she told me always that my father liked to tell her: All you have in the end is how you have treated other people. I have this saying stuck on my wall. Mrs Valerie wrote all the time about love. Now you write to me too and tell me about love. Thank you, Mr Teddy. I love you too and also your lovely family and six children.

God bless you, Mr Teddy, and thank you for listening to old Mrs Hassan.

With love I say, goodbye.

Nawal

All you have in the end is how you have treated other people. Her father. Val's father. And to me, an ancestor – one of whom I feel oddly proud.

Twenty-two

Darshini, Glynnis, Wilma, Nawal, Jennifer, Caroline, Tiffany, and Candice. The night before a trial, especially one that is complex and subject to far more variables than I would like, is always difficult. Sweaty palms. Lump in the throat. Sour knot in the tummy. The irresistible urge to swallow a Xanax, or more than one, pitched against a steely resolve to keep clear-headed. My loathing of the profession, its merciless constructs, is now almost complete. It is a mind game, a game for the mind. Like chess, where the vagaries of luck, of old-fashioned charm, of tears, of song, of gnashing teeth have no useful place. Still, we try it on: bravado, deception, indignation, self-pity. It's all that's left in the ruthless halls of those places that espouse the vaunted rule of law. The sandstone edifice, the enrobed officials, the sycophantic decorum – all fading remnants in support of an old superstition, a fiction that supposes that, at the core of every human being, there is a machine, a computer, if you will, which reasons and computes and calculates with unwavering precision in exactly the same way, with deadening uniformity.

I dared not read another thing about the Smollens. Sick to death of the Smollens!

Sleepless and irritable, I walked through to the cupboard and pulled out Val's box of letters. Her original instructions – no doubt for the benefit of Terry Winstanley – was still sticky-taped to the box. Do NOT open. Or *was* it for Terry's benefit? Perhaps it was for mine.

I picked away at the sticky-tape around the edges and opened the box. Val had kept their letters and handwritten copies of each of her replies.

This was Caroline Beaufort in a letter written in 1986:

My husband is a very keen birdwatcher. Wherever we travel, he always takes with him his bird books and binoculars and his special birdwatching hat! I find it a bit tiresome. I prefer to while away my time reading. Spy thrillers are my best. Although I must tell you that we were recently in America, wandering around some national park or another — I forget which one — and my husband spotted some unusual bird high up in an enormous tree. I could barely see it. But he was enthralled! On our walk back to the car, he explained how birds engage in a rather complicated sort of courtship. Male birds fluff up their feathers, exaggerating their colourful plumage, and offer the most seductive calls to the rather mousy-looking female birds in the forest. He said that courtship, whether it be for birds or humans, is inevitably steeped in all kinds of preposterous deceit!

Of course, I disagreed with him. I might not be an avid birdwatcher, but I am still fond of nature and disinclined to believe that all these wonderful innocent creatures are cavorting about the forest deceiving one another. In fact, we ended up having the most appalling row. He referred to the dog who is threatened and how the hair is raised on its back — designed to make it look bigger than it really is. He pointed to the mock charge offered by elephants and wildebeest and so on (or buffaloes. I don't recall). He described the way a chameleon changes colour so that it appears to be little more than a nodule on a tree. Or the way that a tiny ladybird might flare up with its little red wings as if to suggest that it might be poisonous to a predator. He literally assailed me with a litany of other examples and I can't possibly remember them all. I suppose I'm only really telling you all this because you live in Africa and are surrounded by all those wonderful animals. And I suppose also to ask whether you might have a view on this. I've found it all to be rather unsettling. I've even discussed it with our local vicar, but he's a young fellow and doesn't seem to be a good listener. Do let me know what you think, my dear. I truly want to know. You will write to me soon, won't you?

I sifted through the other letters and, here, I found Val's rather succinct reply:

I'm quite sure your husband is right. Seduction is innately deceptive.

And to Wilma's complaint from 1987 that

what really hurts is the lie ...

Val wrote:

It hurts not because she cannot be trusted, but because you do not trust yourself. Lies would be meaningless otherwise.

And later in the same letter, she added a little lie of her own:

Forgive me if this letter is shorter than usual, but Walter the pig has been unwell and I have the vet coming around any moment.

Had the kind and generous Wilma deceived me? Was she an idle, self-pitying frump who obsessed over her cat? Is that why Tiffany had left her? How could I be sure?

And in 1999, Darshini wrote of her love of music:

It's the space between the notes that captivates my imagination. I know many people have taken it on themselves to say this before, but it's really true!

Darshini seemed excited about expressing this observation and Val replied:

How right you are! The absence of sound is what gives sound meaning. You seem willing to forgive the silence that sound offers us. Forgiveness is yours, Darshini.

This was Candice from 1992:

Do you know that I never cry? I haven't cried in years. I'm sort of proud of it in a way. And it also kind of annoys me.

When I read Val's reply, a sudden, involuntary sob rose to my throat:

I cry. I cry all the time. I cry alone.

Val cried alone. I couldn't bear the thought of it. And was this another aspect of her deceptive bravado? Another aspect of her unusual seductiveness? The brave, stoical, invincible woman with silver hair and a powdered face? Was Val loved? Aubrey, the man who, by her own admission, no one ever thought about, did he love her? Is that why she'd, in a moment of panic, written him down as her next of kin on her hospital admission form? Did she miss him, right through to the end? Even after all those years?

In 1999, Jennifer remarked:

All everyone seems to do these days is talk about politics and politicians. Frankly, they all bore me to tears. They all lie their heads off. None of them seems to have the foggiest idea of what they're doing. I wish we all had something else to talk about!

I laughed at Val's reply:

You're quite right about politicians or people who want to be politicians. There is something rather disturbing about them – mentally so. They do seem to lie their heads off. I suppose it's their own fault, poor things. It's an old trick to make promises – especially promises that purport to solve every last one of our most intractable problems. Properly duped, we tend to obsess over them in the way that we used to obsess over God himself. But, of course, they are not God. They are, instead, in search of God. Perhaps all we can really do is love them. That should settle them down. And then we might at least all get on with the business of living with one another.

This was a truly spectacular idea. A profound indictment of the secular state. A call to anarchy!

I could not find the corresponding letter from Tiffany to which Val wrote:

> *Your anger is yours. Whenever you feel it, you will know that it is your truth. Let it guide you towards an understanding of what, for now, is some unmentionable aspect of yourself. There's no need to express your anger. It's not for me or others to see. It's there for you. Your anger is your anger, as is your love.*

And Glynnis was right when she told me that she had resented Val's first letter in 1979:

> *Allow me to make myself plainly understood: I don't know you and you don't know me and I find your letter to be unduly intrusive, if not even a little sanctimonious. Please do not write to me again. I am quite all right. Thank you very much.*

Val replied:

> *You'll have to forgive me, but, in a strange sort of way, I do know you. And I believe that you know me too. Aren't we all a bit like that with one another?*

And finally, to Val's half-sister, Nawal, in Egypt in 1978:

> *You'll have to forgive me, but, in a strange sort of way, I do know you. And I believe that you know me too. Aren't we all a bit like that with one another?*

These letters. These writers. They are the healer, the sick, the fearful, the brave, the student, the teacher, the glum, and the bright.

With Nawal's letter held to my chest and the other letters spread out over the bedspread, I fell asleep with the lights on – as ready as I would ever be for *Smollen v Smollen & Another.*

Twenty-three

It was cold with clear skies in Pietermaritzburg that morning, and it looked as if it would warm up nicely.

'Thank you, My Lord. I'm Edward Dickerson appearing for the plaintiff.'

Judge Wiseman Ncube gave me a perfunctory nod.

'Thank you, My Lord. I am Fanie Boshoff sc appearing for both defendants.'

Another perfunctory nod.

Someone coughed. Papers were shuffled. The judge made notes. We watched him obediently. He looked up, almost as if he were slightly bored. 'Mr Dickerson?'

I stood. 'Thank you, My Lord. With the permission of the court, My Lord, I may submit an opening statement.'

Judge Ncube's eyes narrowed. He looked at me for what seemed like an awkwardly long time. 'Yes,' he said finally. 'Proceed.'

'Thank you, My Lord. As Your Lordship will see from the pleadings, this is a matter that concerns a brother and a sister. The plaintiff is the First Defendant's sister and the Second Defendant's sister-in-law. Given that all the parties to this matter share the same surname, that of Smollen, counsel for both the plaintiff and the defendants propose that we refer to them by their first names so as to avoid any confusion.'

'That is fine, Mr Dickerson.'

This is what it comes down to: A man, dressed in a black robe with a fluffy silk bib fastened around his neck by a piece of elastic hidden beneath his collar, stands in a room full of people. He speaks to another man, a stranger by all accounts, who also wears a robe and a fluffy bib, and who sits in a decorative chair in front of an elaborate desk festooned with brass fittings. He imparts certain facts. More enrobed people join in. Facts are heaped on facts, one teetering on the other in support of a decision that will forever explain the anguish endured over the life of a dead father.

This was the point of it. A rational explanation. This would solve everything.

The truth was apparently what we were after. An explanation. A list of reasons. And once comprehensively explained, what became of the anguish of the disputants, with their real or imagined suffering? The truth, apparently – this orderly arrangement of credible facts – would set them free!

One day a computer will be able to do this job.

'As it pleases the court, My Lord. The plaintiff is Janet, Janet Smollen. The First Defendant is her brother, Robert, and the second defendant is his ex-wife. Janet and Robert's father, the late Mr Randolph Smollen, whom we shall refer to as Randolph, died in 2009. He was, by all accounts, a wealthy man. In late 2008 he was diagnosed with terminal cancer, specifically stage four pancreatic cancer. Soon after this diagnosis, Randolph executed his Last Will & Testament and deposited this document in the custody of Goddard Fairbairn & Ngubane attorneys, here in Pietermaritzburg. Thereafter, he underwent extensive medical treatment, including various operations, chemotherapy, and radiation therapy. For the most part, he remained at the family home, a farm in the Midlands, until his final two weeks, whereupon he was treated in hospital, which is where he finally succumbed to his illness. He is survived by his wife, Mrs Jill Smollen, whom we shall refer to as Jill, and his two children, Robert and Janet. During the last months of his life, Robert attended to his father every day or very *nearly* every day. We propose to lead evidence indicating that the attention Robert gave to his father bordered on something almost obsessive, much to the exclusion of other visitors and even sometimes compromising the ability of medical staff to provide the necessary treatment. We will also show that during that time, Robert was involved in arrangements to have his father execute a new Will. We will show that on the day the new Will was purportedly executed, there was a dispute between Robert and the two witnesses who ostensibly witnessed the execution of the new Will. We will show that Randolph's purported signature on the new Will is indeed a forgery. Alternatively, we will show, as pleaded, that Robert coerced Randolph, by exerting undue influence on the sick man, to sign the

Will. Either way, the Will was executed or ostensibly executed with the intention of fraudulently depriving Janet and her mother of their lawful inheritance. Randolph Smollen's estate, conservatively estimated at nearly one billion United States dollars, was wound up by order of this court in 2011. According to the provisions of the ostensible testamentary document, Robert Smollen inherited the entire estate. He has moved abroad and lives, by all accounts, in splendid opulence, while Janet and her mother live here in modest rented accommodation, in penury, struggling to make ends meet.

'When these proceedings were launched four years ago, Robert Smollen conveniently and somewhat cynically divorced his third wife, the Second Defendant. We will submit that this was a deliberate attempt to conceal and divest himself of the assets of the deceased estate. Our evidence will show that the divorce was far from acrimonious and that it was little more than a ruse.

'My Lord, this matter has caused, as can only be expected, considerable distress and sadness to Janet Smollen. Janet had a close and affectionate relationship with her father and with her brother. This is about more than just money, My Lord. It is about greed and betrayal. It is betrayal of the very worst kind, betrayal of a family, betrayal of a dying man.

'Janet has undergone psychological and other forms of medical therapy over the past few years to help her navigate the emotional trauma that this affair has wrought on her. She will give evidence in these proceedings, My Lord.

'In summary, My Lord, we will show that Robert, acting individually and in concert with the Second Defendant, connived to deprive Janet and her mother of their lawful inheritance, causing them irreparable loss, and we therefore pray for the relief set forth in the plaintiff's plea. As it pleases the court, My Lord.'

I sat down and Fanie Boshoff stood up. He was a plump, bearded man with thick wiry hair and seemed altogether cheerful.

'Mr Boshoff?'

'Thank you, My Lord.' Mr Boshoff spoke slowly in a gruff Afrikaans accent that was slightly benign, slightly menacing. 'We have no interest in delaying these proceedings any further. Suffice it to say that the defendants will, by and large, prove the opposite to be true.' He paused, took a sour glance at me and said: 'I may add, My Lord, that there is only one Last Will & Testament to be entered into evidence, that of the so-called forged Will. Whether it was forged or not, or whether Robert somehow coerced Randolph into signing it, then the plaintiff is doing little more than asking the court to invent a new will. Based on a few letters and emails and maybe some oral testimony, they are effectively asking this court to write up a will that they like. Your Lordship will be aware that no matter how aggrieved the plaintiff may feel, it is beyond the powers of this court, although considerable, to invent the final wishes of a dying man. If the Will is somehow shown to be invalid, which is something strenuously denied by the defence, the court must find that Randolph Smollen died intestate and according to the laws of succession that applied at the time, the entire estate ought to have devolved on the surviving spouse, the plaintiff's mother, who is notable by her absence from these proceedings.'

He sat down and looked at the papers before him with enviable smugness, pleased with himself, avoiding eye contact with me.

Fanie was accompanied by a team of seven well-fed lawyers. All of them had driven down from Johannesburg the night before in an array of expensive shiny black cars with GP plates.

Ben and I had driven up from Durban that morning in Ben's old Mercedes, accompanied by one of Ben's clerks, a sweet, gangly young man called Moosa with a sensual curved nose and the gentlest hint of a moustache.

Our client was emotionally unhinged, utterly terrified, while theirs was sipping brandy on a balcony overlooking some glittering coastline, waiting for little more than a phone call telling him it was all over.

To any independent observer, it might have seemed we were doomed.

'Mr Dickerson? Your first witness?'

'Thank you, My Lord. We call the plaintiff, Miss Janet Smollen.'

Janet walked briskly to the witness box. She entered the box, placed her handbag on the floor next to her, cleared her throat, and faced the microphone with encouraging assertiveness.

'Orderly? The oath?'

The orderly stood. 'Say after me, please: I swear that the evidence I shall give shall be the truth, the whole truth, and nothing but the truth. Raise your right hand and say: "So help me God".'

Janet raised her right hand. 'So help me God.'

'The witness is sworn in.'

Judge Ncube again took to studying his papers. Janet stood in the witness box, rigid and defiant. I couldn't help feeling a little proud of her.

'Yes, Mr Dickerson, you may proceed.'

'As it pleases the court, My Lord.' Turning to face Janet, I offered her a little smile. She glared at me fiercely, as if I were a slightly threatening stranger. 'Janet, could you give your full names for the record, please?'

Janet took a deep breath and clutched the railings of the witness box. 'I—' She stopped. The back doors of the court had opened and someone had entered the room. I did not need to look. I knew who it was. Blood drained from Janet's face. She leaned forward against the railing as if she might suddenly fall.

Ben and Moosa turned. Ben tugged at my sleeve. I leaned towards him. 'It's him,' he hissed. 'It's Smollen. Robert Smollen. They told me he wasn't going to be here.'

'It was a trick,' I whispered back.

Straightening up and facing Janet once again, impervious to the commotion created by Robert's entrance, I said: 'Janet, are you all right?'

She returned to face me. Her earlier assertiveness had abandoned her and her voice was little more than an anguished whine. 'I … I am …'

I faced the judge. 'I apologise, My Lord, but it seems to me that there is something of a distraction going on. I might ask the court to place on record that, at this point, the First Defendant, Mr Robert Smollen, has entered the courtroom. Janet and Robert have not seen each other since their father's funeral. Given what has transpired between the two since then, it might be that the plaintiff is in a state of shock. Might we have a few minutes to allow the witness to compose herself?'

Fanie stood. 'My Lord, what is this game? Robert Smollen is the First Defendant. Why on earth, I mean *how* on earth could this be a shock? Of course Robert is here. Frankly, nothing should be *less* unexpected.'

'Mr Dickerson?' the judge asked glumly.

'If the relationship between the parties is one of long-standing acrimony and estrangement, My Lord, Janet might be forgiven for experiencing a sense of shock, even if Robert's presence is not entirely unexpected.'

'Hmm,' the judge said. He turned to Janet. 'Are you all right, Miss Smollen?'

Janet gaped at him and then at me. All I could do was stare back at her stiffly.

'Yes,' she said. 'I'm fine.' She looked at her shoes.

I stood. 'Very well. Might we have it placed on the record that Miss Smollen's demeanour was such that she appeared distressed or disturbed, or at least had lost her train of thought when Robert entered the court?'

'Mr Boshoff?'

'Well this all seems a bit theatrical, My Lord. If we need to point out every time a witness loses their train of thought, we might be here for a while.'

'We can enter it, Mr Dickerson,' the judge confirmed.

'As it pleases the court, My Lord.' Turning again to Janet, I said: 'Janet, please give the court your full names for the record.'

'I am Janet Irene Smollen.'

'Thank you, Janet. Perhaps you can start by giving us a description of your relationship with your family, including your late father.'

We'd practised this testimony countless times and Janet acquitted herself in an exemplary fashion. I barely prompted her. I was enormously impressed. So were Ben and Moosa, and even the court seemed transfixed by her tale of a happy childhood. Occasionally she directed a glance at Robert. Yes, she *could* look him in the eye!

She spoke of the time when her mother was ill with pneumonia and how Randolph had bundled them all into the car late at night, driven through the mist and the rain from The Millhouse to Pietermaritzburg and had doted on her like a loving husband. She spoke of the time she was homesick at boarding school and how her father had visited her. They had sat in his car. He had brought her English toffees. They'd eaten the toffees; he'd comforted her and she'd felt better. She spoke about Robert's twenty-first birthday and how Randolph had given a speech to hundreds of assembled guests and how, at the end of his address, he had called Janet and Robert to the stage, describing her as his 'angel'. She explained the contents of an email he had sent her when he was away on business in Malaysia: 'One day, my darling, you and Robert will inherit the family fortune and I pray that you will be happy.' She even recalled incidents where there were arguments – inconsequential family rows, about where to go on holiday (Robert wanted to go to St Moritz, but Janet and Jill had wanted to go to the Caribbean). All was resolved amicably. Even Robert offered a little smile at that one.

Photographs, birthday cards, emails were admitted in evidence without a hitch. Fanie made no effort to interrupt – he almost seemed a little bit bored.

Robert had taken a seat directly behind his team of lawyers. He occasionally scribbled notes and handed them to instructing counsel, who handed them to Fanie. Fanie nodded, seemed deep in thought and then hurriedly penned a few notes to his own papers. But for these interruptions, I suspected that Fanie might have drifted off to sleep.

'Thank you, My Lord. I have no further questions for the moment.'

'Thank you, Mr Dickerson. Mr Boshoff?'

'As it pleases the court, My Lord,' Fanie said, rising to his feet wearily. With his gaze keenly focussed on Janet, he said: 'So you like English toffee, Miss Smollen?'

'I, uh ... yes.'

'Your dad liked English toffee too?'

'Er ... yes.'

'He did?'

'Yes, he did.' Janet brushed her hair back from her face assertively.

'In fact, he liked them so much that anyone who knew him well knew that he liked to travel with a tin of English toffees in the car, isn't that so?'

'Yes. Yes, he did. He loved toffees.'

'Right, so when you said in your testimony that he "brought toffees" to you at school, he wasn't bringing them specifically for you, was he? He just happened to have them in the car, same as any other day – isn't that an accurate description?'

'I ... he ... I mean, he did bring them to me, you know.'

'Yes, but it's important for us to provide a very accurate picture for the court, Miss Smollen. So, just answer the question. He never brought any toffees especially for his little girl at school, did he?'

'No.'

'And, as it happened, you weren't just homesick, Miss Smollen, were you?'

'I was homesick!' Janet looked at him indignantly.

'And?'

'What?'

'And let's see what else you might have left out of your glowing testimony. You had been admitted to the school sanatorium, hadn't you? The nurse had phoned your father saying that you had been unwell. Does that jog a memory?'

'I ... I hadn't been well. That's true, but I was also homesick.'

'In fact, Miss Smollen, you had been *mentally* unwell. Wasn't this your first brush with mental illness?'

'I had been unwell. I'd been depressed. I was homesick.'

'So your father didn't visit you because he just happened to have some spare time on his hands. He visited you because the school nurse had asked him to. He had been called there.'

'Well, he visited me. He visited me. He was concerned, as any father would be.'

'And your mother? Why didn't your mother visit?'

'I ... uh... I don't remember.'

'She used to visit you often, did she not?'

'Yes, she did.'

'So, why did she not visit you on that occasion, when you were sick and depressed?'

'I ... I don't remember.'

'Your mother was in London, Miss Smollen. If she had been in South Africa, she would have visited you, not your father.'

'Oh ... I don't ... I don't really remember.'

'Well, I put it to you that she was and you don't deny it.'

'No. I mean, I don't deny it. She might have been.'

'So, this lovely visit from your father when you ate toffees wasn't because he cared for you like any father, but because there was frankly no one else available when the nurse called. Isn't that so?'

'He did care for me. He *did*!'

'In fact, the only reason why you remember his visit so clearly is because it was the only time he ever visited you during the six years that you were at boarding school, isn't that so?'

'No! I mean ... He ... It ... He loved me very much and came to see me when I was sick.'

'Your wonderful happy family life Miss Smollen – frankly the only way I can describe it is that it was too good to be true. Is that an accurate description?'

'Yes.'

'So, it's not true?'

'No, it's true.'

'So why did you say it was *too good* to be true?'

'Because it was ...' Janet suddenly reddened. Her voice began to shake. 'Because it was good and it was true. Sorry, I'm getting ... You're confusing me.'

'Oh? Confusing you?'

'Yes.' Janet glowered at him and then at me, imploring me to intervene.

'You spoke about your brother's twenty-first birthday, Miss Smollen. It sounded like a happy occasion. But can you tell us about your own twenty-first birthday? Why did you not recount any happy memories from your own twenty-first birthday?'

'I … um,' Janet gulped. 'I … didn't have one.'

'What? No birthday?'

'Well, no party. I was feeling a bit blue at the time.'

'Oh, you were feeling blue? A bit depressed? Another depression?'

'Yes.'

'I see. Funny how during your evidence you didn't mention any sign of any depression. Not even a little bit blue, but now in less than two minutes of cross-examination, you've admitted to two serious bouts of depression, one so serious that the school nurse phoned your father and asked him to come and check on you, and the other so serious that plans for your twenty-first birthday were cancelled.'

'They weren't cancelled. There weren't any plans.'

'No plans? No plans for Mr Smollen's precious angel when she turned twenty-one?'

'No.'

'Do you know why?'

'No.'

'So a lavish party with hundreds of guests was held for Robert when he turned twenty-one, but for you, the one who was depressed, there was nothing, not even a plan.'

'My mother made a cake.'

'Ah! A cake!'

'I … I …' Janet placed a hand to her forehead as if to steady herself. She grew pale, the colour of biscuit dough. She began to sway in the witness stand. She reached for the railing and held it.

'Miss Smollen, are you all right?' the judge intervened.

She looked up at him, her face suddenly shone as if transfixed by some kind of munificent religious deity. The judge recoiled slightly. He'd perhaps never been regarded with such misapprehension.

'I … I'm fine. I … It's all just a long time ago. It's not always easy to remember.'

'I see. Proceed, Mr Boshoff.'

'As it pleases the court, My Lord. Miss Smollen, according to your testimony, the family once argued about where to go on holiday, is that right?'

'Yes.'

'St Moritz for a skiing holiday in Switzerland or to a Caribbean island, is that right?'

'Yes.'

'And where did you end up going?'

'Switzerland.'

'What Robert wanted.'

'Yes.'

'And what happened during that holiday – do you remember?'

'I ... We ... we went to Switzerland. It was, you know, fine. Very happy. We all liked Switzerland.'

'Yes, I see, and how did you react when you discovered that you and your mother had been abandoned at the hotel in Zürich while your father and brother went to St Moritz with their skis?'

'We weren't abandoned!'

'No? You arrived in Zürich in the evening and the following morning, you and your mother were left at the hotel there. You ended up flying back to Johannesburg after two days, while your father and brother had a pleasant three-week holiday on the slopes.'

'It was cold. We didn't ... We did a bit of shopping and were ready to go home.'

'But you just said that you all liked Switzerland.'

'Well, we did. I mean, Daddy and Robert liked it more than we did, but you know. We liked it.'

'But not for more than two days.'

'I—'

'It's okay. The witness doesn't need to answer that, My Lord.'

After a lengthy pause, Fanie shuffled blithely through the papers on his table. 'Miss Smollen,' he said, still looking at the table, 'I put it to you that your description of a happy family upbringing is false.'

'It's ... No ... It—'

'I put it to you, Miss Smollen, that you have deliberately created a version of events that patently misleads the court.'

'No … I—'

'I put it to you that your relationship with your father and your brother was one of antagonism and acrimony and that your father's Will is a proper reflection of that state of affairs.'

'It … No … I … He—'

'No?'

'No!'

'You were depressed, Miss Smollen. You are still depressed. You have been depressed for years. You never mentioned this in your testimony. How much else have you concealed from the court?'

'I have been … I mean, I was … People do get depressed. I mean—'

'We will submit medical records, Miss Smollen. These show that you have suffered from deep-seated anxiety since childhood, Miss Smollen. It explains why your father resented you. You had let him down. Do you know where I'm going? May I remind you that you are under oath? It won't do to tell any more fibs.'

I stood. 'Objection, My Lord.'

Judge Ncube spoke with his usual unflappable manner. 'Mr Boshoff. Please.'

'As it pleases the court, My Lord,' Fanie Boshoff replied with a slight bow. We all looked at Janet. She was biting her lower lip. Her eyes were a dark frightened shimmer. I could see where she was headed; I'd seen it before.

'I put it to you, Janet, that there was a very good reason why your father did not include you in his Will. There was a very good reason why he resented you and why he favoured his son. A very good reason for your constant depression.'

'You …' Janet blanched. She looked down at her handbag, as if thinking about sudden flight from the building.

'Let's talk about what you did to your little sister – your little sister, Norma.'

Janet held onto the rails. She leaned forward. Her long famously bright ginger hair fell over her face as she looked at the floor. Slowly she slid downwards onto her knees, her arms resting against the railing, as if in prayer, sobbing.

I turned and looked at Robert. He was a short, plump man. He had the same blue eyes as his sister, but a round, pinkish face and a head of blond curls. He couldn't have looked more harmless or less like an international playboy. He stared ahead, without any discernible emotion, as if at some distant horizon. And then he turned to face me. It might have been that he had wanted to give me a small friendly smile, but his face suddenly contorted in a reddening, almost wincing frown. It was unmistakeable pain. He abruptly turned away, stood and walked quickly out of the court.

To Fanie, Janet's depression was little more than a useful piece of evidence, a fact that supported the view that she had been resented by her father since she was little. Her sadness was living proof of this unpleasant fact. No, this wasn't a quest for truth. It was a quest for facts.

I stood. 'My Lord, may the court note the witness is in a state of emotional distress and has sunk to the floor, sobbing. My Lord, this is obviously a tormenting account. Might the court grant us a short adjournment?'

'Mr Boshoff?'

'It would seem to be appropriate, My Lord.'

'Very well. Five minutes.'

Twenty-four

We – Janet, Ben, Moosa, and I – stood on the steps of the court so Ben could smoke. Our gentle Moosa had taken it on himself to embrace Janet and offer her comforting words of encouragement.

'You've done great, Janet,' I added. 'You've been a star ... a superstar!'

I was then startled to find dozens of text messages on my phone.

Please call. Urgent. Jill Smollen.

'Excuse me,' I said and strode further away, dialling Jill Smollen's number.

'Mr Dickerson. Thanks. Thanks for calling. How is Janet?'

'She's done amazingly well. Amazingly. It's not been easy, but we're all very proud of her.'

'That's good.' She sounded relieved but continued to speak with urgency. 'I'm glad to hear it. This has all been terrible. Now actually, Mr Dickerson, I might be too late, I don't know, but I have something ... something that might be helpful.'

'I see.'

'I have the Will. The one that Randolph signed when he first got sick, the one that Goddard prepared. I have it. The original.'

'You ... have ...?'

'Yes, I know. You probably could have done with it earlier, but I told you, I didn't want to get involved. And then I saw Janet leave the house this morning, on her way to the court. She had such ... such courage, I suppose, and I felt something. I suppose I never thought this thing would get this far. I don't know, but I now ... I can't just stand by and I ... I've been trying to reach you ever since.'

'Right. Mrs Smollen, could you hold the line for a second?' I turned to Ben. 'It's the Mouse. She says she has the Will. Has had a change of heart. We'll need more time. Get a further adjournment.'

'She has the Will?'

'Yes! The original Will. The one that Goddard did.'

'How the fuck?'

'I don't know. I'll find out. She's still on the line. You stay with Janet. Moosa can come with me as my instructing attorney.' I returned to the phone. 'Jill?'

'Yes.'

'Where are you?'

'I'm at home.'

'Give me the address – we're coming to you.'

I wasn't used to driving Ben's behemoth from the 1980s. I felt as if I were at the controls of a Sherman tank with a slightly loose steering column. Swerving this way and that, I still had Jill on the line. 'Jill, you'll need to explain how you got your hands on the Will. It'll be useless to us without an explanation.'

'Well, I … I mean, the day after Randolph died, Angus Goddard phoned me. He said he had the Will and that he was the executor, and that if I'd like to go over to his office at any time then I could. So, I did. I went that very day.'

'And?'

'We sat in his office. He showed me the Will. We talked a bit about it. Then he took a call. While he was talking, I took the Will, folded it, and put it in my bag. He was oblivious. We said goodbye and then I left.'

'Why did you take it?'

'Because I didn't trust Goddard. I don't trust lawyers, Mr Dickerson – I thought you knew.'

At that point I realised that we'd just barrelled through a red light. And I was talking on a cellphone while driving. I was breaking quite a few laws of my own and it felt rather good.

'Well, that's as good a reason as any. So, Goddard doesn't know that you have it.'

'No.'

'Right, we're almost there, Mrs Smollen. We'll be five minutes.'

Jill Smollen stood on the narrow cement path on the other side of a wire gate. She wore the same flat, scuffed shoes I'd seen before and had the same shawl wrapped around her shoulders. A small, fluffy white dog stood next to her and yapped at us. 'Quiet, Suzy, quiet,' she said as she unfastened the padlock.

'Mrs Smollen, thank you. We're in a bit of a hurry.'

'Yes, of course.' She drew the gate open. 'It's inside.'

It was a small, squarish brick house with flaking plaster and a buckled grey tin roof. What had been a small veranda was now bricked in, depriving the house of any intrigue. It gave a blunt expression of slightly aggressive, slightly shame-faced ugliness.

We followed Suzie and Mrs Smollen into the dark fusty room where the light was shut out by heavy drapes. She lifted a large yellow envelope from a table. 'Here,' she said. 'I hope it helps.'

I drew the document from the envelope: *Last Will & Testament of Randolph Raif Smollen*. I scanned through it as it quivered in my fingers.

'Yes! This is it!' I yelped. I put my arms out to hug Jill Smollen, but she took a step back, startled. Yes, she didn't trust lawyers. Fair enough. So, I turned and hugged Moosa instead. 'We've got it!' I said, stepping back from the two of them. 'Here, it is perfectly plain. You, Mrs Smollen, get The Millhouse placed in trust, plus a cash legacy of one million pounds and the rest of the estate ...' I paused and inhaled the giddying scent of victory. 'The rest goes to Janet and Robert in equal shares! That's it! That's what he wanted!' I reached again for Mrs Smollen and this time she relented. I held the small woman in a long embrace. 'Thank you,' I said at last. 'You've done the right thing. I'm sure of it!'

'I have no idea if I've done the right thing, Mr Dickerson. I've always thought Randolph would happily disinherit us and he'd do it in some murky way. I suppose I was scared that if we contested this awful case, we'd lose, that we just weren't smart enough after all.' She turned and headed back towards the house.

Moosa and I marched down the front path. Suzy scampered around our feet, playfully imploring us to stay a little longer. I turned and saw Jill Smollen standing in the doorway. The hydrangeas on each side of her had grown dry and rusty in the winter. She had a smile, noting our enthusiasm and haste – and what might even have passed for youthful exuberance. It would have been a long time since anybody had accused me of that. And still, in that smile I detected a note of weariness, a suggestion that youthful exuberance is always a little misguided. In time, we might realise how little of this really matters. Before placing the car into gear, I glanced again at Jill as she stood behind the wire fence. I had wanted to offer her a bright smile in return, and a wink, but I didn't. We raced away.

Driving the huge car with tangential regard to the lanes of the road, flying through red lights with gay abandon, I said to Moosa: 'Get Goddard on the line. We need to talk to Goddard. Google him.'

Within a minute, Moosa had Goddard's details.

'Angus? It's Teddy Dickerson.'

'Oh, for heaven's sake, you're not phoning me about that infernal bloody subpoena, are you?'

'Well, yes, I am. But I've got good news!'

'Good?'

'Yes. We'll withdraw the subpoena. We've found the Will.'

'You have it?'

'Yes. You thought you had lost it, didn't you? You were embarrassed.'

'I … I—'

'Well you didn't lose it. Jill Smollen took it from you. The day after Randolph died, you had a meeting with her. Do you remember?'

'I … uh … yes, I remember.'

'She snuck it into her handbag and left, and you've spent every year since fretting over it, not sure where you might have misplaced it. But you didn't lose it, Angus. It was taken from you and now we have it.'

'Well, I … suppose … that it is good news after all!' He seemed suddenly pleased, sprightly. 'Frankly, in all my fifty years as an attorney, I've never lost a single document. I couldn't fathom what the hell had happened!'

'Yes, well, there you have it. An unblemished fifty-year record! You can go ahead and retire in peace.'

'Ha! I suppose I can. It's been a terrible nuisance, this whole thing. I had Robert Smollen sending people over here all the time, telling me not to release it. I always told them that I wouldn't release it, but never mentioned that I didn't even have the damn thing!'

'Well, as I said, there are no flies on you, Mr Goddard!'

He chuckled drily.

I turned to Moosa, manoeuvring the steering wheel with my elbow and shielding the phone with my free hand. 'Look at the Will, Moosa, and give me the names of the witnesses.' Speaking again to Goddard, I said: 'I'm heading back to court right now. Can you tell me about the witnesses?' Moosa held the signature page up to me. Driving at high speed, examining the Will, speaking on the phone, I said: 'Yes, one of the witnesses is a Fulton and the other is a Van Niekerk. Do you know them?'

'Ah, yes, I do,' Angus said. 'They're attorneys, from the firm across the road.'

'Excellent!'

I took long imperious strides back into the High Court of South Africa. Ben and Janet sat on one of the wooden benches in a dark corridor with a flickering fluorescent light.

'Well!' I said delightedly, taking a space next to Janet. 'Here it is!' I waved the envelope at them. 'Your father *did* love you, Janet. No matter what those jokers have said in court this morning, your father did love you and this proves it.' I drew the Will out of the envelope. 'Here, two weeks after your father was diagnosed with terminal cancer, he signed this document. Your mother was to receive The Millhouse and a cash legacy. You and your brother received every-thing else in equal shares. That was your father's *will*!'

Somehow, the excitement of the moment was already beginning to ebb. I couldn't quite fathom it.

'That's ... that's ... amazing,' Janet said, looking up at me briefly, smiling hesitantly.

'Yes,' I agreed, even more flattened by her response.

'Excellent!' Ben joined in. 'Well done, Teddy, and thank God the old Mouse finally agreed to play ball.'

'Exactly. Here's to the Mouse!'

We both chuckled uneasily. The euphoria we were hoping for seemed to be eluding us in that dark, flickering corridor.

'Now obviously,' I added more sombrely, 'this isn't the end of the matter. We'll need to get a postponement. We'll need affidavits from Goddard and the two witnesses. We'll need the handwriting expert to examine this. There's plenty to do and plenty that could still go wrong, but the main point here is that we don't have to prove what your father wanted; we only have to prove that the forged Will was precisely that – forged! Or defective in some way, even some minor way! We don't have to worry about who loved whom, but simply which of the two wills should prevail. This is a major leap forward, Janet!'

'Yes,' she said meekly. 'Yes, I think so. That is good news, Mr Dickerson. It's very good news, of course it is.'

'The court will resume after lunch,' Ben added. 'You might want to ask for a further postponement in Chambers,' he suggested dimly.

'No. I want this in open court. I want Robert there.'

When court resumed, with Robert and his legal team in the room, I stood.

'As it pleases the court, My Lord, allow me to apologise for the unexpected delays this morning, My Lord.'

Fanie looked up at me with grim curiosity.

'As it happens, My Lord, this case has taken on something of a dramatic twist and a further delay might be called for in the interests of justice. We have, this morning, come into possession of another Last Will & Testament, duly executed by the late Mr Randolph Smollen.'

The defence team gasped and shuffled papers and shifted feet and offered one another hushed whispers of outraged incredulity.

'Mr Boshoff, please, you'll have your turn,' Judge Ncube intervened calmly. 'Proceed, Mr Dickerson.'

'As it pleases the court, My Lord. This document was executed before two witnesses, both of whom are available to testify. We are in the process of obtaining sworn statements. Mr Smollen signed this document two weeks after he was diagnosed with terminal cancer. It is markedly different in every way from the Will that the defence team is relying on.' I turned and gave a fiery look at Robert. '*Markedly* different, My Lord,' I repeated, still fixed on him. He blinked, crossed his legs and looked resolutely at the floor. Turning back to the court, I continued: 'The document has not been shared with the defence. It has not been discovered during pre-trial proceedings. The court will be aware of the numerous subpoenas issued on persons who were said to have possession of this document and of the tireless efforts by the plaintiff to bring it to court. It was only moments ago, during the adjournment, that I received a text message indicating to me that it would be made available for these proceedings. For now, My Lord, the essential nature of this trial has changed from one where the wishes of Mr Smollen might have been uncertain, to one where his wishes are *plainly* certain, evidenced in one of two competing documents. This court will be called on to determine which of the two is valid. Thank you, My Lord.'

'Mr Boshoff?'

Fanie stood. He glowered at me, ran his stubby fingers through his bristling hair. 'My Lord, this is a deplorable tactic. We are all experienced officers of this court and we've seen these tricks before. We haven't even seen a copy of this "mystery" document that is apparently so "markedly" different as my learned friend alleges.'

At this point, I nodded at Moosa. He stood and delivered fresh warm copies of the Will to the other side. He returned to our table, literally shivering with nervous excitement.

'Oh well, now I see, we have some copies, so okay.' Fanie dug one of his short fingers under his collar and again brushed a hand through his hair. His instructing attorney tugged at his sleeve. 'If the court will indulge me, My Lord.'

Judge Ncube nodded patiently.

Fanie and his team, with Robert leaning forward from a bench behind them, huddled together, offering one another a highly charged internecine squabble, replete with hisses of exasperation, whispers of infernal damnation, and absolutely no direction.

I smiled grandly at them all. They were in a comprehensive dither. This is what I wanted Robert to see. I turned and triumphantly shook Ben's hand and patted Moosa on the back, congratulating them on a job well done, as if our victory were unassailable (which it wasn't, but still).

Robert saw all of this. It was hard to tell if he was impressed, outraged, or afraid. He saw Janet. She looked patiently ahead, at the judge, with her usual frail dignity, ignoring us all. He gulped and turned back to his team. He whispered something. They all shut up. The court was so silent, we could hear the muffled throb of hip hop from a taxi in the street outside.

Finally, Fanie rose. He cleared his throat as if to signify his displeasure. 'As it pleases the court, My Lord, the defence agrees to a postponement, but submits that the plaintiff shall bear the costs of the day.'

'Mr Dickerson?'

'Costs reserved, My Lord. This was not a delay of the plaintiff's making, as we will make abundantly clear when the trial resumes.'

'Very, well. Costs reserved.'

Fanie scowled at the papers before him. He had wanted to scowl at the judge, at his team, at Moosa, at me, but he dared not. His harmless pieces of paper became the object of his consternation as he rubbed his temples with his fingers, fuming.

The Honourable Mr Justice Ncube stood.

'All rise.'

Twenty-five

Janet had returned home while the lawyers assembled in the car park. We stood by our Mercedes and they stood on the far side of the concrete square next to their shimmering fleet of black cars in what might be seen as a final showdown.

Fanie waddled towards us as if he were a simple, likeable man with nothing else to prove apart from his magnanimity. 'We have instructions to settle, gentlemen.'

His colleagues and his client watched us from their blazing corner.

'What does he have in mind?' I said blithely, placing my briefcase in the boot and folding and refolding my gown over my arm.

'They can have the stud in the Midlands, what's it called? The Riverhouse, or something.'

'The Millhouse.'

'Oh, ja. The Millhouse.'

He smiled at us, interlinking his fingers and stretching his short arms towards the ground, as if he was about to bow before us.

'And?'

'And well, ja, yes, also a cash legacy. Five million for the daughter and the mother.'

'Ten!' Ben interjected hotly. 'At least ten!'

'Pounds, Mr Williamson. Pounds Sterling.'

'Oh,' said Ben. 'Pounds. I see.'

'Well, we'll need to take instructions, Mr Boshoff.'

'But wait a minute!' Ben intervened. 'The estate is worth nearly a billion! And you're offering us five million?'

'We're offering you five, Mr Williamson. Let's face facts, none of them can take much more of this. You want to put that plaintiff back on the stand?'

'Fifteen and I'll recommend it to client. And that includes costs,' Ben stammered irritably. 'Five!' he scoffed and sniffed the air as if it contained a sudden disturbing odour.

'We'll take instructions,' I said at last. 'Give us ten minutes. We'll call Janet.'

Fanie shrugged his ample round shoulders and waddled back to his corner.

When Janet heard of the proposed settlement, she laughed and then began to sob. Laughter and tears were never that far apart with Janet. Perhaps it's the same with all of us. 'Yes. It's fine. It's fine,' she said at last.

'But, but, we could get fifteen, Janet. Fifteen! Or even ten!' Ben protested.

'Five is fine,' Janet said. 'Five is fine.'

It was our turn to walk across the concrete square.

Robert straightened up, tugged at the hem of his blazer, and gave me that familiar steely look – familiar, only because I had seen it in his sister and his mother.

'Five it is, plus the house and the stud.'

'And half a million for costs!' Ben blurted to my surprise and my annoyance. 'This hasn't been cheap.'

Fanie glanced at Robert. Robert nodded, turned and reached for the back door of a black Range Rover. He was eager to leave.

'Sounds like we have a deal, then. Thank you, gentlemen,' Fanie said. He put his hand out. I shook it. 'Quite a little show you put on there, Mr Dickerson,' he acknowledged with a hint of bitterness.

'Well, we all have our moments, Mr Boshoff.'

They all turned towards their cars. Robert was in the process of climbing up onto the back seat of his car, when I stopped and said: 'I'm sorry, Mr Smollen? Robert?' He turned and frowned. He couldn't abide any further delay. 'I just wanted to ask … you know … if, while you're here, visiting from wherever you are these days, whether you might want to pop in and say hello to your mother, say hello to Janet too. I know they would be grateful. Might make everyone feel a little bit better. By God, life is hard enough!' I did my best to offer him a slightly jolly smile.

Robert was about to speak, but he thought the better of it. It was clear that he didn't trust himself. He turned away, shook his head, and climbed into the car, shutting the door.

His Range Rover reversed out of its space and raced down the spiral ramp, heading for his private jet, his ceaseless and aimless refuge. I pictured Robert, landing in some faraway city, hastening towards some outrageously expensive club where he would drown his sorrows by licking Veuve Clicquot off the boots of an exotic dancer while she whipped his butt with a belt – or something like that.

We, the remaining lawyers, all looked at our feet. It was one of those rare moments when we all enjoy some solidarity in privately pondering whether any of us is any good … at anything.

Twenty-six

We'd asked Janet and Jill if they would join us for dinner. 'We're going up to Hilton. Having dinner at the hotel. A little celebration!'

'No,' they had said. 'We don't much care for going out these days, or for celebrations, but thank you.'

So, it was Ben, Moosa, and me, relentlessly determined to have a *good time*, who sat in the long lounge room in wingback chairs, drinking whisky by the fire. Well, Moosa had a Fanta.

'I don't drink, Mr Dickerson,' he had said gently, firmly.

'And you want to be a lawyer?'

He'd grinned and suckled at the straw of his drink, unpersuaded.

By the time Moosa was on his fourth Fanta (he was actually starting to *look* slightly orange), Ben and I were incapable of counting the number of whiskies. Over dinner we'd conquered what might have been two rather good bottles of Pinotage. It was hard to tell.

There was only one other diner in the dining room. A solitary figure in a brown jersey sat at a corner table, nibbling his food, and looked as if he might die of boredom at any minute. Perhaps our jovial quips helped to cheer him up (or might have made him feel worse – like a lot of things that night, it was hard to tell). The solemn, almost dismal silence of the dining room and its lone patron were hardly enough to dampen our ebullient spirits.

With much in the way of high fives and thunderous roars of laughter, we ate our dinner and clinked our glasses and declared how good we felt about ourselves, about our client, about justice being served and the world, yes, the entire world, being a fair and orderly place after all.

'And half a million in fees! In *sterling*! That's ... that's what? What's the exchange rate?'

'Ten million rand!' Moosa offered.

'Ten million!' We cheered and chinked our glasses and then Moosa quite abruptly told us that he'd best be off to bed.

With Moosa gone, we looked about. The lone diner in the corner had also disappeared. For all we knew, he might have already electrocuted himself in the bath. Two staff hung lazily about the doorway to the kitchen waiting for us to leave. It was almost impossible not to notice how swiftly our raucous merriment had plummeted into brooding despair.

It was Moosa. He was our foil. The delicate young man with soft pinkish cheeks and a lofty dream of growing up to be just like us – two middle-aged lawyers who'd won an unwinnable case (or extracted a half-decent settlement out of a sociopathic millionaire – which was more to the point). Now, with Moosa gone, an unmistakeable gloom had descended on us with stunning clarity.

'I suppose we'll never know about Norma.'

'Norma?'

'The one who died.'

'Oh, yes,' Ben said gruffly. 'The sick one.'

'Fanie had said that Janet had *done something* to her.'

'Yes. I heard that. One shudders to think.'

'Killed her?'

'Jesus, Teddy! What's with the morose speculation all the time?'

Despite Ben's protest, I knew he was thinking the same thing.

'Well,' Ben said finally. 'Like you say, I suppose we'll never know.'

Ben ordered two more whiskies. The waitress could barely contain her irritation.

'I suppose we'll never know about Toby either,' he mused sadly.

'Toby?'

'The investigator we had in London. The one who was shot. Or who shot himself.'

'Oh yes. Toby. Shot with the mystery gun.'

'The funny thing about that gun was that the police knew when it was made. It was a Smith & Wesson, made in the US in 1983. It was sold to a dealer. The dealer sold it to a customer. When the police investigated who the customer was, they discovered that he didn't exist. There was no record of the customer ever having existed. Isn't that extraordinary? Strange that Toby should have shot himself with such a gun.'

The gloom was now vibrating around us, inside us.

Our whiskies arrived. Ben drained his. 'Enough of this shit. The problem with these small towns is that you have to drive a hundred miles to find yourself a decent hooker. And it's a cold night too.'

'Too far to drive for a hooker on a cold night,' I agreed readily.

I couldn't drain my whisky in the way that Ben had drained his. I would have thrown up.

We left for our rooms. As Ben sloped up the steps, I stopped him. 'Hey, Ben. Give me a cigarette, would you? Or maybe two?'

'You smoke?'

'Occasionally. Only when I'm sober.'

Ben grunted half-heartedly. He drew a box of cigarettes from his pocket and tossed them to me. 'Not all of them. Just two.'

'It doesn't matter,' Ben said, turning to face the stairs. 'I've got a carton in my room and another in the Merc, just in case.'

Ben shuffled upstairs and I took the back door out into the thin, icy air of midnight towards the pool.

The Hilton Hotel was so named because it was in the small town of Hilton, perched on the hills overlooking Pietermaritzburg (and not, most emphatically *not*, because it had anything to do with the American chain of hotels). Built just after the war in what some would despairingly call a 'mock Tudor' style, it was a place I remembered as a boy. Clarah had attended boarding school not far from there and occasionally, for a school function – a variety play, a choir performance, a sports day – my parents would travel up from Durban to attend. I was at boarding school too, further inland towards the Berg, and was relieved of the tedium of school weekends by joining them. Whatever the event might have been, the parents and their children congregated at the old hotel. I remember standing in the front room as all the parents milled about, eagerly conversing, sipping brandies, smoking cigarettes – the sheen of tweed, the shimmer of silk, and the gleam of jewels all swimming in a golden hue. The fireplace roared in the winter. And in the summer the windows were flung open, mosquitoes feasted on our ankles as the ceiling fans lazily stirred the air above our heads.

Now, as I walked outside, my feet crunching over the frost, smoking a cigarette (my first in, what, half a decade?), I thought about my father. I remembered him standing there, at those events. He stood so stiffly and yet laughed so amiably. He was taller than most men, a fact that I regarded with some pride. His more rotund companions swayed back and forth around him, their tongues loosened by the first pleasing pings of insobriety. They joked and gulped and smoked, while my father stood among them, eternally aloof. They spoke of guns and money and women and how pleasing it was to be cunt struck. My father grinned and always seemed as if he was on the cusp of leaving.

The cigarette was good. I was reminded of how my father seldom drank, how quiet he was, how he nodded and smiled, clinging to the same glass of brandy all night. He said so little. To any of us. He hardly ever said a thing. I was reminded of that.

I drew aggressively on the cigarette as if it might warm me up. My fingers were stiffening with cold.

Twenty-seven

It shouldn't have surprised me (but it did) that I awoke with a cracking head-ache. It was already noon. Time to check out.

Wincing with each step, I made it to the lobby. Moosa sat in one of the wingback chairs. He sat upright, rather primly. Hair brushed. Suit and tie. He broke into a broad smile. It almost made me want to cry.

'Hello, Moosa,' I groaned.

'Good morning, counsel!'

He'd been sitting there since dawn. Waiting. I couldn't stand the discipline, the vigour.

'Ben down yet?'

We heard him growling from the corridor, his giant frame thumping across the carpeted floorboards. 'I'm here. Let's press on.' It sounded as if he'd swallowed a chainsaw (or an angle grinder).

Driving back to Durban, I blamed the hangover for my melancholy. I was still keen to put on a show for Moosa, to demonstrate how youth had not abandoned me, how I was still enjoying myself. But the hangover was as good an excuse as any to sit in despair with my eyes closed as we hastened along the freeway listening to the radio and its dire warnings of a cold front moving in from the south. 'Strong winds and rain along the coast tonight with sleet and ice warnings on higher ground and heavy snowfall on the Berg' – so the weather lady predicted. Then they played 'You Can Leave Your Hat On', by Joe Cocker.

'Turn that fucking thing off,' I snarled.

Moosa grinned. Perhaps my frailty was something comical after all. Perhaps he genuinely liked me, even if I was miserable.

At Chambers, I was vaguely heartened to find two letters. One from Wilma (which was excellent because she'd been on my mind ever since her last letter, and I had been worried about her ... and her cat) and one from Darshini (which was also excellent because she was the one who had told me about the scratching of the pen on the paper, and I'd been conscious of it ever since, every time I wrote anything down).

I took the letters home, planning to read them when I recovered (*if* I recovered – hangovers increasingly presented themselves as a terminal condition and I had the distinct suspicion that I might not survive this one). At home, there was only one thing for it. An ice-cold can of beer. I sat at my dining-room table and surveyed my letters. It was a dining room with six chairs and a view of the city that no one ever used.

I had my letters, my letter *writers*. Val had given those to me. Nasty old Val.

I took another beer and stood in the hallway, staring at the purple satin box that contained Val's remains. I recalled a line from one of Candice's letters: 'It's unbearable if we don't go around and thank people for their stories.'

Val's funeral at the Manning Road Methodist Church had been a sham, a compromise intended to indulge the most banal fantasy of all, the idea that when we die, no matter how we may have behaved when we were alive, we were still *liked*. It's easy to say that about the dead. It's as easy as some remote double click. No, the ceremony was not a little treat that we offer the dead. It was an obligation – one we owe to ourselves.

I'd had those ashes on the shelf ever since Val had died. If there was one way to thank Val, it might have been to deposit them into the sea, as she had requested. If I was truly thankful, this was not something I would get around to *when I had time*. This was hardly the kind of thing I could delay.

I placed the purple box on the passenger seat (the thought had crossed my mind to fasten a seatbelt over it – Val had always insisted on seatbelts) and headed up the coast. The last few silvery shards of light played on the surface of the sea before the flat grey sky slid in above us and a strong wind began to batter my car as it raced along the freeway.

I drove to Tinley Manor, a tiny, decrepit resort town just north of Estantia. I had hoped to avoid Estantia. It would have been easier to park at the gates and walk alongside Ray's shiny new fence, on to the path through the cane fields and down to the beach, but I didn't want to bump into Ray or Marsha. And I needed a curry. Nothing like a curry on a stormy day (with a hangover). Tinley Manor served a decent curry.

At the Impact Restaurant and Bar I took a table for two and placed Val's box on the table mat opposite me. We were the only customers. The manager, a thin Indian man with a sagging face, promptly turned off the boxing and put on a CD of romantic Hindu ballads which I found to be wondrously soothing. He handed me a laminated menu, taking a slightly suspicious glance at the satin box.

'Expecting someone special?' he said smiling, exposing a set of very loose teeth.

I looked at the box. He might have thought it contained a gift for my sweetheart – a piece of silver jewellery on a little maroon cushion or a bottle of perfume. 'Uh, no, not really. Not especially.'

Val would have thought that mightily funny.

I ordered a mutton bunny and a quart of beer. My day was looking up. I had something to do. I had a plan. It was late afternoon and I still had time to walk down to the beach across the sandbar between the lagoon and the sea and to the little rock pools that Val had spoken about in her letter. I would sprinkle her ashes there, offer some kind of solemn commendation to the heavens, and drive home.

With that settled, I enjoyed my curry and ordered another beer and then a brandy. I sat contemplating the white flecks on the heaving metallic grey sea. The rain arrived, whipped around by the wind, crackling against the window panes.

'I'll take another brandy,' I said to the manager.

He gave me a sad look, perhaps he'd assumed that I'd been stood up by my sweetheart.

'Two for the price of one,' he said with a smile when he returned.

'Ah! A double. Thanks.'

It was mid-afternoon and they had turned the lights on.

At some point, I lost count of the brandies, and the manager and I were discussing the storm. 'She's a big one,' I said a little pompously, as if I knew something about coastal storms.

'A monster!' he agreed. 'The biggest of the year!'

We sat in silence for a while. 'Another brandy, sir?'

'Yes. Why not?'

He delivered another and then again eyed the box. 'So ... eh ... sir,' he said hesitantly. 'She didn't come?'

'Who?'

'Your ...' He gave me a sly smile. 'Your special companion!'

'Oh that!' I looked at the box. *My special companion.* I had the urge to tell him that my special companion was there, *in the actual box.* But no, that might have unsettled him. Might have been too macabre. 'No. She didn't come. It doesn't matter.'

Now I knew that it had to be done.

Twenty-eight

We have a cold snap every year. It's fierce. And it always takes us by surprise. I've never understood this about Durban people — myself being one of them.

I drove to the end of the road. Val sat quietly on her seat, perhaps a little expectantly, as if taunting me to go on into the storm. I stepped out. Icy splinters of rain flew at me with an almost gleeful violence, stinging my face. I wore only a thin cotton shirt, my work trousers, and shiny black shoes. In a moment of misguided inspiration, I hurried to the boot of the car and drew out my court gown — the huge pleated black garment with its symbolic ribbons and pouches. It flapped and tugged at me with wild indignation. 'Sorry, old chap, you'll have to do.' From my briefcase I took out a long piece of ribbon and fastened it around my waist. 'There! All set!'

I returned to the cabin of the car and picked up Val in both hands. 'Here we go, Aunt Val. Into the storm!' Slamming the car door shut, facing the wind, I held her in my hands. 'The biggest storm of the year!' I shouted. The wind snatched the words from my mouth, crushing them in its roar, never to be heard. I proceeded down the path to the lagoon. The tide was up, as was my mood, and the frenzied ocean thumped against the shoreline, all muscle and froth. The lagoon was normally sealed from the ocean by a sandbar, but now the sea had broken through it, opening a chasm in the sand, about ten feet wide. The water gushed through it in brown sinewy threads, swirling upwards, inland, and then flexing and gurgling as it was sucked back out into the ocean. It offered a choice of drowning in the lagoon or drowning in the sea.

But I wasn't thinking about drowning; I was thinking about my shoes. I sensed that Val was thinking of the same thing. 'They'll be ruined!' I complained. I looked down at them. They were already ruined, soaked through; still, you can't wade through the water with courtroom shoes on. It would be ridiculous, improper. I sat on the wet sand, hugging Val under an armpit, unlaced my shoes and removed my socks. I looked at my slender, pale feet in the sand, admiring their unusual elegance.

'The Zulus used to run around barefoot all the time!' Was that me or Val? Who said that?

I stood and slid down the sandbank into the water. It immediately ensnared me, seized me in its grip and tugged me out towards the sea. I tried to push on, holding Val aloft. 'Everything is fine!' I said to her as I was inexorably sucked out to sea, just my head and arms above the froth. A sharp granular thing scraped against my foot. 'I'm fine! Fine!' I said, pushing fecklessly against the current, trying to stand. A wave pushed me back up towards the lagoon. 'No problem at all! Almost there!' I regained something of a foothold and pressed on against the torrent. The current reversed suddenly and swept me in the other direction. I floundered, fell again. The water was over my head. I broke the surface gasping, but still I held Val high up above the maddening tumult. The current was drawing me towards the sea and also towards the other side of the chasm. I let it take me. As the shoreline flattened out on the other side and the water grew shallow, I saw my chance and leapt forward, clambering up onto the beach where I lay on the sand, Val still there – grinning, no doubt. I looked at her. 'Done!' I said with a laugh and I heard her laughing back. 'Now, onwards to the rock pools, just like you said.' I rose to my feet. Yes, one of them had been cut – a surface wound, a scrape. Tiny speckles of blood seeped from it. 'A mere scratch!'

I trudged on. The ribbon that I had fastened around my waist had disappeared and my gown flapped stubbornly in the wind, trying to free itself of my long angular limbs. I headed up towards the forested edge where the wind was less violent. 'Only a mile or so to go,' I said to her.

'Honestly! I've never seen such buffoonery!' she said.

'Oh, Val, that'll be you and your last word.'

She said nothing further for a long time. The sky had darkened. The day was coming to its end. The horizon offered a glum sulky glow. 'We'll need to pick up the pace to find the rock pools,' I said.

Val said nothing. Or maybe she said: 'Hmph!' I couldn't be sure.

I trudged faster, still pummelled by the storm. The sand was rough against my soft feet.

The sight of me and Val would have made any observer blink as if they'd spotted a phantom, some horrendous mythical creature.

But there were no observers on that stretch of beach that night.

The wind weakened and my plod through the sand became more urgent. Was it here? Or further still? Have I passed it? I couldn't make out the rock pools in the gloom. I'd last been to this beach on a sunny day, decades ago. The wind whistled about me; its diminished bluster reminded me of the cold. I wrapped my wet robe around me, pressing it against my sides with my elbows. 'Come on, Val, help me out here. How am I supposed to remember where the bloody rock pools are?'

Val remained silent. My spirits sank. I should have had more brandy at the curry restaurant. The wind and rain still stung me, burning me, chilling me – I could not tell. A fresh squall plucked the lid of the box away, sending it spiralling up into the air. It fell to the sand and cartwheeled along the shore. I ran after it. I didn't know why. But it seemed wrong – to think of how far we'd come – that I should lose the lid. I ran back, in the direction from where I'd come, chasing after the lid. 'Come back! Come back here!' I yelled. The lid came to a sudden rest. As I drew nearer, the wind picked it up again and it travelled further down the beach. 'Come back for fuck's sake!'

I stopped as a wave crashed onto the shoreline, snatched the lid in its hissing, frothing grip and sucked it into the sea. I sat down and began to sob. 'Sorry, Val, I lost the lid.'

Val said nothing.

My gown had stopped tugging at me. Instead, it seemed stuck to me, wrapped loyally around my loins with sudden coy remorse. I looked up. In the dim light, I detected the murky whiteness of the breakers as they rolled towards the shore. There was a strangeness to their shape as they drew nearer. Their distinctive luminosity seemed to crumble and curve in different directions. I leapt to my feet. 'This is it! Val! Here! This is it! The rock pools!'

She laughed.

I hobbled towards the water. 'Oh, Val! Here we are!'

'Here we are!' said Val.

The water fizzed around my feet as I sank slightly into the softening sand. I could discern the rocks now, black jagged shapes hunkered in the spume.

I looked down at the box. The glass jar that held Val's ashes had a coppery coloured lid. 'Well ...' I said as I drew her from the box. I had nothing further to say. This was to be a good ceremony. Good in every conceivable way. And I had nothing to say. My mouth was full of words, but they were all the wrong ones. A lump ached in my throat. Val offered me no clues. It was now only her silence that urged me on.

I unscrewed the lid of the jar. The dying wind picked up the first few specks of ash, carrying them into the remnants of that violent night. 'Here,' I said. I turned the jar upside down and her ashes fell freely into the swirling fringes of the sea.

'Thank you,' I said at last.

I remained on my knees as the saltwater sucked and gurgled around me, drawing Val's ashes into the dark sea.

I was there for a long time. The rain still fell, but with less sharpened fervour. It came from above, not from the sides. My foot throbbed in the sand. I stood. I ached. Cold. Tiredness. Endless damn frailty.

'Here we are.'

I knew what she meant.

Twenty-nine

I turned to face the forested edge of the beach and began to hobble along the sand in search of the path. I had no reason to think I would find it – a dark opening into a darker forest on the darkest night of the year. But I did find it, strangely, with a vague sense of accomplishment, fully undeserved. I crept forward, crouching beneath the low branches, my gown constantly caught by the twigs and vines of the forest floor. A gust of wind sent heavy droplets pattering through the leaves, but it was still drier under the trees. The sand path was fine and powdery beneath my feet. I stepped blindly forward, feeling my way through the forest. Occasionally I wandered into a thicket, crashing and snapping through a sudden tangle of branches that crowded around me, lacing cobwebs about my head. Cursing, I'd retreat and fumble about again for the path as it twisted over the lumpy dunes. I finally reached a clearing and found the edge of a cane field. At last! Straight up the hill and I'd be there! The rain fell in a rhythmic deluge and my bare feet slipped on the wet grass of the track. But the track soon began to lead downwards towards the river. No, this can't be right. I followed the track anticipating a turn, up the hill. But the turn never came. Further down it went. Without any clear purpose, I decided to veer into the cane itself, find an upwards trajectory. The silvery wet stalks tore away at me with their serrated fronds, cutting my face and hands while my elegant mutilated feet trudged through thick mud. Just keep going upwards, I told myself. The house is at the top of this hill.

I became very lost and at one point found myself on my knees. I might rest here. I might just lie here and fall asleep and be eaten by wild pigs. There are worse ways to go. I paused and thought about that. What might be worse than being devoured, one limb after the next, by a wild pig? No, I couldn't think of anything. So, I plodded on. I couldn't quite tell if I was heading down the slope or up the slope. It didn't matter any more. I needed to get out of the field before it drained me of my blood, reduced me into the untraceable bits of a lawyer who went missing on a famously dark and stormy night. Find another track. I began to suspect that I was trapped in a circle of my own making. Why can I not find my way out of this field, this famous English sugar plantation, with its towering stalks, slicing at my soft hairless skin? I stopped again. I was reconsidering my options with the wild pigs. Disappear without a trace. Even my skull would be crushed and chewed into a mush, squeezed out the back end of the animal, transformed into little more than an indistinguishable lump of pig shit. They might find a bit of the gown. And maybe a small metatarsal that had been swallowed whole. But why would they find it? Why would they suspect that I might have been blithering about the middle of this plantation in the middle of the night? They'd find my car. They'd talk to the sad-looking man at the Impact Restaurant and Bar. He'd tell them about the brandy and about my being stood up by my sweetheart. It was obvious. I had drowned in the sea. Suicide. He was always a bit of an oddball anyway, so the witnesses would say. They'd look no further. Case closed.

The idea of not being found, of having disappeared without trace, frightened me more than the simple act of dying. There was no meaning to a random disappearance, alone with nothing other than the earth. I drew some comfort from the idea of having people around – even if they were strangers, doctors and nurses, wearing surgical masks, monitoring my vitals – while I discreetly slipped away. No. Anonymity – retreat – isn't all it's cracked up to be. 'Somehow, we're all connected,' I found myself gasping. I trudged on. That's where all the meaning is. I kept my head down and ploughed on through the cane with a potent bloody-mindedness. It was just me and my breathing and my tattered robe, tearing through the field like a maddened beast in pursuit ... not of mere survival, but of something far more inexplicable: *life*.

I felt the wind grow stronger. The rain came at me from an angle and I was reminded of the cold. I looked about me. I was in a clearing! I'd made it through the cane. In front of me, I could make out a distinctively man-made arrangement – a flat surface, tall poles sticking rigidly out of the ground. The grass was long and thick around my legs. I approached the poles and found myself at a fence. It was the tennis court! I held onto the fence and pressed my face against it. I could almost hear the pop and whizz of tennis balls. I began to sob, clinging to the fence, like some piece of detritus flung on it by the storm. I could even make out the strange white markings on the surface, like some sort of landing strip for an alien ship. Here, I thought, moving along the perimeter, on the other side of the court is the *garden*. That'll lead me to the house. I waded through the thick grasses on the edge of the court and soon found myself on flat ground, a trimmed lawn. I limped upwards, through the black lumpen swathes of foliage on either side of me — Val's vaunted garden, her lilies and hydrangeas, bougainvillea and wild bananas. Reaching higher ground, I caught the gleam of Ray's new security fence. I hobbled forward, trying to break into a jog, but all I could do was totter ahead with a sort of demented glee.

The house was just a dark rectangular shape, a strangely geometric forma-tion among the trees. I leapt at the fence. 'I'm here!' I wanted to shout, but my voice was just a dreamlike gasp. 'I'm here!' I began to wail and shake at the fence as if I might tear it down. 'I'm here!'

They appeared out of nowhere. I only caught sight of them the moment they were pounding at the fence. I saw their muscly silken heads and the glint of their reddish gums as they snarled and roared and pummelled the fence. I fell backwards. I'd forgotten about the damn dogs. The good old Rotties! I rolled onto my knees, ready to flee, sobbing again at my foolish-ness. Then I was trapped in light. Floodlights from the house. It was as if I was about to be beamed up to some other planet, a place full of pigs and dogs. I ducked and crawled behind some of Val's lilies. I heard a man's voice. It was Ray — the little Ray of sunshine.

I crawled further away, over the wet grass, back down the slope. In the shadows I got to my feet and staggered back to the court. I pushed open the wire gate and hobbled towards the practice wall. There I fell. Pressing myself against the wall and covering my head with the remains of my robe, I lay still, listening to the rain and the distant gibbering yelps of those enraged dogs. He'll release them, I thought. They'll scamper down, sniff me out, and tear me into a thousand pieces with playful abandon. It didn't matter. I'd had enough. At least someone, some other self-absorbed little human being would know what happened to Teddy Dickerson that night. I felt so sleepy suddenly. And hot. The wind was cold against my skin, but I felt as if I might be boiling alive under my robe. I shifted it away from my head and there, standing in front of me, wearing his baggy shorts and a thin wet T-shirt, was Fernando in all his ribald glory. I crawled towards him. I hugged his ankles. 'Oh, Fernando,' I wept at his feet.

I detected the flicker of a torch light across the cracked surface of the old court. That'll be Ray, I thought, overwhelmed by dread.

'Who the fuck? What the fuck?' he stammered as he bounded towards us on his stocky legs.

He shone the torch at me. I pressed my face to Fernando's feet. His beautiful shapely feet.

Looking up at the light, offering Ray my glistening face at last, I said: 'It's me. It's Teddy … Dickerson. Teddy Dickerson. The lawyer.'

'Teddy who?' he bawled, torch in the one hand, revolver in the other, but he'd lost the threatening fearful notes to his voice. At least I was white. Probably harmless.

'I came to see you here a few months ago. My aunt died.'

Fernando stepped back and I released his legs at last. The last bit of warmth on earth.

'Ja, I remember you. What the hell are you doing? It's the middle of the night. In a storm, for Christ's sake.'

'I … I … got lost. I got lost in the storm. I'd come to release my aunt's ashes into the sea and I got trapped in the storm. I'm sorry. I must have alarmed you.'

'Alarmed me? Jesus, buddy, I nearly shot you.'

Ray was calling me 'buddy'. It was insufferable. Once again, I had that short man looking down at me.

'I'm sorry,' I said at last. 'I've been terribly lost.'

'You're not exactly in great shape,' he remarked with a surprising note of tenderness.

He walked towards me and took me by the arm. It hurt. I winced. 'I … I'm not sure I can stand,' I said.

'Come on, Fernando, help me here.'

Fernando took me by the other arm and they raised me to my feet. I *could* stand, but only just. My knees felt as if they were made of sponge. The rain had eased and I began to shiver from the heat, the blood pulsating sluggishly through my veins. Might it have been that curry?

I wasn't sure if I was walking or being dragged up to the house, towards that blazing white light.

I felt myself being placed on one of the plastic chairs on the veranda. I saw Marsha's terracotta pots, heard her voice coming from the yellowish light of the front hall.

'It's that lawyer!' Ray said proudly. 'The Dickerson. The one that came to see us a few months ago.'

I heard her voice again. A shrill murmuring sound full of anguish from behind the thick walls.

'I don't know. He got lost in the storm.'

Marsha finally appeared. Her blonde hair tousled by a restless sleep. She too carried a gun. A shotgun!

'Should we call the police?' she said, turning to Ray.

'Nah!' He dismissed the idea with manly confidence. They both looked at me while I looked at my bruised and bloodied hands.

'What's he *wearing*?' she said as if I weren't there, as if I were just some enfeebled apparition that had landed up on her veranda and wasn't even that scary.

'It's my gown,' I muttered weakly. 'My court gown. It was all I had.'

The remnants of the shredded wet robe clung to me.

'We'd better get him out of those wet things. I'll warm up some soup. Ray, you go and get one of your jackets. Maybe we should get him into a hot bath.' With unsettling decisiveness, Marsha marched back into the house. I remembered now that she would have had her two sleeping children in that building. Marsha. Marsha the mom. Marsha and Jesus.

Ray left too. 'I'll get you an anorak,' he said.

It was only Fernando and me. He stood, shivering on the steps of the veranda, his muscles hardened, his eyes glowing like distant unknowable jewels.

'You probably saved me,' I said. I tried to smile but felt only another sob welling up inside me, slowly throttling me. I held it back stiffly.

What must he have seen?

He saw another strident Dickerson, one of the last, who'd finally run out of ideas, his robe in tatters, ready to hand himself in, admit finally that nothing was ever really solved. Is that what *they all* saw?

'It's okay,' he said.

I looked up and he'd already skipped back into the cold night to his room, troubled no further by my peculiar state.

I stood up uneasily from the plastic chair. With trembling fingers, I removed the robe and let it slither in a wet heap to the floor. I walked into the house. There was no one in sight. I could hear the whistling of a kettle calling from the kitchen at the back.

With one hand against the wall, I walked unsteadily and yet with deliberate care along the smooth stone floor. Through the hallway, and into the dim passage. It was the third door on the left. The door was open. I patted the wall in search of a light switch. I flicked the switch. It wasn't what I expected. I saw a room with a long table against the far wall. I saw a clothing rack with half-finished dresses hanging, malformed, from the railing. A sewing machine. Rolls of pale fabric leaning in the corner. Of course! It was her sewing room. Marsha liked sewing. Yes, I had forgotten. I surveyed the room again.

There was no sign of him, my father.

I flicked the light off again and my memories of that endless night rushed at me in a sudden torrent. All of them compressed into that infinitesimal point where the light vanished and the darkness returned. I leaned against the door frame. I could not stand, and I began to slide downwards with my cheek pressed against the thickly painted doorjamb. I could see the entries written there.

Tilly 2 November 2014 136cm
Jenny 2 November 2014 130cm
Tilly 3 October 2013 131cm
Jenny 3 October 2013 124cm
Jenny 7 October 2012 122cm
Tilly 7 October 2012 119cm

It went on. Back in time. I was growing smaller. I couldn't keep up. On my knees, leaning against the door, I peered into the dark. I saw him then. His head at that odd angle, abruptly forward and to one side. His arms splayed out stiffly, as if he were about to embrace me. His feet in black lace-up shoes, swaying gently in mid-air on that breathless night, as if he might still want to dance. The radio was playing. And then I saw the rope – taut from the back of his neck, receding into the darkness above his head.

Released once more into that cool and vivid space, I faced the darkness and the truth it concealed.

'Thank you,' I said. 'Thank you, Dad.'

I vaguely heard Marsha utter something from the kitchen.

Thirty

O ut for eighteen hours. Down and out. Out cold. Out.

I woke up in the same hospital in which Val had died only six months earlier. Pneumonia. From head to toe. The lovely Doctor Hoosen (whose teeth seemed whiter than ever) had even popped in. He and his colleagues concurred that I might have died in the midst of that legendary storm. I was gravely ill.

People came to visit. Thandi came each morning before heading off to work. I know that I have truly loved her. How did she let me do that? I can hardly even say that I knew her. Ben arrived too, accompanied by his wife – the one he liked to complain about. Other colleagues from Chambers popped in, some bringing gifts – overpriced decorative trinkets from the gift shop in the hospital lobby.

Sidney Ngwenya was one of them. But he didn't bring a gift.

'What? No gift? No flowers?'

He laughed with his usual ease. 'You've been really sick,' he said.

'Yes. On the brink of death, apparently.'

We talked a little about the banal happenings of his working week, my illness, when I might be discharged – usual hospital bedside fare. When he rose to leave, I said: 'Do you ever think about retiring? You know, throwing it all in? We don't get to live that long as it is and we seem to waste so much of it working these dead-end jobs.'

'I think about it every day.'

'Me too. And the thing that scares me about retirement is that you get to face a simple, rather brittle proposition: you'll never be young again; that all that's left is a less and less intriguing future, a future that grows old too. I mean, I'm sure in your dreams you want to return home. You know, the rolling hills of Zululand?'

'The rolling hills?' He briefly looked up at the ceiling with a vague and distant smile. 'I don't care about the rolling hills. But you know what I miss?'

I shook my head, giving him a half-smile in return, always slightly anxious about what he might say next.

'I miss people,' he said at last. 'I miss being with people.'

Even though it should not have, it surprised me that Terry Winstanley also found the time to pay me a visit. On his departure, he managed to offer a bit of his very finest advice: 'You've made a Will, haven't you, Teddy? I mean, you're not getting any younger and, you know, you never know.'

'You're right, Terry. I may never know.'

He left my room and I turned to look out of the window.

There was a litchi tree outside and occasionally I'd spot an Indian myna perched on one of its branches. It busied itself, preened its breast feathers with its beak, squawked randomly at nothing in particular, and occasionally stared at me for a few intense seconds at a time before flying away. It returned often, that bird. Grateful as I was for the attention of my visitors (including the bird), my head was suffused with ungainly thoughts. They moved through my vast mind – an endless unexplored landscape – with sluggish aimless intent.

The body is its own best doctor. Val had said that. I found myself nodding vaguely – yet again in agreement with that caustic old woman. And so I willingly indulged my bleak solitary imaginings as if they were leading me through some sort of opera, the ungraspable movement of colour, the formation and dispersal of patterns, the essential interplay of light and shadow, of exertion and exhaustion, all of it together producing a kind of numbing rhythm.

As I slowly emerged from my disease-induced, drug-induced, dream-like stupor, I detected a word – unfathomable at first – stirring deep inside some long-neglected region of my mind.

Music. The word was music. As I stared at the tree outside, waiting through the afternoons for my bird to arrive, I found myself asking: What happened to the music?

This is my story. It is my opera. My colleagues would chastise me for saying this, but it is *my truth*. That we seek an objective truth, a truth to be grasped, unwavering through all times and circumstances, properly fixed within the confines of empirical knowledge, is not an indictment of the elusive nature of truth but an indictment of the impossible rigidity of knowledge. The information age. The knowledge economy. How deflating this is for the human experience.

I might mention that Val would have berated me for writing this story. 'Far too much information,' she would have said. I might counter: Perhaps not enough. This would have left us in a state of palpable silence whereupon she would have returned with her most appalling retort: It doesn't matter if I'm right or wrong; at least I'm right.

So what of the truth? What of it did I get right? And what of it did I get wrong? The answer to both of these questions is: All of it.

Let me start with the Smollens.

About a year after being discharged from hospital, I received a call from Janet.

'Mum and I would like to invite you to dinner,' she explained. 'I suppose we've never really thanked you.'

'Well, that's hardly necessary, Janet,' I said with my usual guarded charm.

'Well, it might not be, but we also have something to tell you, Mr Dickerson.'

'Oh, please call me Teddy.'

'All right, but please … please come to visit. Come and have dinner. It'll just be me and the Mouse.'

'Right. I'd love to. You're back at The Millhouse?'

'No. We're still here in the little house, in Maritzburg.'

'Oh?'

'We sold The Millhouse. We're okay, Mr Dickerson.'

I drove up to Pietermaritzburg. Indeed, there they were, standing behind that sagging wire fence in front of the small house with its bricked-in veranda that they'd lived in since Randolph had died. The house still had the same vexed, affronted expression. Little Suzy sprang and wiggled about, nearly demented by the commotion of my arrival.

Inside the same dark room, we sat at a table and ate a vegetable bake – something the Mouse had prepared. 'I've never been very good in the kitchen,' she explained, as if ashamed of her culinary efforts. 'We're both vegetarians now. Poor Randolph must be spinning in his grave. He was a voracious meat-eater!' She let out a sudden shrill yelp that might have been intended to pass for levity but sounded more like terror.

Randolph was long dead, yet he still seemed to enjoy a conspicuous presence in that house. I could feel it too, and to my mind it was not particularly malignant – a little acerbic perhaps, a little grumpy, and even a little forgiving.

'Vegetarians!' I said grandly. 'A damn good idea!'

Janet reached across the table and filled each of our glasses with some not-very-good wine.

Jill said: 'We heard what you did when the case was finished.'

'What I did?'

'Yes, what you said to Robert when he was about to leave.'

'Oh … I … I don't really remember.'

'You told Robert to come and visit us. Do you remember?'

'Oh yes, good heavens, so I did!'

Jill and Janet looked at each other and then, with surprising warmth, they smiled at me. I picked up my glass, drained it, and put it down again.

Jill continued: 'I wrote to Robert a number of times after the case. I had asked him in each letter to please let go of all this terrible nastiness. We didn't hear from him for months and then, suddenly, three weeks ago, we received this!' Jill leaned back and lifted a letter from the sideboard. She unfolded it carefully and read a passage:

> *Your lawyer was a bit of an unusual chap, although I can't say I didn't rather like him. Odd thing to say about a lawyer. When the case was over, he suggested that I pop in and visit you, that it might make everyone feel a bit better. It rather galls me that I couldn't reply to him, but to be honest, I've thought of nothing else ever since. I suppose I could say that I'm sorry, but I'm not even sure if that's true. What I will say is that I've missed you …*

Jill paused and wiped away a tear. With a distinctive, almost delightful quaver she continued:

> *I've missed you and I do plan to visit, if it's all right with you. As your lawyer said, 'Life is hard enough already'.*

Jill stopped reading, wiped her eyes and looked at me.

I looked around the room. For some reason I couldn't quite face her. 'I might have another glass of wine if that's all right.'

Janet promptly refilled my glass and I gulped it down as if it were some sort of emergency measure. I was, for the sake of completeness, very close to crying.

'You write to each other? Letters?' I said at last.

Jill smiled and reached across the table to take my hand. 'Thank you, Teddy.'

The wine, glass after glass (and as dreadful as it was), steered me towards an agreeable state of slight oblivion, of *not knowing*. Booze. It can't be all bad.

So Robert was reunited with his mother and younger sister. And I was surprised to learn that poor Robert was no fraudster. I had forgotten one of the cardinal rules of the profession: believe no one, least of all your client. Randolph had indeed changed his Last Will & Testament and had indeed excluded Janet and Jill from the remains of his earthly riches. There was no 'undue influence'. There was no forgery. Robert's defence of the lawsuit might have been factually astute, indeed quite proper, yet it was still an evasion of the truth.

Why had Randolph changed his Will in his final hours? No one knows. Not even Robert.

And Robert had indeed divorced his third wife after being summoned to court, but he'd done so for the same reason he'd divorced the first two: he was sick of her. It was only poor timing that suggested an ulterior motive. And what a fuss we lawyers might make of poor timing!

Pictures hung from the walls of their small house. Family pictures. There was Randolph and Robert down at the lake at The Millhouse. They held fishing rods and Robert beamed at the camera, holding up a plump-looking rainbow trout. There was a picture of Jill and Randolph – in all their finery – at the races. There was a picture of Janet. It might have been the early eighties. She stood next to a cabriolet sports car, she herself sporting a giant pair of sunglasses, her hair vast and lustrous, flowing over her shoulders. She smiled at the camera in a way that I'd never seen her smile in real life.

I felt her standing near me. She was dutifully refilling my glass.

'That was my first car.' She laughed. 'A Triumph TR 7. I don't think I've ever looked so cool!' She laughed again.

My first reaction was that the photograph could have been used as evidence in the trial. We might have shown that her father had bought her an exotic sports car. He did love her! He did!

But no. What would I ever know of the Smollens?

On the sideboard in the living room was a photograph of Randolph in his military uniform. Mysterious soul, old Randolph. An unknowable man. I found myself scrutinising the picture for clues – for latent signs of cruelty, remorse, rage, tenderness. What might this image, this flat, fading image representing one thousandth of a second in the life of a man, tell me?

I was slightly transfixed.

'His loyalty to the last governor of Rhodesia cost him friends in the 1st Battalion,' Jill explained. 'There were only so many hushed silences in the officers' mess he could take every time he joined them for a drink. He eventually resigned his commission. One day, at a race meeting in Salisbury, he met a fellow called Heiser. They drank Scotch together and became rather chummy. That was unusual enough for Randolph. Soon enough, Heiser had recruited him. Mercenaries. They called themselves the Copperheads. They were involved in a campaign in Zaire, took on some sort of rebel group – the People's Democratic Liberation Movement of a Free Katanga, or something like that. It was impossible to know what Randolph did up there. What he felt. He spoke once – and only once – of bodies without limbs, the limbs without bodies floating down brown rivers, nuns raped and dismembered, the babies with teeth smashed out of their mouths. He could never say – not even to himself – if he might have been complicit in those atrocities.'

I turned away from the photograph – that harmless image. I sat in an impossibly low and spongy sofa, slightly unsure if I'd ever be able to get out of it.

Janet was in the kitchen washing the plates.

Jill sat opposite me, holding a large glass of brandy in her small hands. She continued: 'He left Rhodesia and headed to Johannesburg. He had a bit of money, I suppose, but he *was* unemployed. Unemployed and with no real plans.' Jill paused and smiled – there was something in that smile that revealed a lovestruck young woman, still so enriched by those distant memories. 'I suppose I should have taken that as a clue, but he was a good-looking man who didn't say much and I liked that about him. While the rest of the world moaned and bleated over the pettiest trivialities, Randolph presented an unshakeably firm character – square jaw, clean-shaven, upright posture, wondrously untroubled. Oh, military men!'

Partial to a man in uniform myself, I knew what she meant. If you're to be stuck in a trench with rockets flying overhead – and let's face it, life is quite often like that – there might be nothing more comforting than having a square-jawed, clean-shaven, upright military man by your side.

'On the night that Robert was born, Randolph walked into the hospital room, looked at me and at tiny Robert, and he turned without saying a word and ran off. I didn't see him again until I was discharged. We returned home and he was sitting in an armchair reading the newspaper. I held Robert in my arms. He looked at me as if he had no idea why I might have been carrying a baby.

'I knew then that the idea of producing a child utterly appalled him. It was the future – a future that would survive him, out of his control. His horror of an unknowable future was complete.'

And so did Randolph hate Robert? Did he hate Janet and the Mouse? Or was it a hatred born out of love? Are all relationships love-hate relationships? Which aspects of these experiences do we indulge? Which notes of that opera are the best? And which are the worst?

'One night, in the bar of The Diplomat – Randolph often went to bars on his own – he met James Plunkett,' Jill said. 'It was quite by chance. "You'll never make any money out of killing anyone," James had said. I suppose this was a comforting idea for Randolph. "What matters is what's under the ground, not above it. And what's under it is a drug. An obsession. And if you want to know anything about obsessions, you'll know they're worth more than the planet itself." I remember these words because Randolph had repeated them so often.'

Thus, began Randolph Smollen's rather surreptitious partnership with James Plunkett. From prime-ministerial residences and boardrooms in Europe, they flew to presidential complexes and mineral-rich land concessions in Africa, connecting them all with signatures along dotted lines (and, as some observers claimed, the occasional veiled threat). Eventually, they would do the same for China. They were the darlings of the world's most eminent banks, mining houses and energy companies – lending a shimmer of sophistication to what were indubitably nefarious deals.

Business was booming and Randolph, ever a solitary country boy, decided to move to the Midlands – The Millhouse. There, Janet was born and Norma too.

Speaking of those early years at The Millhouse, Jill said: 'It was isolated. Miles from anywhere. He was increasingly paranoid and suspicious, and felt it proper that we should stay as far away as possible from other human beings. He offered so few words. He became impossibly inscrutable. I complained: we're stuck out here on this damn farm, all on our own! Whenever he flew away to some godforsaken place, I used to arrange parties. We had helicopters fly in from Johannesburg. They landed at The Millhouse and I sent bow-tied waiters shimmying out over the lawn to offer guests flutes of chilled champagne!' Jill seemed a bit surprised when she laughed, as if laughter had abandoned her a long time ago. She took a firm swig of brandy and I did the same.

It seemed to me that Jill felt as if she'd been had. Randolph's manly silence had slowly evolved into a scathing taciturnity. It was not a happy marriage.

And Norma?

Randolph had given Janet a horse for her tenth birthday – the famous Blackforest. Janet was told that she wasn't allowed to lead the horse without the help of a stable hand. She wasn't supposed to mount the horse in its stall. Randolph had been perfectly clear – the Mouse as his witness. But as Janet's confidence with the beautiful Blackforest grew, she took it on herself to go down to the stables one afternoon, accompanied by little Norma, her six-year-old sister, and Robert, her twelve-year-old brother. Placing her feet on the stirrups that hung from the side of the stall, she swung herself onto the giant beast.

Robert pleaded with her, reminding her that this was against the rules. Janet dismissed him haughtily, saying she knew exactly how to control Blackforest and, in any case, Daddy loved her more than him because she had a horse and he didn't.

While Janet sat happily astride her beloved animal, Norma looked up and burst into a terrible wail. She wanted to mount the horse too, so it seemed. Janet reached down to lift little Norma up, but neither of them was strong enough. The wailing and fussing and slipping had aggravated Blackforest, and with a sudden jerk he violently threw Janet from his silky back and began to kick and stamp his giant hooves in the narrow stall.

Robert ran away screaming.

What Randolph saw when he arrived at the scene was probably not unlike what he'd seen in Zaire – a child with its teeth kicked in.

Janet was remarkably unhurt, but Norma was killed instantly.

As one might expect, this was a seminal moment for the Smollen family.

Randolph never forgave himself. Each day, as Janet grew older, he must have looked for signs of the demented rage that afflicted his own mind.

He shot the horse and had its body burned.

Janet had found Randolph in that very stall trying to make a noose. 'Everyone should know how to make a noose,' he had said. Randolph did not hang himself that night. Janet had stopped him.

There was no escape for the man.

Poor Randolph was trapped among the living; they had him producing his own offspring – coerced him with their usual tenderness, to keep living. What Jill saw in him might have been an expression of chauvinistic power. What Randolph saw might have been an expression of helplessness. Both were true.

When I drove back to Durban that night I was struck by Janet's remarkable courage – to know that she still holds a job teaching street kids how to love and take care of horses at the horse-riding school. This, despite her ordeal. And she'd stopped her father from hanging himself from the rafters of the stable. Her father. My father. Beholden to this feminine earth!

And I found myself thinking of letters: the perfect medium for a species that cannot trust itself. Think of the spaces *between* the words, of what is not said. Think of how these squiggles and symbols on a page, arranged and re-arranged, this way and that, reveal as much as they conceal. Think of the silence of the written word!

Why had Janet and the Mouse not moved back to the The Millhouse? I'd put this question to them as I was leaving. Janet had said: 'We couldn't abide the deception. The worst thing to do with suffering is to betray it.'

They'd sold The Millhouse. They'd bought a new car. They'd repaired a leaking roof. They'd bought flowers for the garden. They'd kept a small amount of the cash in a savings account – enough to earn a modest but sufficient amount of interest – and donated the rest to charity.

And Robert! Why had the man been so callous? Why had he defended the lawsuit with such calculated malice? I never got to know. Perhaps he felt he was right, that the facts were on his side. Perhaps that was all that mattered. I suppose, as I contemplate what I have witnessed, what my letter writers witnessed of Val and she of them, I can conclude that knowledge will fail me. There is only that to share: our shifting perceptions, our arcane passions, our inexcusable neediness and inescapable pain.

Thirty-one

So, where am I now? I have resigned from the legal profession. No, I haven't left the continent. Many people asked me this, but it was Val and her strange love of the place that has compelled me to stay. Riddled with tension and ambiguity, fraught with complexity, there remains in my troubled heart an unbending, almost haunting affection for the place. Yes, I intend to be the very last Dickerson in Africa. I hope I am. I'm quite sure that this land couldn't possibly be expected to handle any more of us.

Now I live in Maputo. It is a suitable wreckage of colonial rule with a hint of modern madness all bound together by an easy-going rhythm.

I remember in the old days, when this place went by that strangely exotic name of Lourenço Marques, how they used to speak of holidays in Mozambique. They spoke in awe of its many illicit pleasures. There was the gambling and the interracial boxing, the chance to listen to mildly subversive music. There were the lavish hotels and bars that served liquor on Sundays! And there was also the sex. Back home there were policemen bashing down doors, running into bedrooms while naked men covered themselves in bedclothes and their lovers hid in wardrobes. Blacks screwing whites. Whites screwings blacks. Prosecutions followed. Suicides followed.

Mozambique, for all its violent upheaval, its bloody conflict, is a place of life-on-the-streets, of hookers, thieves, jaded chancers and jilted lovers, where our fear of one another is immediate and proximate, and yet our greatest guide, our inner reflection and our outer reflectiveness. I am at last accepted in this African place for what I am: an expat. I surrender to her story, her voluble and comforting outrage, where my humiliation is transformed into humility, a fitting end for a prodigal son.

And at least it's hot. And sunny too! I even play in a cricket team for old codgers and, for now, I am the youngest codger in the group, so I play the game with a wild sort of youthful abandon that pleases me.

I have taken a job as a late-night radio host, broadcasting my favourite hits from midnight to 4 a.m. My show is called 'The Darkest Hour' and I broadcast under the name 'The Midnight Aunt'. I live in a ninth-floor apartment in Avenida Vladimir Lenine. When I first moved here, I spent most of my weekends hanging around the pool at the Clube Naval on the Avenida de Marginal, which is where I met Tiaro, a smooth thirty-year-old with just a hint of a beard – the look that has always provoked me with such exhilaration.

Tiaro is a musician. He is the drummer in a band that plays at Club Quattro downtown. *The drummer in a band!* I am almost tearful – in my usual girlish, romcom way – whenever I muse over the sheer romance of it. Good old-fashioned luck, I'm sure.

The girls love Tiaro. But Tiaro has never been so sure about the girls.

He is the son of a fiercely socialist Portuguese engineer and a Shangaan mid-level commander of the Resistência Nacional Moçambicana. His father returned to Portugal in 1988 after yet another outburst of violence (one of many and more than he could cope with). Tiaro remained to be raised by his mother on the seventeenth floor of what was once a luxury townhouse and that had no functioning elevator. Somewhat protected by his mother's political connections, he was better educated than most, obtaining a degree in civil engineering from the Universidade Eduardo Mondlane. But then, Tiaro did what I never could – until now. He abandoned his promised career so that he could hang out in bars and play music.

We live discreetly together. We spend many of our waking hours in bed, under a thin sheet. We watch TV. We eat snacks. We hold each other and snooze. At night, we go to work, Tiaro at Club Quattro and me at the radio station. On Saturdays, we have Tiaro's mother over. She eats. She says nothing. And she would shoot anyone in the head at point-blank range if anyone tried to harm us. I'm sure of it. Ah! Military men! And military women too, I suppose.

If we ever go to the market together and people frown, I introduce Tiaro as my houseboy and everyone seems fine with that. I think this is enormously funny. Yes, it's a funny old world. Master and servant is quite proper. But two lovers? Not so much.

Perhaps the most profound aspect of living here is when I hear Tiaro speak of his parents, his starkly black and white ancestors, their history of deception and violence. I see him, this slender, dreadlocked man, born of ancient conflict, now – so fragile and for the briefest time – bearing the promise of love. I yield with relief to this unyielding yet forgotten truth.

Val had often exhorted people to love one another. What I hadn't realised was that the exhortation in her last letter to me was subtly different. 'Be loved,' she had said. 'That is your only real responsibility.' What Val had been trying to say (for seventy-nine years) was that we owed it to ourselves to *deserve* love. Whether we *were* loved or not, well, that was everyone else's problem.

I still have my letters. I keep up my correspondence with Nawal, Wilma, Darshini, Caroline, Glynnis, Candice, and Jennifer. I wrote to Tiffany only once more:

> Dear Tiffany
> I'm sorry.
> With my best wishes,
> Teddy.

I have never heard back from her, but one day I suspect I will.

As for Wilma, she woke up one morning and Prunella was dead on the bedspread. As one might have expected, Wilma was distraught. After some weeks, she wrote to Tiffany to tell her that Prunella had died. They'd bought the cat together when they were still young lovers. 'I just thought you'd want to know,' Wilma had written. The letter affected Tiffany in a way that must have surprised her. After days of what must have been anguished prevarication, she sent Wilma a text message: 'Sorry about Pru. Hope u r ok xxx Tiff.' And then she said she had to run off to a meeting.

I did eventually find a picture of Val and I sent it to Nawal Hassan, her half-sister. It was a black-and-white photograph of Val sitting at a Christmas table. She wore a paper hat, was smiling brightly, and had her head turned to the side, offering a clear profile of her celebrated aristocratic nose. Nawal was delighted and immediately stuck it up on the wall of her room. She then sent pictures of herself and her family – four middle-aged children – and insisted that I send pictures of my own brood of six. Our correspondence endures and I simply pretend to forget – just as Val had done.

Caroline got up late one morning and walked downstairs to find her husband in an armchair with a large, hard-covered pictorial book on tropical birds face down on his lap. He was perfectly dead. Caroline's daughter immediately boarded a plane in Yangon (or Rangoon) and flew to London to comfort her mother. After the funeral and the tea party at their large house, in which Caroline was now consigned to rattle around alone, she prevailed on her daughter to disclose whether she might have met someone *special*. Her daughter was pleased to announce that indeed she had – an Iranian doctor who'd studied at Cambridge. 'Cambridge!' Caroline had cried. 'How wonderful!' Caroline wrote to me giving me the news. 'So, I suppose all's well that ends well,' she said. 'Our precious girl is to be married to a man from Persia!'

Just as well the poor fellow wasn't from Turkey, otherwise she might have described him as man from the Byzantine Empire.

Caroline was also slightly disturbed to learn that I had moved to Mozambique. 'Mozambique?' she asked. 'And they have High Court judges in Mozambique, do they?'

Candice landed up as a millionaire. She married an octogenarian Cambodian tycoon who'd made his fortune out of air-conditioners. 'Now that I'm rich, it's so weird how nice everyone is these days. Assholes!' She still insisted that I visit her in Phnom Penh. 'We've got aircon! Aircon!' But I've not yet been. 'The thing about wealth, Teddy,' she wrote in her last letter, 'is that it gets you the club, the house with the high wall and the razor wire, the car with blackened windows. We get to be distinguished. We get to be exclusive. Invariably, we get to be lonely. It's just another way of admitting how defeated we are by one another. That's why everyone wants some. That's why there'll never be enough. Heck! I'm still a nurse, sticking tubes up people's asses. Rich or poor, it's still a hell of a way to live!'

Darshini confessed to staying up late and listening to my radio show over the internet.

Oh, Mr Teddy how I love your voice. It is the voice of stars! It is a voice of romance and love. I know our Val will be so happy to hear your voice on the radio. You know, my mother loved all music. She played the piano and the guitar and the violin. My young life was filled with music. I love music very much. More music, Mr Teddy, or should I call you my Midnight Aunt?? This is a most amusing name for me. I know what aunt you are speaking about, Mr Teddy. She is our lovely Val!

Moosa came to visit. He was pleased to see me and to show off his new fiancée, a pale, almost insipid girl with very thin arms.

'I just want you to know, Teddy,' he said during our first meal, pausing over the peri-peri prawns with reddish oil glistening on his lips, 'that I'll never forget the Smollen case.' He turned to his bride-to-be and said: 'Best lawyer ever!'

I blushed and frowned and took a sip of beer – funny old self-deprecating me. 'And you, Moosa? Finished your articles? Soon to be admitted to the Side-Bar?'

He smiled with his usual ebullience. 'Not at all, sir. That's why the Smollen case was so important to me. I knew then that I'd never want to do that kind of work.' He laughed readily. 'What the teacher teaches is never what is taught!'

Moosa had plans to join his future father-in-law's business – something to do with car imports.

'Well, that's excellent!' I declared, unaware that I was patting Tiaro on the leg in a way that was just slightly more than affectionate. 'What the teacher teaches is never what is taught! An excellent line, Moosa.'

Jennifer continued to write by candlelight from Harare.

> *Yesterday, Riaan and I went down to the supermarket. Riaan commented on how many Chinese people there seem to be these days. I suppose it will end for them in the same way it has for all the other prodigal sons. They'll be left gasping with shame just like the rest of us. Perhaps, to be loyal to the parable, Africa will allow them their place here with her usual indignation and continue with her measured plod through the centuries that remain.*

I sigh in a dispirited kind of way when I contemplate Africa's future. True, I like Chinese food, but how many times did this have to happen to the Mother Continent before the rest of us realised how little we have learned? Is that why Africa is trodden over so easily? Have we forgotten some essential aspect of ourselves? Will she eventually remind us of our insufferable folly? Do we not already suspect it through each pointless day?

Glynnis grew ever smaller. 'It's funny how you said that we grow smaller,' she wrote in one of her letters. 'I've never really thought of that. But we do grow, Teddy. That's exactly what we're doing when we get smaller. We grow.' A few weeks later she wrote to tell me of a burglary. 'They took everything, so I'm told. Fortunately, they never harmed any of us. I can barely tell what's gone and what's still here. I muddle about on a wheelchair, along the familiar passages and through familiar rooms. I am blessed in a way. Blessed by what I don't know.'

As I returned the letter to its envelope, I thought once more about what made these letters so important. Yes, there is the slowness, the deliberation, the quietness of writing. One is automatically compelled to be more thoughtful when writing instead of speaking. That can't be a bad thing. But more than that, there was in handwritten letters an obscure kind of tactile suggestion that they carried with them. The writer physically touched the paper, leaned over it, crunched up previous drafts because there was a mistake at the bottom of the page and rewrote it. And of course there is the *handwriting* – the curve and slope, the narrow points and looping arches, each some sort of unique expression of the writer. How much is concealed by the uniformity of printed text. How machine-like! How well we hide! I appreciated this as I stored my letters in a box, just as Val had done.

I should mention – and I should do so emphatically – that I do not miss my days as a lawyer. I am happier to be known as the Midnight Aunt on Avenida Vladimir Lenine than I was to be known as Teddy Dickerson of Chambers. Sitting on my balcony with a view of the old Delagoa Bay, readying myself with a gin and tonic for my next show, I recently mused: there'll never be enough rules with this many truths.

Later that night, from the studios in downtown Maputo, I couldn't resist it: 'Good evening, Maputo, Inhaca, Inhambane, Komatipoort, Malkerns, Mbabane, and beyond. The time for talk is over. If there is such a thing as a universal truth, it'll be a lie. It's time for music. It's time for the Darkest Hour ...'

I often think of Val's words – those she had penned in her last letter. 'I'm proud of my Teddy,' she had said. I know she is. And I'm proud of her too. It'll never just be about me. It'll be about us – the last Dickersons to hail from the eastern shores of Africa.

ACKNOWLEDGEMENTS

My sincere thanks to Kate O'Donnell (linecreative.com.au), Barbara Stowe, William Lorentz ('You can't live in the air'), Serge Selbe ('All you have in the end is how you treated other people'), Louise Liebenberg (for nakedly dramatic purposes I might not have followed all her tips on the law), Andrew Eather, and forever and always, my dear Tia.